KU-031-721

All Sorts of Possible

rupert Wallis

SIMON & SCHUSTER

First published in Great Britain in 2015 by Simon & Schuster UK Ltd
A CBS COMPANY
This paperback edition published 2016

Copyright © 2015 Rupert Wallis

This book is copyright under the Berne Convention.
No reproduction without permission.
All rights reserved.

The right of Rupert Wallis to be identified as the author of this
work has been asserted by him in accordance with sections 77
and 78 of the Copyright, Design and Patents Act, 1988.

3 5 7 9 10 8 6 4 2

Simon & Schuster UK Ltd
1st Floor, 222 Gray's Inn Road
London
WC1X 8HB

www.simonandschuster.co.uk

Simon & Schuster Australia, Sydney
Simon & Schuster India, New Delhi

A CIP catalogue record for this book is available from the British Library.

PB ISBN 978-1-4711-1893-7
eBook ISBN 978-1-4711-1894-4

This book is a work of fiction. Names, characters, places and incidents are either
the product of the author's imagination or are used fictitiously. Any resemblance
to actual people living or dead, events or locales is entirely coincidental.

Typeset in the UK by Hewer Text UK Ltd, Edinburgh
Printed and bound by CPI Group (UK) Ltd, Croydon, CR0 4YY

Simon & Schuster UK Ltd are committed to sourcing paper that is made
from wood grown in sustainable forests and supports the Forest Stewardship
Council, the leading international forest certification organisation. Our
books displaying the FSC logo are printed on FSC certified paper.

All sorts of Possible

Also by Rupert Wallis

The Dark Inside

For YOU

'. . . a human being is a being who decides – who still has to decide – what he or she will be in the next moment . . .'

Viktor Frankl, TV interview, Buenos Aires, 1985

https://www.youtube.com/watch?v=-wf6DAQQVno

The Moon
at the End
of the Tunnel

1

When the sinkhole opened, there was no time to brake or turn the wheel, and the old green Land Rover was snatched off the dirt road over the smoking rim.

The teenage boy in the passenger seat blinked as blue sky was ripped from the windscreen and trees launched themselves like rockets.

He was a raggedy doll thrown forward as the car was swallowed down into the world.

2

The boy's eyes flicked open and he panicked, thinking the Land Rover was still falling, but it wasn't. The car was stationary, pointing down, his seat belt braced across him and his chin buttoned tight to his chest.

'Dad?'

His hands wouldn't stop trembling until he gripped the seat to turn and look.

Trussed in the seat belt, his father could have been asleep.

'Dad? Can you hear me?'

The boy edged closer, stopping when he heard stones popping out from beneath the tyres and the Land Rover groaning, wanting to move.

'DAD?'

He kept watching the drumbeat in his father's temple until every sound around them had died away, too afraid to do anything else.

3

The windscreen was shattered but not broken. Through the open window next to him the boy could see between bars of dirty sunlight all the way to the other side of the sinkhole.

The hole was huge. Black. Like the filthy inside of some industrial flue.

He could smell the cold.

Hear damp crackling on stones.

He kept breathing slowly until he had focused clearly on what to do next.

But his phone wasn't in the pockets of his shorts or the plastic well between their seats. Not even in the side of his door. When he tried thinking back to where it had been before the sinkhole had opened, all he kept remembering . . .

. . . was the sunlight flaring in the windscreen as he tried to tell his father one last time that he didn't want to go camping, shouting . . .

__It__ was a waste of time, __not__ the PlayStation.

That he was __too old__ for camping now.

That he was __done being a kid__ and should be able to do whatever he wanted.

And then the road had opened up as if answering him back.

He clicked out of his seat belt, using an arm to brace himself against the glove compartment as he leant forward to search for his phone, hunting for it like a cat in the space under his seat. But all he found was an old shopping list written on the back of an envelope in his father's hand.

'I __hate__ you, Dad.'

That was the last thing he had said, after being told his PlayStation would be thrown out if he carried on complaining.

The boy shivered. He was only wearing a T-shirt. Somehow, even the marrow in his bones felt cold. He reached back into the rear seats for his North Face jacket and managed to slip it on, the Land Rover creaking as stones tumbled unseen around them, until he realized it was just their echoes. It made him wonder how deep the sinkhole might be and how far they had fallen, whether he could climb out and get help.

He peered out of the open window, just a little way at first.

The car was a long way below the level of the road, sunk into a dark scree that looked like mining spoil piled against one side of the hole. Tiny stones streamed out from around the tops of the Land Rover's tyres as if the rubber was slowly melting.

Daring to lean out further, the boy realized the sinkhole was even bigger than he had first thought. As wide as a football pitch, but far deeper than the length of one. He could see a stream at the bottom, as purple as a vein in the low light.

In the cool, dank updraught, he smelt wet stone and petrol and soil.

'Hello!' he shouted, looking up at the rim of the sinkhole and the fat crescent of blue sky above it. '*HELL-LO!*'

A dark hole of his own suddenly appeared inside him as he wondered how many people drove down the dirt road in a single day.

Ducking back in the car, he gripped the door handle, imagining the PlayStation version of himself clambering out of the Land Rover and wading through the thick dark scree, then climbing the wall of the sinkhole and disappearing into the blue sky for help.

He thought hard about everything.

About what might go right.

And what could go wrong.

And then his iPhone rang.

4

He pushed his head out again, looking all around as the sinkhole tried to trick him with its echo, its walls ringing too. He remembered now. He'd been holding his phone, his elbow resting on the open window, the trees blipping by as he shouted at his father.

He worried it would stop ringing, that he would never find it, and then he saw the phone some way below him among the dark stones, daylight catching on its screen.

Clicking open the door, he heard the car's suspension bushes twang and the tyres straining, wanting to move, and he whispered over and over that he was lighter than air. But the scree swallowed his foot like murky water, and then sections below him sheared off, sending the phone clattering deeper into the hole, the ringtone mewling as it fell.

When the Land Rover suddenly lurched and started to slide, he yanked the door shut and turned quickly, clasping his right arm round the back of the driver's seat, and his left one across his father's chest, to try and keep him safe.

5

The Land Rover had fallen further, about halfway into the hole, and was lying lopsided. Its faded green paintwork was dappled with gold where spots of sunlight caught it.

The boy was already slip-sliding his way down the loose dark rubble, plotting a route to the iPhone below as the voicemail rang.

One bar on the phone was enough to make the call to the emergency services, but the woman's voice at the other end was faint, foamy with crackle, and it was like talking to the spirit world. He told her his father was breathing but unconscious. That they had been on the dirt road going towards Farnham's Wood. But he didn't know the road number when she asked him for it, saying it was just called the 'Back Road' by everyone who knew it. He told her to *sendsomeonequickly*.

'Just hurry!' he shouted. 'My dad's trapped in the car.'

'Someone's already on their way,' she said. 'They'll be there as quickly as they can.'

He nodded as though she was beside him, then whispered he was scared.

'I'll be with you till someone comes, I promise,' said the woman on the phone. 'I'm Mary. Tell me who you are. Tell me all about you. Keep talking to me so I know you're OK.'

'My name's Daniel. I'm fifteen. There's just me and Dad because my mum died when I was born. I'm just a normal kid, nothing special.'

'You're being brave now and that makes you very special indeed.'

A loud cracking sound made him look up and he watched the sinkhole's mouth opening wider by a couple of metres as a chunk of wall fell away from the very top. It broke apart in the air and crashed down against the side of the hole. The scree hissed. Rubble clattered on to the Land Rover. Daniel had to dodge and twist and cover up as stones rained down around him.

When he looked up again he saw huge, jagged cracks appearing in the walls and he realized that far larger sections of rock were going to fall.

'I can't wait,' he shouted into the phone as he started slogging his way back up the slope towards the Land

Rover. 'I've got to get him out of the car.' Static furred the line and Daniel pressed the phone harder to his ear. 'Hello?'

'Daniel?' came her faint voice back, and then the line went dead and the single bar was gone.

It was harder work than he thought, climbing up the slope, and Daniel soon saw that there was no way of reaching the Land Rover and pulling his father out before the black, crooked columns of rock above him came crashing down. Even so, he wanted to keep going anyway, just to try and be with him. But, when the light began to dim more quickly, he panicked and some ancestral working in his brain took over, telling him there was nowhere to go except down, because he would be safer there. He felt something tear in his heart as he turned round and went stumbling deeper into the hole.

He moved as fast as he could, slipping and sliding down the dirty scree, frightened of being hit from behind with rocks constantly falling. He told himself his father would be OK in the Land Rover because it would protect him, saying it over and over like a prayer to make it come true, as the crack of stone on stone went caroming louder and louder round the sinkhole.

Reaching the bottom of the hole, Daniel shone the light from his phone screen over the stream, splashing over the slippery stones, hoping it might show some-where to hide.

He found an opening into which the water vanished, cut into the bottom of the rock wall and framed by an overhang. Daniel crouched, breathless, and shone the phone, lighting up a narrow gully down which the stream ran into a chamber of sorts, but how big he could not easily see.

For a moment, all he could think about was his father as the huge pillars of black rock began to collapse like blocks of dark ice. He shouted above the great tearing and rumbling sounds that he was going to come back, and then rocks were bullocking down the slope towards him, leaving him no choice but to turn and slide head first into the gap in the wall. He held the phone aloft like a lantern, its light skittering madly as he wriggled like an eel in the wet flue, trying to slip his shoulders through.

Stones thumped the soles of his trainers and Daniel struggled harder, the water splashing up into his face and the cold iron smell of it making him gasp.

He thought he would never move.

And then he did . . .

. . . just as the light from the phone screen went out, leaving only the sounds of the water and the rubble crashing into the wall behind him as he slipped down the smooth, ancient gully into the dark, the fingers of his free hand bobbling over rock and trying to grab hold, the nails burning at their nubs.

6

He thought he heard voices. Helicopter blades chopping the air and a rope dropping on to the rocks. But it was a dream. He shouted himself awake into the dark and clutched his phone, pressing the home button and casting the light from the screen round the small stone chamber, expecting someone else to be there.

Not a sound, except for his breathing and the stream running in the stone guttering beside him.

According to the time on the phone, Daniel had only been dozing for a few minutes, but he had been waiting in the same space for over an hour, a place barely big enough to let him stand up and stretch out his arms and legs when he needed to, to keep out the cold.

After scudding to a stop, he had crouched, dripping, in this chamber and flashed the torch on his iPhone round the walls before wriggling the few metres back up the flue, to the hole he had squeezed through.

But the hole was gone.

He had tried pulling the stones away as the stream trickled through gaps too small to see, but they were jammed so hard together his cold fingers kept slipping. When one did come free, another dropped into its place like some party game being played by an unseen hand.

It was difficult not to imagine how much rubble might be piled up at the bottom of the sinkhole now and Daniel breathed as slowly as he could, telling himself to keep calm and wait. That he would be found. That Mary had sent help. So he slithered back into the chamber and took off his North Face jacket and squeezed it dry, and then did the same with his damp T-shirt and then his shorts and underwear, before putting everything back on.

He checked the time on his phone again. It had definitely been a couple of hours now. Tricksy thoughts whispered to him.

Had they come already?

What about his phone? Could they find him with that?

What were they doing that was taking them so long?

What had happened to his dad?

Daniel tried shouting again, but his voice cannoned round the chamber, as trapped as he was.

His forehead ached where he had bashed it, a bump like the start of a horn in the centre of his head. His nose hurt too and he picked away a dark red crust that had grown like mystery coral round his nostrils.

He shone the phone up the flue again and stared at where the hole had been. And then he turned away and sat down again, wrapping his jacket tighter round him, his breath misting the air, before the light on the phone screen went out and he closed his eyes.

Daniel stirred when he thought he heard voices for definite this time and kept hollering until his throat felt raw. But no one answered.

Every time the light from the phone screen went out, he was starting to feel himself falling away into the dark and it scared him so much he kept pressing the wake button. He tried not to think about how long the charge in the phone would last. Or what the damp and the cold might do to it.

Or to him.

He hugged himself harder to keep warm. But it wasn't enough. Stiff and cold, he managed to stand to three-quarter height, then crouch back down, then up again, exercising for as long as he could to pump himself warm. Out of breath, he sat back down on the cold rock floor and it sucked the heat right out of him in an instant.

He checked the phone, but there was no reception. He hit the call key anyway and pleaded with the silence on the other end.

He sat in the dark for a little longer, trying not to be scared, listening to the water until he played the light from the phone screen over the stream, turning the clear water orange.

'Maybe the stream leads somewhere,' he said to the phone. But the phone said nothing. 'Mary sent help. They'll find Dad. Help him. But what if they can't find me? What if they think there's no point?' Daniel sat in silence for a few moments more. 'We should take a look just to see,' he said.

He shuffled forward, keeping his knees either side of the stream, the water dancing on down the ancient flue into the dark, and the damp walls shining golden as he held out his phone.

When the guttering became narrower, he leant lower, his weight on his elbows, and the water dancing centimetres below his chin, creeping forward until he came to a ledge he could peer over. The stream went rushing on down the wall of a large cave in which lay a silent lake made of clear, shimmering green.

The screen light from the phone frayed quickly in the vast dark, so Daniel switched on the torch and spotlit a wide channel of water running out of the far side of the lake, through a natural archway as big as

18

the entrance to a church. But what was beyond that he could not see.

He turned off the torch. Listened to the water again. And then he manoeuvred around on the ledge and crawled back against the stream, until he had returned to the small chamber from where he had started.

'Help!' he shouted. 'HELP! *HELL-P!*' But there was no one to hear him. 'It's very cold,' he said to the phone, his words turning to white vapour in the screen's light. 'We've been here longer than I thought we would be. I don't know how long they'll go on looking. What if they find Dad and give up on us?'

When the screen went out, Daniel sat in the dark, listening to his breathing.

'I don't know what to do. Is there anyone who can help us?' he whispered.

But the black was silent.

'I'll die if I stay here.'

And the black did not argue back.

'What should I do?'

He waited for an answer.

'OK then. We follow the water.'

7

Ripples appeared mysteriously across the surface of the green lake and moved without a sound. The water was so clear that when Daniel held up the phone he could see into the shallows and it looked like a sledgehammer had been taken to a concrete floor. The ceiling of the chamber soared above him, folding and unfolding like a vast sheet being shaken out.

He stood by the edge of the lake, watching the water flowing out through the archway.

'All that water's got to lead somewhere.'

But the phone wasn't sure. It didn't say a word.

'It must do,' said Daniel, nodding.

He started to pick his way round the shoreline towards the arch, levering open the vast dark with the torch on his phone.

*   *   *

A river at first, the water seeped away quickly between the rocks to nothing more than a small stream, which led him into more caverns and caves, and through tunnels, some so small he had to wiggle through them on his belly, splashing and swearing at the rock until he came free. There were other times when the walls closed to narrow passageways that forced him to haul himself sideways with tiny breaths.

His damp trainers were like deadweights, rubbing his heels until he peeled them off and left them sitting in the dark. And then he padded back in his socks and tied the laces together and hooked the trainers over his shoulder. 'We're all getting out together,' he whispered.

He checked the clock on his phone from time to time, promising himself short breaks at intervals of his choosing. Whenever he stopped, he thumbed through photos on his phone to remind him of the world above.

'They've found you,' he whispered, stopping at a picture of his father. 'You're at the hospital, waiting for me. That's why I have to get out too.'

When the stream vanished suddenly beneath the stone floor, Daniel tried not to panic and kept following its musical sounds, stopping whenever the echoes looping round him threatened to become too confusing.

Worried about losing his way, he picked up a stone and scratched a chalky number 1 on the rock. And a few minutes after that he scratched the number 2.

Soon he was into the hundreds, striking out numbers whenever he found a dead end that forced him to retrace his steps.

When the stream eventually bubbled up again through the floor, he whispered *thank you* and knelt and drank, the pure cold making him gasp.

After a few hours, the short breaks started becoming longer. He was colder. More tired. He sat in the dirt, his chin bumping him awake each time he dozed off, the fragments of his dreams skittering back into the cracks and crevices of his brain, giving him just glimpses at first.

. . . His father smiling . . .

. . . His mother holding out her hands and calling to him.

But, as the cold drilled into him and he rested more and more, those dreams of his crept out as rich dark stories.

. . . His father cursing Daniel for leaving him behind in the car, saying it was all Daniel's fault the sinkhole had opened because he'd said that he hated him . . .

. . . His mother not being gone at all but living secretly with another family, telling him she had never wanted him and that was why she had left the day he had been born . . .

And so real did each dream seem, with their bright colours and clear sounds, that Daniel shouted himself awake from each one into the dark.

Once, he was so scared and cold and confused after waking, he held up the phone to his ear, thinking it was ringing, his face lit ghoulishly by the screen's glow.

'Mary?' But the only noise was the stream. 'You promised,' he whispered when he realized he had dreamt the ringtone.

On one occasion he stopped when he thought he heard voices and wondered if there might be people looking for him and he shouted out again and again.

But no one answered him back.

The only noise Daniel heard was the stream.

When he found a thermal spring in a chamber, bubbling up into a small pool through the rock floor, he undressed and crept into its warmth and floated in the dark.

He swallowed as much warm water as he could before going on his way, telling the phone they could not stay.

Daniel knew he had spent over ten hours following the stream, according to the phone, its torchlight casting an eerie moon glow around him.

He kept whispering to his phone, promising he would find a way out. But, as more time passed, he heard his voice beginning to falter. He spoke less and less for fear of promising something that might not happen, that it might not believe him any more. He said nothing when it prompted him with a message that told him its battery had only twenty per cent remaining.

When he took a dump, squatting like an animal, he was careful not to dirty the damp shorts pooled round his ankles. Afterwards, he hovered close above it, feeling the warmth on his bare skin, until the rancid mess turned cold.

Ten per cent.

Daniel cursed out loud that he should never have left that first chamber and followed the stream. That he should have stayed and waited to be found.

He stopped when he realized he had lost his trainers from around his neck and panicked. But he soon gave up on ever seeing them again.

Five per cent.

He croaked orders at the stream to show him the way out, casting the phone's light around him. But there was no magic door in the stone, only the damp walls shining golden.

One per cent.

Daniel pleaded with the phone not to give up. He stumbled on, bumping off the rocks, grazing his cold hands as he held the phone out, promising it they would find a way out.

Running now, he splashed through the water, barely aware it was rapidly becoming deeper until his legs were chopped away in the brutal cold and he was bobbing like a cork, his arm aloft and the phone in his fingers. He shouted at it, telling it not to die, but he could hardly hear himself above the roar of the fast current spinning him, the phone's light whirling shadows round the walls. When he saw that the water ahead was backcombed into a white, frothy curd, he knew there was a drop coming. It was the last thing he saw before the phone died, its after-image still there as he was swept towards it.

The dark was filled with the roar of water as Daniel was washed over the edge, bellyflopping into clean air and falling weightless into a void that took his breath away, the phone snatched clean from his fingers.

8

He crashed through a pane of cold water that lay below.

He did not know which way was up, his breath bubbling all around him, until he broke through the surface into a cold black he inhaled greedily. He steadied himself, fanning his arms and listening to the sound of the waterfall. Keeping it behind him, he floated forward and cried out when his freezing fingers crumpled against stone. Feeling around it, his hands told him it was a rock jutting above the surface of the water.

It was too cold to keep swimming so Daniel hauled himself up and lay shivering, his teeth chattering.

'I don't want to die,' he whispered. 'I don't. If there's someone there – anyone?' With the noise of the waterfall ringing round him, he imagined he must be in some large cavern. 'I don't want to die!' he shouted as loudly as he could. But he was all alone.

The darkness was so all–embracing, he could not tell if his eyes were open or shut. The feeling made him giddy. Scared of falling back into the water, he held on tight to the rock, whispering to it. He told it how he wished to live a normal life and have a family and grow up to be a person. Anyone. Maybe even *someone*. His wet clothes creaked. The cold felt strong enough to split his fingers. When he started shivering less, the parts of him he knew as being Daniel began retreating further into his body, looking for warmth.

Loose stones skittered over the rock and fell into the water as he moved. He managed to pick one up with death-cold fingers and scrawled a word beside him, seeing each letter in his mind's eye.

HELP

He did not know if anyone was watching him. Or, if they were, whether they cared. But he needed to ask one last time, to be sure.

'Please.'

A moment later, Daniel thought he was falling off the rock, as if the cold had finally prised him loose. But it was the dark that had shifted, lifting and retreating, and in bone-coloured light he started to glimpse the stone chamber around him, its walls gathered like grey wool.

He was beached on a large boulder adjoining the shoreline, with the black water lapping round him, having fallen over the lip of the waterfall like he had done. And, painted across the dark pool, a white stripe, wimpling as the water rippled.

It was moonlight.

Daniel looked up and saw a gently sloping tunnel bored through the rock wall on the other side of the water. And right in its centre was a full moon.

It was a hole in the rock to the world above. A way out, his cold brain slowly told him, that he had missed because it was now night outside.

The moon was already disappearing behind another veil of cloud and the chamber was darkening again.

Daniel lurched forward and managed to sit up, his cold arms like stumps because he could no longer feel his hands. When he wobbled forward and slid down on to the shoreline, his knees clicked and his arms flailed as he tried to stand up. But he was too weak to keep his balance.

In the last dregs of moonlight, he plotted a route over the pale, rocky rim round the water.

And then it went dark.

He crawled painfully through the pitch-black, from stone to stone, until he bumped against the rock wall of the chamber and began to follow its slow curve round. The dark tried to spin him about, but he kept going, the noise of the waterfall a pivot around which to crawl.

31

A couple of times he thought he had found the tunnel and then had to backtrack when he discovered a dead end. But, eventually, he found a wider opening and he kept crawling forward, battling up the gradual slope, the waterfall becoming quieter and quieter, his breathing louder. He collapsed on his front from time to time, crying out as he hit the rocks, so cold it felt like bone on bone.

He stopped, frightened, when he heard a different sound above him until he realized what it was: the hiss of leaves in a breeze.

When his hands touched a fringe of silky grass, he gasped and lay on the ground at the mouth of the hole to try and gather more strength.

There were woods to his right.

In front of him was a large meadow, like a sheet of black ice without the moon to light it.

The night was dark. But it was a dark he knew by smell and sound. It was a dark that warmed him.

10

Gradually, it began to grow lighter, the world turning blue in the dawn.

Daniel found the farm after crawling across the meadow and on through a field of wheat that led to an adjoining lane, picking a path through the prickly hedge because he was too weak to climb the gate. But he found enough strength to totter down the asphalt towards the farmhouse when he saw it, mud cracking and falling from his bare knees.

The light from the kitchen window drew him like a moth into the yard.

When the door opened, he smelt coffee. Toast. Bacon frying in a pan. And it was too much to bear.

As the farmer's wife knelt down beside him in her dressing gown, he told her in between his sobbing that he was sorry for dirtying the floor, but the words came out slurred because he was so cold. She stared at this poor wretched thing and silently prayed *thank you* for his return before shouting at her husband to phone for help.

11

The paramedics handled him very gently as if wary of breaking or tearing his skin. They listened to his heart and wrapped him in silver heat blankets and warming pads. When Daniel tried pleading with them to sit in the front of the ambulance, they didn't seem to hear him. He thought it was because his speech was so slurred he could not make himself properly understood.

When the vehicle started moving, he cried out as he lay strapped to the stretcher, imagining the road was going to catch him out again if he wasn't watching it. Gradually, his sore red hands relaxed as the tarmac held and the tyres kept rolling, but all the time he was lying there, staring at the ceiling, he kept wondering about what was beneath them, his heart jumping every time the vehicle braked. Sometimes his brain felt so cold he forgot where he was until another bump of the tyres jerked his thinking back and he recalled what was happening.

Daniel tried to ask questions whenever he remembered.

'Where's my dad?'

'He got out, right?'

'He's OK?'

But the words came out of him quiet and muddled and meaningless, and he gave up trying to ask anything else when a paramedic placed a mask over his mouth to give him warmed oxygen to breathe. As Daniel lay there, trying to think clearly through the cold, an IV was pricked into a vein in his arm and warm, soothing fluids crept into his body.

The paramedic stayed focused on warming Daniel, checking his vital signs, telling him he was going to be all right because he was a strong, healthy boy.

'We're taking you to Addenbrooke's Hospital,' she said. 'It's in Cambridge. It's not far.'

When they pulled into the bay at the hospital and the driver cut the engine, the paramedic leant in closer. Daniel squirmed, trying to grab her hand, because he wanted to ask again what had happened to his father, but he was too weak and the mask was still on his face anyway. All he could really do was stare at his panicked face reflected in the woman's eyes.

*　　*　　*

The hospital staff cut away the rest of Daniel's dirty clothes and wrapped him in new blankets and heat pads. They injected more warm fluids into his body as he kept inhaling oxygen. He was taken to a ward and he drifted in and out of consciousness for the next few hours, falling into dreams where he was still underground with the water flowing beside him. Sometimes, when he woke up, he thought he was still there, crying out for a moment, his fingers flexing as he wondered where his phone was until his brain caught up and told him what was going on.

He recovered gradually through the day. Nurses and doctors monitored him and he began to understand what they were saying. They told him he was suffering from acute hypothermia, but that he was young and strong and was going to recover. The farmer and his wife had helped save his life by handling him very gently, knowing what not to do to make his condition worse. Daniel nodded, as both his body and his mind came back to him, as though not one single piece of him had been left underground.

Eventually, he found enough strength to ask a nurse where his father was and she bent close and whispered to him. 'They found him. He's here in the hospital too. That's all I can tell you though. Wait until you're stronger.'

But it was enough for Daniel and he nodded and said thank you because knowing such a thing made his heart glow, and the warmth coming off it was stronger than anything the doctors or nurses had given him to help him get better.

Later in the afternoon, he felt strong enough to sit up and he inspected the dressings that had been applied to the cuts on his arms and legs. There were bruises like blooms of lichen on his white skin.

Soon the IV line was removed and Daniel lay on the bed in his gown, sipping soup, its heat turning his stomach golden.

No one told him anything he didn't know already. That he was lucky to be alive. That he had no broken bones, but was battered and bruised and still recovering from being hypothermic. That he needed time to rest and recover. He asked again about his father, but no one said anything more than the nurse had told him before. Finally, when the consultant and nurses had run out of things to examine and questions to ask and forms to fill in, Daniel swung his legs round and stood up beside his bed, wobbly as a newborn lamb, and stared at them.

'If you don't tell me what I want to know about my dad,' he said, 'I'm going to walk through this hospital shouting until I find him.'

The silence deepened. But Daniel kept staring. And then the consultant helped him out of the cubicle around his bed and on through the stares and the whispers in the rest of the ward.

They walked slowly down corridors, Daniel's ill-fitting hospital slippers slapping the floor. When they passed a ward with its double doors open, Daniel saw elderly patients frocked in green tunics, like some weird cult seeing out its end of days together.

They came to a quiet corner of the hospital and the doctor spoke into an intercom on the wall and they were buzzed through. Then on into a ward of eight single rooms linked in an octagon, each one with floor-to-ceiling glass that faced on to a nurse at her station in the centre, light from her desk lamp splashing on to the paperwork piled in front of her.

Standing beside a door to one of the rooms, Daniel could see through the glass that somebody was lying in a bed, their two feet like tiny tent poles beneath the sheet.

Before he could ask anything, the consultant pushed the handle and waited for him to go in.

His father was lying, tubed and silent, wearing a white smock just like Daniel's, his arms resting on top of the sheet. His head was bandaged. A ventilator was breathing for him.

Daniel touched the top of his father's hand and felt the warmth coming off it.

'He's been placed in an induced coma,' said the consultant. 'That means he's being kept asleep for now. Your father needed life-saving surgery because his brain was bleeding and now it has to have time to recover. The team on the ward here will be able to tell you more.'

Daniel squeezed his father's hand harder. 'Can he hear us?'

The consultant shook her head. 'He's heavily sedated. Daniel, your father is very poorly. Who would you like us to contact? There doesn't seem—'

'There's just us.'

'No other relatives?'

'Only my aunt. But she lives in America and I've never met her. My dad doesn't speak to her because they fell out, so I don't think she'd come. Can I stay with him for a bit now?'

The consultant was about to ask something else, but then she just nodded. 'For a little while. You need to rest as well. Get yourself stronger too.'

When the consultant closed the door, Daniel looked round, shocked by the gentle click.

'Dad?' The walls began fraying at the edges of Daniel's eyes because it was always his father who had told him about the important things. 'Dad, I'm here. But I don't know how.'

12

When the nurse from the station opened the door, Daniel was curled up asleep on his father's bed, twitching like a dog in its dreaming. She stood watching because she didn't have the heart to wake him up.

But then he cried out, clicking his teeth together, catching the cuts on his lips and scattering gobbets of blood over the sheet where they bloomed like tiny roses around him. When he woke himself up, the nurse hugged him as hard as she dared, feeling his heart thumping against her chest.

'It was just a dream, Daniel. You're safe now. You came back.'

He looked at her with big, blinking eyes, sucking up the blood from between his teeth, nodding as he remembered where he was.

His father had not moved.

Not one centimetre.

Daniel screwed up his face. Pushed knuckles into his eyes to stop himself crying. 'Do you think he's going to be OK?'

'Daniel, when a patient like your father turns up unconscious, there's no way of knowing early on if they're going to make a full recovery or not. All we can do is wait and see what happens. He'll be kept sedated for now, in what we call an induced coma, to help give his brain time to recover. When the doctors think it's time to try and wake him up, we'll start to know more about his condition.'

'We were supposed to be going camping. And the last thing I said was I hated him because I didn't want to go. I wanted to stay at home and be on my stupid PlayStation.'

'What happened wasn't your fault, Daniel.'

'Then why did it happen?'

The nurse shook her head, unsure what to say. She took hold of one of Daniel's hands and ran her thumbs across his palm, stroking the skin as though reading a secret in the lines.

'When I heard you'd been found, I thought it was payback for all the kids who've gone missing in the world, for the ones who never got to grow up. I said to myself, "Finally, the world's given us one back." And, even though it's still waiting on what to do with your father, I'm hoping it's going to bring him back too.'

Daniel thought about what she was saying. 'I've got to wait and hope he gets better, haven't I?' He wiped his eyes when he felt them getting hot again. 'But . . .' He paused until he was ready to try a second time, his voice stuttering as he spoke. 'But . . . how do I do that?'

The nurse hugged him close and whispered to him. 'I know how hard it'll be. I do. But you're one of the bravest people I've ever met, and I should know because you get to be an expert about a thing like that working here.'

The Fit

13

In those few days afterwards, staying in the hospital and growing stronger, the corridors were a strange comfort to Daniel. White and bright and dry with signs that took him wherever he wanted to go. He mapped them, and the walkways and stairways that connected them, by heart, grateful he could never become lost, always returning to his father and sitting with him whenever he was allowed. Whispering to him that he was there. Stroking his arms. Helping to wash his hands in a bowl of warm water after the nurse had shown him how.

He noticed the doctors and nurses nodding when they passed him in the corridors. Occasionally, they paused and asked how he was. Patients did too. Sometimes those who looked the most ill touched his arm as they spoke to him, as though he was a charm that might bring them good luck.

Daniel smiled it off at first.

But, on the morning of the third day after arriving in the hospital, he passed by the shop on the ground floor and stopped when he saw the newspapers calling his survival a 'miracle'. The word was written in a headline next to his photo, and the longer he stopped to look at it, the more it sent his mind whirring. When a man bent down to ask if he was all right, Daniel reeled away, flushed with embarrassment, until the corridors were winding him back exactly where he wanted to go.

He sat by his father's bed in his hospital dressing gown, then closed his eyes and asked for another miracle. Over and over he repeated it inside his head, like a prayer, or a piece of magic that would only work if he really believed in it, trying to remember exactly how he had asked for help underground.

But, when he looked, nothing had changed. His father was still lying there in exactly the same position. Eyes closed. The ventilator inflating his lungs, then sucking them small.

Daniel studied the small undulations in the rubber floor, trying to imagine how many people had walked in and out of this particular room and what their stories were.

'I hate seeing you like this,' he said quietly. 'I'm scared you won't wake up and be like you were, that things aren't ever going to be the same again.'

Daniel leant forward in his chair until he could see the pores in his father's nose. 'You have to make sure you get better,' he whispered. 'Please. I don't know what to do if you don't. I don't know how long I'll be staying here or what'll happen when I go home. The social worker who came to see me yesterday was talking about getting in contact with Aunt Jane.'

When the door opened, Daniel sat back abruptly in the plastic chair. But it wasn't a nurse or a doctor. It was a man, wearing a dark, single-breasted suit, with wide turn-ups resting on the laces of his brown shoes. Beneath his jacket was a white shirt and a dirty yellow tie, dangling like a strip of flypaper as he set his black brief-case on the grey rubber floor where it stood like a low headstone.

14

'It's Daniel, isn't it? We met downstairs in the shop.'
The man held up one of the newspapers and tapped
his finger beside Daniel's picture on the front page. 'I
didn't mean to frighten you earlier.' Daniel couldn't
remember anything about the face that had bent down
and looked into his. 'You were busy chewing things
over. I understand.' And the man smiled as though he
could see right inside Daniel, at what he was really
thinking.

Daniel watched the tops of his feet winking in their
hospital slippers as he thought about leaving. But the
nurse had vanished from her station, and abandoning
his father with someone he didn't know felt wrong,
however ordinary the man might look in his suit, his
dark hair flecked with grey. Like any businessman who
had just stepped off a train.

'Do you know my dad from work? Is that why the

nurse let you into the ward? Are you an accountant like him?'

The man just smiled. 'How's your father doing?'

'No change.'

'No worse then.' And the man grinned as though it was the best news in the world. 'I'm sure he's going to be fine, Daniel.'

'Not even the doctors know that yet.' Daniel took hold of his father's hand quickly, afraid of having said something not meant to be heard.

'It was a terrible thing to happen to you both. You must have been very scared down there in the dark.'

Daniel nodded and pressed his hands together, making his fingers click.

The man placed the newspaper down on the bed and Daniel shook his head at the headline.

'It wasn't a miracle,' he said.

'How do you know?'

'Because what was the point if it was?' Daniel glanced at his father's pale face. Not a flicker.

'Actually, I have a theory about that that I wanted to talk to you about,' replied the man, producing a business card from the inside pocket of his jacket and holding it out between two fingers as slender as chicken bones.

Daniel reached forward and took the card. Written in fine black print was:

'I'm retired now,' said Lawson. 'But I'm very interested in speaking to you about what happened. If you turn the card over—'

But Daniel tore the card in half and threw the pieces at the bin. Lawson just kept staring at the boy, as if nothing had happened at all.

'I think you should leave,' said Daniel. 'My dad isn't into God. Neither am I. It was luck I got out, that's all.'

Lawson shook his head. 'I think you might have been rescued . . . saved, to go on and do things you could never have dreamt of being able to do before.'

'I'll call for the nurse,' warned Daniel, stretching out a hand for the bell beside the bed. But, before he could reach it, a golden spot of heat blossomed suddenly behind his ribs, making him stop. It was ticklish, not uncomfortable or painful, but odd enough to make a hand fly to his chest in a panic and he looked up at Lawson to tell him that something was wrong. But the man was smiling, nodding gently as if he already knew. His body was straining slightly, the muscles around his eyes twitching.

'The talent you have is very powerful, Daniel. I saw it downstairs in the shop, as bright as a star inside you. I can look right into a person and see things about them. That's why I know what happened to you down there in the dark. I know you asked to be saved, that you whispered to the rock you were lying on and told it you wanted to grow up and be someone. I also know you scratched a word on it too, which none of the newspapers have mentioned. I wrote it down on the back of that business card after we met downstairs so you'd believe me.' He gestured at the two pieces on the floor.

Daniel's fingers pressed harder on his chest because he wanted to touch the wonderful golden heat inside him. 'Who are you?' he whispered.

'A man with my own talents too. Daniel, there's so much more to the world than people realize but I'm willing to show you everything I know. We have a chance to make the fit, you and I.' He glanced at the door, head cocked as though listening to something outside the room. 'I think I can show you what I mean, just a flavour, if you'll let me.'

Before Daniel could ask anything more, Lawson's face began to tighten and, as it did so, the boy felt the golden spot inside his chest expand, making him gasp, but not from pain because the sensation was too calm and gentle for that. He felt light-headed. Relaxed. All the tension that had been in his neck and shoulders melted away.

'Can you hear them?' asked Lawson, the muscles in his face twitching and his brow lit by a sheen of sweat. 'Tell me if you can.'

Daniel nodded when he heard the distant sound of voices somewhere inside him. 'Who are they? What's going on?'

'They'll be here in a few minutes. They're coming to see you and your father to tell you what's going to happen next. I know that because your talent allows me to see and know things that my own gifts wouldn't ordinarily allow.'

As the voices grew louder, Daniel began to feel dizzy. He started to panic. Shook his head. 'I don't like it. Stop it. Please. It feels too strange. I'm scared.' As his fear grew, he felt the warm golden spot in his chest begin to dim.

Suddenly, the strain in Lawson's face eased and the sound of the voices inside Daniel disappeared, and the heat in his chest vanished, leaving a cold dark spot.

Lawson was already picking up his briefcase and heading for the door as Daniel began to start thinking for himself again. Lawson turned and looked at the boy before he left. 'Daniel, if we're to make the best fit we can then it's up to you. You're going to have to trust me, open your heart to me. The fit can only work properly if two people want to work together. You and I have the chance of doing incredible things, perhaps even helping your father. That's what you want most of all, isn't it, to help him? Making a fit might be the only way. But it's up to you to make it happen.'

The door closed with a *thunk* and Daniel heard Lawson's footsteps ticking quickly over the tiled floor. Gradually fading. By the time they were gone, Daniel felt strong enough to stand, and he pulled his dressing gown closer and walked a few wobbly paces until he was bending down and picking up the two pieces of Lawson's business card. He laid them face down on a small table in the corner of the room, spelling out a single word written in black ink on the back:

HELP

Daniel kept staring at the word on the torn bits of card because it looked like he had scrawled it there in his own hand for a second time.

Thoughts clicked and ticked.

He was only dimly aware of the door opening again as he put his hand to his chest, wishing for the cold, empty spot beneath his ribs to be warm again, wondering how Lawson had done that.

He thought he heard someone saying his name.

When a hand touched his shoulder, Daniel flinched and gripped the table. Something sweet and lemony prickled his nose as he looked round into the face of a middle-aged woman.

'Daniel?' she said with an American twang in her voice. He opened his mouth and then closed it. 'Daniel, I'm Jane. Your aunt.' But all he could think about was Lawson. About the questions he had for the man. 'Daniel, what's the matter? Are you feeling ill?'

'Nothing. Please, I want to go.' He swept up the

pieces of Lawson's card from the table into a cupped hand. But when he tried to walk away his aunt grabbed his arm, staring at him with grey eyes that looked like tiny rings of granite drilled through from the inside.

'But I've just got here. Don't you have anything to say to me? I've come from the other side of the world. From California. To look after you.'

Daniel thought about that.

'But you and Dad hate each other. I've told everyone at the hospital that.'

His aunt glanced at the doctor and the nurse standing by the door and then took Daniel's hand in hers. She squeezed his fingers and he squeezed back, but only because he wanted all this now to be a dream, so he could wake up.

But he didn't.

'I know you're upset,' said his aunt. 'That we don't know each other too well because of what's gone on between your father and me. But I'm the only family you have. And right now you need someone looking out for you. So how do you feel about me taking you home? The doctors think you're well enough. I bought you some clothes at the airport because I came here as soon as I landed. We'll come visit your father every day, I promise.' And she kept staring at Daniel, waiting for him to say yes as she felt his fingers squeezing harder and harder.

15

'There's nothing to be scared of,' said his aunt as she drove the rental car.

'I'm OK,' said Daniel, unhooking his hands from the edge of the seat and flexing his palms pink again. But when he stared at the road ahead he imagined it falling away, remembering how the sinkhole had opened like a magic trick. 'I don't know what's happened to our car,' he said when he realized his aunt was still glancing over at him and trying to drive at the same time. 'Where all our things have gone.'

She nodded and smiled and cooed that she would buy him anything he needed.

Daniel wound down the window to keep himself cool and breathed in the day, all the sounds and the smells and the sunshine, until he was calm and clear-headed.

'I want to know more,' he whispered into the world. 'About the fit and what to do.'

But there was only the wind in his ears.

16

'I know we're like strangers right now,' said his aunt, dumping her bags in the hallway, 'so we're going to have to take it a day at a time. We're flesh and blood. We must have things in common.'

But it didn't seem like it, not when she opened her arms to him and they hugged, their elbows bumping awkwardly and Daniel treading on her toes.

'Now,' she said, fixing him with her pale grey eyes, 'it must feel good to be home at least.'

Daniel took a deep breath, then let it out and nodded. But there was a photograph of his father on the dresser and when he caught sight of it he couldn't look away.

His aunt clucked like a hen. She steered him round to look at her. 'Your father's almost as tough as me,' she said and smiled. Daniel nodded, but his brain was ticking faster and faster as he stared at her. He didn't know who she was, this woman who said she was *tough*. He had never met her before in his life and now here she was, standing in his house, because the sinkhole had opened and the world had changed.

'Daniel? What's wrong?'

'Dad always said . . .' He stopped and thought about it. 'Dad always *says* that you and Mum were identical twins, but only on the outside.'

His aunt shifted in her flat black pumps, the leather seams creaking. 'Whatever your father's told you about me and your mother can't be all true.'

'Why not?'

'Because you've only heard his side of the story.'

Daniel thought about that. He heaved up her bags over his shoulder. 'I'll put these in the spare room for you,' he said. But she caught him by the arm.

'That's a nice photo of your mother.' She pointed at another photograph on the dresser, smiling as if remembering a younger, happier version of herself. And for a moment Daniel looked at the picture . . .

. . . and then at his aunt . . .

. . . and back again . . .

'When was it taken?' she asked.

'Just after they met,' he said, heaving her bags higher and heading for the stairs. 'When they were still at college. Dad told me she came top in every class.'

'I could tell you things too, you know. I knew your mother for the whole of her life.'

She watched him pounding up the stairs, her mouth opening as if to say something.

Then closing without a sound.

17

After seeing her room, his aunt knocked on Daniel's bedroom door and asked for a tour of the house. But Daniel said he was tired, one hand drumming his chest, his mind on his father and the strange man Lawson. So, when she insisted, he walked her round as fast as he could, starting upstairs.

She carried a notebook, filling a page with spidery writing as she clucked her displeasure at the state of the ancient boiler, and wondered how his father had let the damp in the bathroom spread so much in one corner.

But she just nodded and smiled faintly when Daniel could not bear to open his father's bedroom door.

'I know it must feel very strange without him here,' she said and Daniel could only nod and look at the floor. The shirt and chinos his aunt had bought for him at the airport felt tight and uncomfortable. They weren't the sort of thing he would have worn at all, and he wanted to rip them off and change into his own T-shirt and jeans. He wanted to open all the windows in the house too and flush out the smell of her lemony perfume.

He took her downstairs, through the dining room and living room, wafting his hand about and barely saying a word. She watched him in the kitchen, opening and closing the drawers so quickly the cutlery crashed about, yanking the cupboard doors open and then slapping them shut.

'There, we're done,' he said. 'I'm going to my room now.'

'How about we get some dinner?' she suggested, looking at her watch.

'I'm not hungry.'

'Daniel, you've been on hospital food for the last few days.' She took a breath and folded her arms. 'I know it's hard. I know it is. It's all very different for me too. But I want you to know you can tell me anything, anytime. I'll listen. I thought we could sit down and eat and talk about practical matters to start with. How things are going to work until . . .' She paused, tapping her foot as if annoyed with herself for not saying the right thing. 'I mean, how things are going to work for now.'

Daniel's fingers played with the two pieces of Lawson's business card hidden in his trouser pocket. He was desperate to know more about the man and what he had done in his father's hospital room. The warm golden glow that had appeared as if by magic in Daniel's chest was the first time he had felt anything good in the last few days. He wanted to feel it again. He wanted to know what Lawson had meant by the fit and what it could do.

'How about a takeaway then?' he suggested to his aunt. 'Me and Dad use that Indian all the time.' And Daniel pointed at a menu pinned to the refrigerator by a silver star. 'It's a twenty-minute drive, but it's worth it. I'll stay here and hold the fort.'

'Isn't there anything nearer?'

'I bet you haven't had a decent curry in years. Not in California. The rental car has a satnav, so if we put in the postcode it'll take you straight there. I can ring ahead with the order. I know exactly what I want.'

His aunt chewed her lip as she stared at him for a moment. And then she flipped her notebook shut and clipped the pen on to the white spiral binding at the side. 'If that's what you want then of course I'll go.'

He watched her pluck the menu from the refrigerator door and scrutinize it. 'Tandoori king prawns and pilau rice for me,' she said as she pinned the menu back under the star and turned round. 'You're sure you'll be OK?'

Daniel nodded. 'Thanks,' he said.

'You want some time alone, I understand.'

'No, I mean for flying all that way.'

As she picked up her handbag from the kitchen work-top, she smiled. 'Daniel, like I said, we're family.'

18

Daniel laid out both pieces of Lawson's card on the desk in his bedroom, staring at the word ⧵ℇⵏ↾. It was as though the man had reached inside his head where all his secrets were hidden. When he turned the pieces over, Daniel realized there was only Lawson's name, no address or telephone number or email.

'Hello?' whispered Daniel in the quiet. 'Reverend Lawson? Are you there?' But there was no reply. 'How am I supposed to open my heart? What do I do to show you I want to make the fit?'

Ever since Lawson had left the hospital room, there had been an empty space inside Daniel, cold and dark, unknown to him before. But Lawson had known about it and he had mentioned helping Daniel's father too. Somehow, the strange man had given him hope about his father that no one at the hospital had been able to provide.

Daniel laid his hands one on top of the other over his ribcage, trying to feel for something different in his chest. But there was just bone and gristle and the beating of his heart.

When he closed his eyes, all he could see was a black that was bottomless, into which he could fall forever. He forced himself to keep staring into it, as though it was a test to face the dark again, as he tried searching for what was different inside him. His eyes kept popping open at first, whenever he was spooked by noises in the walls, afraid the world would disappear if he wasn't watching out for it and he would find himself back underground. At the hospital there had always been a gentle hum of voices, and the sounds of people doing things to reassure him, so it was scary closing his eyes now that he was on his own in the empty house. He kept remembering how cold it had been in the dark too, and a chill crept stealthily over his arms and up his neck. Finding that it was too difficult to ignore, he wrapped his duvet about him and sat in his desk chair until gradually he got used to staring into the void, reassuring himself he was still above ground, that being on his own was OK.

He sat still and quiet for some time, looking inside himself for any clue. But, when rain started pattering against the bedroom window, Daniel struggled to keep his eyes shut tight. The burble in the guttering outside

66

made him gasp and tremble, reminding him of the sounds of the underground stream, and his eyelids flew open of their own accord.

His aunt was standing in the doorway, her damp hair shining. 'I knocked,' she said softly, as if the rain had washed most of her voice away. 'When you didn't answer I thought you might be asleep.'

She stood waiting for Daniel to say something, but he didn't. When she saw the pieces of Lawson's card on the desk, spelling out the man's name, she studied it for a moment and then nodded towards the stairs. 'Dinner,' she said, before disappearing back on to the landing.

Daniel sat for a moment longer, until the rain began pounding the windows, and then he sloughed the duvet on to the floor and quickly switched off the light, and followed the warm waft of curry coming up the stairs.

19

After his aunt had taken a sleeping pill and gone to bed to try and battle her jet lag, Daniel googled Lawson, but found nothing online about the man. As his mind wandered, Daniel surfed the Internet, clicking the mouse, trying to find out anything about the fit Lawson had mentioned and what it might be. But there was no explanation of the term that seemed to match what he was looking for.

He had Facebook messages from people he knew at school asking if he was all right. Some of them had posted pictures of the newspaper headlines and YouTube news clips of the sinkhole. A message pinged through from his best friend Bennett saying he would be back from holiday in a couple of days so they could meet up then.

When Daniel typed the words 'induced coma' into the search engine, his finger hovered over the return key as his mind ticked over. And then he deleted all the text and logged off.

After shutting the computer down, Daniel's mind was too alert for sleeping, like something hard and brightly polished, so he paced round his room with the light on. When he stopped he found himself staring at the PlayStation on the shelf beneath the TV screen. He took a tartan blanket from the chair in the corner and covered the console with it.

When the landline rang, Daniel rushed out to the phone on the landing to answer it, thinking it might be the hospital. But a rough form of English conjured itself out of the crackle on the line, pleading with him to pray for a sick relative, saying he had been blessed. Daniel listened, trying to interrupt, not knowing what to say, before giving up and clicking the phone back down.

The phone rang again before he had reached his bedroom door and when he answered the line was too distant and crackly to hear much of anything except that it was the same voice as before.

When it rang a third time, he clicked it off quickly as his aunt emerged on to the landing, hugging her nightie round her.

'They're just crank calls,' said Daniel as the phones started ringing again. 'I'll pull out the point.'

He disconnected the phone in the kitchen and the one in the hall at the bottom of the stairs, but he soon realized that the main point was in his father's bedroom. He stood in front of the door for some time, his hand resting on the handle. But, when he heard the phone start to ring again, he walked straight in and yanked out the cord and stood there, breathless in the silence.

His father could have been away on a business trip or staying with a friend. When Daniel thought of that, something in his heart trembled and broke and it felt like angry red drops were rattling down inside him, spreading into the soles of his bare feet, making the carpet hotter and hotter.

A fly was lying dead on its back on the windowsill, lit by the street lights. Daniel picked it up and dropped it into the bin, cursing it for being there, for dying in that room, then reassuring himself it meant nothing at all. But whisperings started up in his head, telling him it was no coincidence, that it was an omen of what was to come for his father, and to drown them out he plucked a tissue from a box on the dresser and wiped down the dust from the windowsill, lobbing it like a dirty snowball into the bin as well.

But the whispers were still there.

He turned on the light and started cleaning everything he could find. Peeling off dust in woolly strands from the blinds. Wiping down the chest of drawers and the bedside table and the top of the headboard. He went into the bathroom and cleaned the basin and then the bath. He rinsed the toilet bowl with bleach, turning the water into a tiny blue lagoon.

He didn't want to stop. But, eventually, there was

nothing left for him to do and crying was the only way to drown the whispers out.

He lay down on his father's bed and sobbed into the pillows, inhaling the faint notes of aftershave left on the linen.

After he had finished, it seemed enough just to lie there in the quiet, being as close to his father as he could be for now, remembering all the good things they had done, until a memory from long ago came back to him which felt very different in a way Daniel had never thought of it before . . .

. . . Standing with his father on a vast moor, watching a peregrine falcon fold its wings and fall out of the blue sky like a grey droplet and flatten into the purple heads of heather . . .

. . . And his hand creeping into his father's as the bird rose again, a baby rabbit hooked in its talons, the soft fur catching fire in the sunlight as the rabbit screamed.

It was difficult for Daniel to fall asleep. So he wrote down every word that described how he was feeling on the notepad his father kept on the bedside table for his 'wide-awake' moments in the middle of the night. To help him, Daniel remembered what their lives had been like together. All the sounds and the colours. The arguments and the smiles. The love and affection. The down days. The up days. And the somewhere in between. It was only when the page had become so black with ink that the words could not be read that he managed to fall asleep, as if some poison had been drawn out and put on paper.

Daniel dreamt about meeting Lawson on the doorstep of a 1940s, red-brick house set back from a quiet lane, surrounded by fields of wheat.

'What's the fit?' asked Daniel in a voice that was buttery, melting in the warm breeze, as he stood looking at Lawson.

'Do you really want to know?' whispered Lawson.

'Yes. I've opened my heart like you wanted.' Daniel held up the notepad to show him, the page black with words which began to peel off from the paper and float around them like rooks swirling, startled from the trees.

And, when Lawson had read every word, he leant forward and whispered to Daniel the address at which he lived.

When Daniel woke up in the morning, he knew it had been a dream and yet not a dream too because he could remember the address quite clearly.

He wrote it on a fresh page of the notepad and stared at it with a sense of comfort he had not known since before the sinkhole had opened and his world had changed. Somehow, he was certain that everything that had happened with Lawson the day before at the hospital was finally going to be explained.

20

When Daniel remembered that both their bikes had
gone to the shop for a service, he looked out his dad's
old one. It was tied to the wall of the shed by cobwebs
that crackled when they tore. The chain was stiff, golden
with rust, and the gear cassette at the rear looked like
the bloom of some long-dead flower.

He found an oil can on a shelf in the shed and eased
the upturned bicycle back to life in the garden until the
wheel was turning like a spinning wheel as he wound
the peddles round.

'Where are you off to?' asked his aunt as she stood by
the back door, arms folded, the morning sun pooling on
her auburn hair in patches.

'Bennett's. He's my best friend.'

'Really? Didn't he want to come here?'

'No.'

'After all you've been through?'

Daniel didn't know what to say to that.

'Daniel, where are you really going? We need to sit down and sort things out. Go shopping. What about going to see your father?'

'We'll go later. I need to go to Bennett's first,' he said again, more urgently.

'Wait there,' she said, ducking back into the kitchen. She reappeared, holding out three twenty-pound notes. 'In case you get hungry or see anything you want. If you need a new wallet then we can choose one along with anything else you lost in the car. I thought we could make a list before we go shopping.'

'Sure,' said Daniel. 'Thanks.' He took the notes and put them in his pocket.

He turned round, wheeling the bike over the grass towards the door in the fence. When he lifted the latch and glanced back, his aunt was still standing in the doorway, watching him. For a minute, he imagined her as someone else, not the person his dad had told him about. And then Daniel whispered to himself that she wasn't that person at all and went on his way.

21

Lawson's house was just how Daniel had dreamt it: a 1940s red-brick affair, standing on its own about a mile outside Cambridge down a potholed lane. Fields of tall golden wheat shimmered all around it.

Daniel opened the gate and wheeled his bike down the concrete path. Through the front window he could see what the house was like inside. Tidy. But tired. There was a sofa and two armchairs, all covered in a severe grey fabric that made the seats look hard and uncomfortable, as if designed to make a person sit upright. The arms were stripped down to bare wooden struts. The wallpaper was densely patterned with precise rainbow semicircles, geometrically arranged one behind the other in rows, seemingly overlapping like fish scales.

The front door opened before he had time to knock and his hand took fright and retreated, his arm upright like a cobra ready to strike. Lawson beamed as if he had been expecting him.

'What's happened to me?' Daniel asked immediately. 'What's the fit?'

Lawson beckoned Daniel into the hallway. 'You can leave the bike outside,' he said. 'It's safe. No one ever comes down here.' But Daniel stood his ground. Lawson squinted in the daylight as if he had just awoken from a long sleep. 'The best way to explain it is to show you.' He backed away from the doorway and held out a hand again. 'Please.'

'You said we could help my dad?'

But Lawson just kept his hand out. 'Please,' he said again. 'I promise I'll show you what I know.'

Daniel felt the sunlight on the back of his neck, and it seemed all the warmer as he looked into the cool, dim hallway.

He rested the bike against the red-brick wall and then his feet were moving, stepping into the house, taking him with them because they knew he was desperate to know more.

22

The house smelt vaguely of incense, a smell that grew stronger as Daniel stood in the sitting room and watched Lawson light a series of white candles, then draw the thick patterned curtains, making the walls shrink in the stuttering light.

'Your talent,' said Lawson, 'can only be used with someone else, somebody who has their own talents too.'

'What's inside me?' asked Daniel. 'Where has it come from?'

'It's something you were born with, like me. My own capabilities began to surface in adolescence too.' Lawson blew out the last match and tossed it into the empty fireplace. 'It could be that the trauma of what's recently happened to you acted as a trigger to release it. Whatever the reason for its appearance, you're very lucky. Some people think we're all born with abilities, which only a few of us are lucky enough to get the chance to use. Daniel, would you like me to show you your particular talent? Tell you more about what's inside you?'

'Yes.'

Lawson nodded and closed his eyes and began to breathe more deeply, making the little flames around them flutter. He pursed his lips as if he was about to whistle and then blew out a breath. All the candles went out together, plunging the room into darkness.

Daniel gasped as the dark crowded round him, pushing at him, trying to creep down his throat and into his ears.

'I know how scared you were in the dark,' whispered Lawson. 'But there's no need to be now. I'm here to help you. You're quite safe here.'

A faint orange light spread slowly round the room as the wire filament in the naked bulb hanging above them began to warm. It was bright enough that Daniel could just see the shapes of the furniture and the dark squares of pictures in their frames on the walls.

Lawson was standing upright, his eyes like holes, until gradually the light grew stronger and pushed back the dark. He blinked and looked down at Daniel, his bony white fingers outstretched like a wizard about to cast a spell.

'I'm a psychic, with just the barest of telekinetic powers too to make things happen.' And he wafted a hand at the bulb and the still smoking candles. 'My talents mainly give me the ability to see things other people can't. It lights me up just like that light bulb when I hit the switch inside me. But if I'm the bulb, Daniel, then you're the electric wire, the power that can make me burn brighter than I'd ever imagined. That's what making the fit means: two people connecting and combining to do wonderful things. I've read about it, heard whispers, but I never thought I would meet some-one like you who could make it happen. We need to find out more. Explore little by little what we can do together.'

Lawson's face began to tense and Daniel immedi-ately felt a sensation in his chest, like a butterfly trapped behind his ribs. It shifted for a moment and then settled, warming one small spot.

'Can you feel what's different?' asked Lawson.

'Yes.'

'Now let me use your talent. Let me see what I can do with it. Don't be afraid like last time in the hospital. Don't panic and shut me out. You have to trust me. It's up to you to make the fit happen.'

Lawson raised a hand and pointed at the light bulb, his hand shaking. Daniel felt the warmth growing gently in his chest and he told himself not to panic. Little by little, it grew stronger and then he gasped as the bulb began to rise, the white cord from which it was hanging bending to form a loop through which the light bulb itself passed, before dropping down and creating a simple knot in the cord. Still lit, the bulb swayed slightly, hanging a few centimetres higher than before, sending the dark corners of the room bobbing up and down.

Lawson lowered his hand. He was breathing heavily and stumbled a few steps back into the arm of the sofa behind him and perched there, recovering, as if having expended a great amount of effort.

Daniel felt his jaw and throat relax, and he began to breathe more deeply too. His mind was sharp and bright, like some dial had been turned up, sensing the secret hollow in his chest that Lawson had filled with a golden heat. But it was growing cold already. He put a hand against his ribs to try and make a difference, but the warmth from his palm only sat on the surface of his chest, the space inside him somewhere he could not touch.

But somehow Lawson had reached it.

'You see?' said Lawson, pointing at the bulb, his breathing more normal again. 'You see what we can do together? How we can make the fit? Making an object move without touching it is something I've always struggled to do. And now I've done it easily because you let me. The fit might allow us to do anything we want the more we explore it.'

'Can we help my dad like you said?' asked Daniel. 'Could we really do that too?'

'I'd like to think so, Daniel. I really would. If we can make a good fit then we might well be able to do anything we want.'

'I want to try again. I want to see what else we can do.'

'Give me a moment,' said Lawson, nodding up at the bulb. 'What we just did took something out of me.' He wiped his glistening brow and smoothed back his peppery hair, patting its damp strands down. There were dark half-moons under the arms of his bright blue shirt.

As Lawson rested, Daniel blinked at the bulb, staining his eyes with orange spots. 'Do you really think it was a miracle I was saved?' he asked.

'I know what I'd like to believe. But what feels right to you? What makes the most sense?'

'I don't know,' said Daniel. 'It's difficult to remember everything exactly the way it happened. I was very cold. I wasn't thinking straight. I don't know if it was luck I got out or not.'

Lawson nodded and wiped his brow. 'Perhaps you'll work out what to believe when we find out more about the fit and what we can do, whether we can really help your father. It might help you to decide if you were saved in order to get your life back to how it was before.'

'But why would someone save me to do that?'

'Why wouldn't they? Isn't it what you want? To have your father back?'

Daniel nodded. 'Yes, more than anything. Do you feel ready to try again and see what else we can do?'

Lawson cleared his throat. His face looked so white it was almost grey.

'I think I could do with a glass of water first,' he said. But before he could stand up they both heard a loud knocking on the front door and then it was opened with such great force it was banging against the wall. A voice shouted into the house.

'Lawson! Where are you?'

Lawson tottered to his feet as a huge, bald man wearing a tight-fitting blue suit appeared in the doorway.

He peered at them in the low orange light from the bulb, blinking, as laughter suddenly erupted behind him out of sight in the hallway. It was the sort you might hear late at night in the street and not want to glance up in case you caught the wrong person's eye.

The bald man beamed, pointed a finger at Daniel. 'You're that boy, the one who came out of the ground, the one in the papers and on the news.' He rubbed his big hands together and took a deep breath of the incense-flavoured air, observing the curtains were drawn. 'What's going on here, Lawson? What magic are you dabbling in now? Is it something to help with finding that antique flask I want, the one that's going to change my life forever?'

Lawson just stood there, his pale face glistening, as if struggling to work out what was happening and why.

'COME ON, LAWSON!' shouted the bald man, spit flying like sparks off his lips. 'I haven't got all day.' He peered at him as though trying to spot him through a fog. 'What's wrong with you?'

Lawson seemed to think about speaking and then he turned quickly and picked up the metal bin near him just in time before throwing up into the white plastic liner.

The bald man wrinkled his nose as two other large men edged their way into the living room, all three of them watching Lawson as he set the bin outside in the hallway.

'I hope it's not catching,' said the bald man, making the other two laugh. He plucked the immaculate white handkerchief from the top pocket of his jacket and threw it at Lawson.

'I'm not myself,' Lawson managed to say, after wiping his mouth. 'And the boy was actually just leaving.'

The bald man smiled. Put his arm round Daniel's shoulders and gave him a squeeze. 'No he wasn't.' He stooped like a bear to look into Daniel's eyes. 'I'm Mason. There's no need to be nervous. There's no sinkhole to fall into here. This is my house. I say what happens here and what doesn't, including Lawson paying me rent and doing what I say.'

He grinned and waved a big hand at the two suited men sitting themselves down on the sofa. 'These are my acquaintances, Frank and Jiff. Useless, both of them. Don't do anything without my say-so either. No brains, you see.' When he laughed, the two men grunted a laugh too. The one called Frank had a cleft lip, with a raggedy scar like a zipper up to the bottom of his nose.

'What are you gawping at?' muttered Frank, and Daniel looked down at the floor, his heart thumping.

Mason's black patent shoes shone like bricks of wet coal.

'So then,' he said. 'Tell me what's going on here. What's got Lawson so peaky and out of sorts?'

'I'm fine now,' said Lawson and tried handing the handkerchief back. But Mason just wrinkled his nose and shook his head.

'I think you'd best be keeping that, don't you?'

When Daniel looked at Lawson, wondering what to say, Mason steered him back round. 'Just keep your eyes on me,' said Mason quietly. 'So you can tell me what I want to know.'

Mason's giant hands cupped Daniel's shoulders like tiger's paws.

'It's the fit,' whispered Daniel.

'The what?'

'The fit.'

Mason grinned. 'And what's that then? What's the fit?' he asked, clamping his hands even tighter round Daniel's shoulders.

23

Mason clapped his hands like a giant toddler too excited to speak until he had managed to calm down.

'Daniel, this all sounds perfect,' he said. 'You're a godsend.' He winked at the boy and then produced a silver signet ring from his jacket pocket and held it up in the orange light oozing out of the naked bulb. 'I drop by so Lawson can solve a little problem of mine, because he's my go-to guy for anything I can't sort out, and discover you're here too. Daniel! The . . . the . . .' He wafted a hand in front of him as if trying to catch the right words eluding him. 'The . . . "magic boy" . . . who can help Lawson do even more wondrous things than he ever could before.'

Mason slapped his thigh so hard that Daniel flinched. 'This is all meant to be. This is . . .' he drummed a big finger against his lips, '. . . fate.' He beamed and shook his head. 'You have to marvel at the way the world works, don't you? About how things always pan out the way you need them to.' He held out the ring to Lawson. 'I want to see you two at work solving this problem of mine. I'm fascinated to see what you and the boy can do with this connection of yours. This . . . this . . .'

'. . . fit,' finished Lawson.

'Precisely. So tell me what you can about the man who owned this ring for starters, Lawson. Think of it as a test for you both. I want to know if this fit can help you find the flask you know I'm so desperate to have. Tracking it down is your top priority after all, and you've been working on it for weeks.'

But Lawson shook his head. 'Our last effort took a lot out of me. I don't know how hard we can push making the fit for now. About what might happen if we do.'

But Mason didn't seem to hear. He just grabbed Lawson's wrist, popping the fingers open, and put the silver ring in his palm, then perched himself on the seat of the armchair and took out a small black notebook and a pen.

'Lawson, you work for me, remember? Or would you like me to remind you some other way? I could ask the lads to help with that,' he said, jolting a thumb towards Frank and Jiff.

Lawson stood staring at Mason for a moment and closed his fist round the ring and shook his head. 'We'll see what we can do.'

'He's gonna nick that ring, boss,' giggled Frank, licking the scar above his lip.

'Yeah, it'll vanish right in front of our eyes,' said Jiff, who shifted about to get comfortable on the sofa. Daniel noticed that the man had a hunched back, the top portion of his spine humped like something had been stuffed beneath his jacket.

Mason raised a hand and the two men stopped laughing and the room filled with quiet. The only sound was the hum of the naked bulb above them.

Daniel looked at the floor when Mason stared at him, unsure what was going to happen or what he should do. And then he felt that warm golden sensation flicker up in his chest again.

When he looked up at Lawson, the man's white face was already strained, the little tendons standing out in his neck like lengths of cord pulled tight. Lawson nodded and managed to smile. 'Just focus on me, Daniel. Don't be scared. Let's just do what we did last time and see if I can connect with you even better than before.'

He closed his eyes. He clenched his fist harder round the ring, the knuckles shining whiter. Mutterings started rolling off his lips in whispers that could barely be heard.

Mason leant forward as if trying to listen, flipping open his notebook and readying his pen. Frank and Jiff were watching intently too.

When Lawson's voice began to rise a little louder, Daniel felt the sensation in his chest increase. Like a hummingbird flitting, caged behind his ribs. The golden shimmer inside him grew brighter and warmer, filling out the secret space even more than it had done before.

Images wafted at the corners of his eyes, drifting round the dull-lit room, vanishing if he looked too closely at them.

The body of a man, lit by a street light . . .

. . . lying in a pool of blood in a quiet road bordered by shops shuttered up for the night . . .

. . . the silver signet ring on his little finger.

Silver boot tips beside the dead man's head and then somebody's hand reaching down, the fingers hooking round the handle of a leather briefcase lying in the road.

A white car disappearing down the street into the dark.

He could hear Lawson describing these things as if he was seeing them too behind his lidded eyes. Lawson told Mason it was his money in the briefcase. That it had been taken from the man who had been wearing the silver signet ring after he had been knocked down by a white car. Mason was nodding as he listened, jotting down details in his notebook, his tongue darting out between his lips as he concentrated on what Lawson was telling him.

'Who took it, Lawson?' he asked. '*Who* took my brief-case full of money?' Lawson's face twitched harder, the muscles dancing in his cheeks, his lips bleaching as he tried to see more. 'Who was it, Lawson?' growled Mason, his pen poised. 'Tell me the number plate of this white car at least. Something I can use.'

As Lawson's voice grew louder and more garbled, repeating the things he had already said, Daniel felt the wonderful warmth in his chest start to burn and become painful. It felt like the flame from a match was being held against his skin. As Lawson's voice became more frantic, the pain worsened.

'Stop,' said Daniel. 'Stop. Something's not right.' He wasn't sure if he had said that loud enough. Or said it at all. His mouth felt like it was turned inside out. 'Something's wrong,' he said again, but all he heard was a mumble in his throat.

'What's that, boy?' asked Mason. 'What did you say?'

But Daniel ignored him, focusing on Lawson instead, who was starting to shake, one of his eyes rolling up white into his head, like a pebble had been placed in the socket.

'Let go,' said Daniel with all the strength he could muster in his voice, the pain in his chest increasing as if someone was turning up a dial. 'This feels as far as we can go.'

Lawson wiped his nose with the back of his hand and there was a tiny stripe of blood across it, wet like paint.

'Don't panic, Daniel,' he said. 'You need to keep your heart open. We need to see how much of a fit we can really make.'

'Attaboy, Lawson,' said Mason. 'Keep working it. Tell me who stole my money.'

'But something's not right,' replied Daniel, shaking his head. 'It's painful. It's not like it was before.'

'Don't shut me out,' shouted Lawson, his face waxing and waning, shining with sweat. 'Don't you want to know what we can really do? If we can help your father?'

There was a painful knocking in Daniel's forehead now. Each time he blinked, he saw Lawson's face inside him and it felt as though the man was trying to take over his body with his very being, reaching deep down into him. He could sense how scared Lawson was of Mason. How desperate he was to find out what the big, bald man wanted to know.

But, as the burning sensation in Daniel's chest became more intense, he gritted his teeth and tried to ride it out because he wanted to know what the fit could really do too, whether it might be powerful enough to bring his father back.

'I won't shut you out,' he gasped. 'I want to know. I want to see what we can do.'

Mason whooped. He muttered and swore and wiped his brow with the back of a meaty hand.

Daniel heard a strange sound starting up inside him, a clicking, like someone flicking a light switch on and off. Slow and regular at first, then steadily becoming faster and faster, until it was just a constant buzzy sound, warbling inside him. It pounded his ears like an alarm. When it stopped suddenly, without warning, Daniel felt a jolt, as if a wire had been cut, and the pain in his chest vanished immediately too, leaving just a hole again, filled with cold, gleaming dark.

Everyone in the room saw Lawson's fist explode like a grenade.

The stump of his wrist was left raw and red and white. Like something still oozing blood on a butcher's slab. The hand itself was nothing but mess on the walls and the ceiling.

Frank picked a bloody finger out of his lap and held it up, making a face to Jiff, who was laughing hysterically.

Lawson dropped to his knees and his head lolled forward on to his chest, the stump of his arm still outstretched as though being offered up for inspection. He began to shake and cough and he raised his head, and, when he opened his eyes, he smiled, apparently unaware of his missing hand.

But then, slowly, his smile reversed, becoming the mirror image of itself, and he began to shake, his cheeks draining whiter and whiter. He tried clutching his arm to his chest, cupping his remaining hand round it, below the stump, and rocking it like a baby.

'Help me,' he whispered. 'Help me.'

But no one moved as Lawson's stump pumped more blood down his arm.

'Who's got my money, Lawson?' asked Mason calmly.

Daniel *knew* that Mason's white handkerchief was on the floor beside Lawson. He *knew* he was kneeling down and picking it up. And he *knew* he was wrapping the handkerchief round the man's arm, fumbling with both ends of what was to become a simple knot to try and stem the flow of blood.

But he did not seem to own these movements. They just seemed to happen of their own accord.

As soon as it was tied, the handkerchief was already soaked, leaking crimson drops on to the floor. When Lawson put out his good arm to try and steady himself, it collapsed at the elbow as soon as he put some weight on it and he hit the carpet with a grunt. He lay on his side in the shape of a question mark, a fierce line pumping in his throat, looking up at Daniel through narrow-slitted eyes.

There was so much blood it was eating up the carpet.

And sitting in all that red was the silver signet ring.

When Mason crouched beside Daniel and touched the top of his shoulder, the boy flinched, and Mason had to grab him tight with one big hand so he didn't topple over. The man picked up the ring from the floor with a tissue he had plucked from a box on the sideboard. 'Go and get a glass of water from the kitchen,' he said softly. 'We'll ring for an ambulance.'

24

When Daniel reached up a shaking hand for a tumbler in the cabinet, his mind was scrambled with different thoughts.

There was blood on the back of his hands and he set the glass down so he could rinse them off under the cold tap. He scrubbed the skin with a washing-up brush until it was red and sore. The pain focused him down to a single thought that was clear and bright and hard, just like the tumbler beside him on the worktop catching the daylight.

He shut the kitchen door as quietly as he could and pulled out a wooden chair from the table and wedged it underneath the handle.

Go, said a voice inside him. *Run*. But Daniel made himself walk slowly to the back door and open it quietly . . .

. . . birdsong and sunshine and a long stretch of lawn.

The garden was bordered by a tall wooden fence on all sides and he searched for the best way to climb it.

'DANIEL?' shouted Mason from the hallway.

Daniel stood with his foot raised like a tightrope walker waiting for the right moment to step out on to a high wire as he looked for a way out.

'DANIEL!' came Mason's voice more urgently. 'Don't go doing anything stupid now.' Behind him the door handle wiggled vigorously, but the chair held it fast. And then a great force thumped against the door and the whole frame shuddered as the chair legs wobbled. Another crash came and two bright splinters popped out like fangs from the white painted wood around the top hinge.

Daniel spotted a compost bin positioned beside the fence and knew it was his way up and over.

'Daniel, I know who you are. Everyone does after what happened to you. And I know where your dad is. Addenbrooke's Hospital, right?'

Daniel put his foot down. The sunshine warmed his face, but he was deathly cold inside.

'I'll have to pay him a visit if you don't open this door. So let me in, little piggy, or I'll huff and I'll puff and I'll blow it right down.'

Daniel wanted to step out on to the grass. To run home back to his aunt and tell her everything. But he couldn't. Not after Mason had mentioned his father. So he pulled the back door shut and turned round and picked up the tumbler from the worktop and filled it from the tap. He carried it in a wobbly hand and pulled away the chair.

Mason was standing in the hallway, hands in his pockets. So casual was his stance, he could have been waiting for a bus. He took the tumbler, drained it and put in on the sideboard, wiping his mouth with his hand.

'Lawson's dead,' he said simply and then he turned round, making for the front door. 'You're coming with me.'

Daniel grabbed the edge of the sideboard to steady himself. He opened his mouth to ask if Lawson was really dead. About what had happened to the ambulance. But he found himself asking a different question. 'Where are we going?'

'I thought we'd visit your dad now. Say hello.' Mason opened the front door and he seemed to grow even bigger in the daylight that flooded in from outside.

Daniel walked towards him, glancing into the sitting room as he did so. Lawson was on the floor, staring up at the ceiling, not blinking. Daniel looked away quickly. His legs were nothing but air. But he managed to make it out through the open door where he drew in great looping breaths that tasted of sunlight and green leaves and warm red bricks.

'Don't worry about your mess,' said Mason, shutting the front door. 'Frank and Jiff'll clean it up.' He cupped a big hand to his ear. 'What's that?'

Daniel said nothing. Mason leant further towards him as if he was trying to hear something very quiet.

'Thank you,' whispered Daniel.

And Mason beamed. Slapped him on the shoulder.

'You're welcome.'

25

'He's being kept in a coma for now,' said Daniel as he sat beside the bed. He clutched his father's hand tight because he was afraid that death might drag him away at any moment like it had done with Lawson.

Mason nodded approvingly. 'So the papers say. I saw a piece about you both on the local news too.' He clamped a big hand round Daniel's shoulder and squeezed gently, like a caring uncle might, then leant forward to observe the calm face looking up at him from the pillow. 'I'm jealous he's getting so much rest. It's hard work being me.'

Mason slumped into the chair opposite, lifting up his feet and placing one over the other on the bed. The pale leather soles of his black shoes were dimpled with black and green marks. He smiled and waved to the nurse at her station and she looked away.

'How much do you think a nurse gets paid?' Daniel shrugged. '*Not enough* is the right answer.' And Mason sighed as if he was managing all the worries of the world.

'What do you want?' asked Daniel quietly.

'Blimey, how long have you got?' Mason laughed at his own joke and then he plucked the silver signet ring from his pocket and held it up, his right eye scrunching tight and the other one staring through it at Daniel. 'I want you to tell me where my briefcase of money is for starters.'

'I'm not like Lawson.'

'Neither of us is. Not now.' Mason turned and looked through the ring at Daniel's father like a jeweller inspecting something of great value. 'Not even your dad.'

'I didn't do anything to Lawson,' replied Daniel softly. 'It wasn't my fault.'

Mason hid the ring in a big fist. He looked around the room and then smiled and nodded as if another person was sitting to his left. 'I'm afraid I don't know what you're talking about, officer. The last time I saw Mr Lawson he was with a boy about so high with mousey brown hair. I recognized him too, you know; he was the one who fell down that sinkhole. The one in the papers. Sad business that. And with his dad too. Do anyone's head in, something like that. Least it would me. Send me la-la. I might go and see a psychic too, a charlatan like Lawson, a defrocked vicar who dabbled in the occult, to try and find some hope in such an awful situation. Anyway, officer, maybe you should speak to the boy if you're looking for Lawson.'

Mason grinned at Daniel, pleased with himself as he rubbed at an itch through his trouser leg. 'Now,' he said, 'I think that means we have an understanding, don't you?' He raised his eyebrows and waited for Daniel to say something, but the boy kept quiet. 'Marvellous. So tell me again about you and Lawson, how it worked.'

'I don't know any more than what you saw or what we told you.'

Mason licked his top front teeth like they were made of barley sugar. 'Then run it by me again. Let's see where we go from there.'

'Lawson told me we could make the fit. He said I could help him do things he hadn't done before. I don't know anything about it except there's something inside me. Right here.' Daniel tapped his chest. 'Lawson plugged into it like a power cord, and when he did I could feel it happening, warm and golden inside me.'

Mason's mouth flickered. 'And that felt good, you said.'

'Yes. Like everything felt better all of a sudden. Like the fit was something really special and meant to be.'

Mason nodded and then his eyes narrowed. 'But whatever happened to Lawson means you didn't fit as well as he thought?'

'I don't know why. One moment it was all OK and then the next it . . .' Daniel tried not to remember how it had been or what had happened to Lawson. He put his hands together to stop them shaking. 'It just shut off,' he said quietly.

Mason tutted. 'I told you Lawson was my go-to guy for the weird. The strange. Whatever you want to call it.' He raised his hands and clasped the back of his head. 'So I guess that means now you are, Daniel my boy.' When Daniel looked up at him, Mason just shrugged. 'You're going to fill the vacancy on my books.'

'But I'm not like Lawson. I told you I can't do the things he could. I can't tell you where your money is.'

'So find someone else like him. Someone who can plug into you like Lawson did. Somebody else to make a fit with, but a better one.'

'I don't know anyone like that.' Daniel felt a black panic rising in his stomach that was making it difficult to breathe. He glanced at his dad and wished he would wake up so everything could be normal again. But the machines just went on blipping and beeping and his father lay there as if nothing untoward was happening at all.

'You'll find someone,' announced Mason. 'I have every faith in you, Daniel. There are other psychics in the world. My mum was one. She did things you would never believe. And believing it all keeps me top of the pile because people in my line of business tend to be cynical about such things. Lawson was a marvel who helped me no end, bless his cotton socks.' Mason clicked his teeth as if he was remembering a favourite pet and then sat back in the chair. 'I'll give you three days to find someone else.'

Daniel shook his head. His body drooped as he turned away.

'Look at me, Daniel.' And Daniel dragged his eyes back to the man. 'You want your dad to wake up, don't you?'

'Yes.'

'And I want my money back, which means we can do a deal.'

'You can't do anything to help my dad.'

'No I can't.' Mason's big hands made a boulder in his lap. 'But *you* can keep him safe while he's lying here by working for me.' Mason smiled when Daniel's jaw began to tick. 'So that's what you're going to do. You lost me a good man, someone I relied on to help with certain things, little projects of mine. So it's only fair you take up the slack. Lawson was using his talents to search for something very special I want. An antique flask. So, as soon as you find someone to make a fit with and locate my money, then I'm hoping you can get a fix on that flask too. The money can just be a test. A way for you to learn more about this fit and how it works.

You want to know as much as you can, don't you? About this talent of yours?'

Mason braced himself against the chair and something in his spine crackled. 'Course you do. Back at the house, you and Lawson mentioned making the fit to help your father. So don't try telling me you don't want to find someone else now that Lawson's gone.'

Mason moved forward to the edge of his seat and inspected Daniel's father again, tutting and shaking his head.

'If your dad has to stay on a ventilator after the doctors try to wake him up, they'll start asking questions about what's best for him. They'll want to know what he would want to happen and talk to you about what's in his best interests. They'll listen to you. But it'll be their decision about what to do, not yours. They have the power of life and death.'

Mason sat back in his chair and grinned like a toad. 'I've seen how it happens on those documentaries on the telly. I've got a plasma screen. Fifty-two inch. You can learn anything watching that. I love tucking into a takeaway in front of it and expanding more than just my mind.' He slapped his gut. 'So how about it, you working for me for a bit? Finding my money? That antique flask too? And helping your dad. We can both get what we want, Daniel.'

The boy stared at Mason, saying nothing.

'Tell you what,' suggested Mason brightly. 'You find someone and I'll break the bad news to them, tell them they'll be working for me too, do the hard part for you. I'm good at that. Telling people what to do.'

Daniel shifted in his chair, but stayed silent.

'I'll take that as a resounding yes then, shall I?' Mason tousled Daniel's father's hair. 'You've got a good son there. Isn't that right, Daniel? You're a good lad, aren't you? Do what you're told.'

Daniel looked from Mason's grin to his father's soft white face. 'Yeah,' he said quietly. 'I'm a good lad.'

Mason nodded. And then his voice dropped. 'Stay away from Lawson's house. There's no need for you to go back there now.' He kept staring until Daniel nodded that he had understood. 'Good lad.' And Mason clapped his hands and laughed. 'See!' he shouted at Daniel's father. 'I told you!'

26

His aunt was sitting in the kitchen with a cup of tea. The sink was a bright tub of chrome. Daniel could smell the bleach. There were lilies on the old oak table, sitting in a tall green vase he had never seen before.

It was like coming back to her house not his.

'We're going to have to get you another cellphone,' she said, pulling the sleeve of her cardigan down over her watch. 'I was getting worried. You've been out all day.'

'Me and Bennett lost track of time.'

'Well, I'm glad you've got someone you can speak to. I'd worry if you didn't.'

Daniel stayed sitting at the table as she prepared supper because he did not want to be alone. He watched as she went round the kitchen, never going to the wrong cupboard or drawer for anything, which made it seem even more like her house. They talked about her work in California. She said she had her own start-up that could tick along without her so she could be in Cambridge for the whole of the rest of the summer holidays if necessary.

'What's it like there?' asked Daniel as they sat down to eat.

'Maybe you'll come see for yourself one day.'

Daniel kept asking as many questions as he could think up about her life on the other side of the world because, whenever there was a lull in the conversation, he imagined Mason peering in through the window, grinning at him, or Lawson lying on the floor beside him, the bloody stump of his arm raised.

'What's wrong,' asked his aunt when she noticed Daniel staring at his empty plate yet again.

'Nothing. I'm just tired.' He pinched a lily petal between his fingers and felt how smooth and delicate it was. 'We've never had flowers before,' he said.

His aunt just smiled and nodded and then she cleared her throat. 'I had a call from the hospital today, updating me on your father. There's been no change. But then I suppose you know that. The charge nurse said you went to see him. She said you looked so sad sitting there on your own.'

Daniel nodded, remembering how Mason had whispered something to the nurse at her station to make her laugh before handing over a fold of twenty-pound notes and telling her he wasn't really there. It made a lock click shut in his stomach, trapping everything about Mason inside him.

'Daniel, did you really see your friend today? I'm only asking because I don't want to think you can't be here with me, that you're uncomfortable with me being around.'

Daniel put his hands flat on the table to help himself breathe. 'No,' he said. 'I didn't see Bennett. I'm sorry I lied.'

'So what did you do all day?'

'I just mooched around town,' he said quietly, his toes flexing so tight inside his trainers he thought the seams might pop.

'On your own?'

Daniel nodded.

Before she could ask anything else, the phone rang and Daniel sprang up to answer it and listened for a moment, and then shouted down the line in a rage that it was nothing to do with miracles at all, that he had been cursed instead, before slamming the receiver back down in its cradle.

'I'm having the number changed,' said his aunt. 'They just keep ringing.' She poured another glass of red wine and took a sip. Cleared her throat. 'Daniel, it doesn't matter what anyone else thinks. Let people believe what they want about what happened. All that matters is you. How *you* process it. So you can start to come to terms with it all.'

'I don't know why any of it happened.'

His aunt nodded as if she understood. 'I can't even begin to imagine how terrible it must have been for you down there. But if you want to talk to me, about anything, then you can because it's not healthy keeping everything bottled up. It'll rot you on the inside. That's what bad experiences do. Hollow you out and fill you up with all the questions you can never answer.'

She reached forward and lifted up his dirty plate and stacked it on to hers. 'We're family, Daniel. We're all we've got. So we need to stick together. If you want to tell me anything, you can.'

'I don't think I'm ready to talk just yet,' he said, picking a loose thread from the edge of the tablecloth.

When Daniel clicked his bedroom door shut, he caught sight of himself in the mirror and placed his hand on his chest, trying to feel for the secret space that Lawson had shown him. But there was only the thump of his heart and his serried ribs, like the rungs of a ladder leading to somewhere mysterious inside him.

After finally falling asleep, he dreamt of a world where death was a long sleep from which everyone awoke, wide-eyed and smiling, with all the answers to how the world works and how to live peacefully and well. *You have to die to know*, they said when Daniel asked them the secret to being happy, for they had all sworn not to tell a single person the truth.

The Man
in the Mackintosh

27

Bennett was all tanned after his holiday. It looked like his teeth and the whites of his eyes had been freshly painted. He was goose-stepping over puddles on the path, making every cloud in them shimmer, as Daniel wheeled his bike beside him, talking everything through, right up to the day before with Mason.

'So?' asked Daniel when he had finished. 'What do you think?'

Bennett stopped to peer down at his reflection in a puddle, a cigarette between finger and thumb.

'What do *you* think?' asked Bennett, bending closer to the water as if expecting his reflection to answer for him. When it didn't, he sighed and shook his head and looked up at Daniel. 'That you can't tell anyone else about Mason, but then you know that already. Also, that you should be glad you're not me. Because I'm the one who's supposed to tell you everything's going to be

113

OK. But I can't do that. I can't lie. Otherwise, I wouldn't be acting like a best friend should. It wouldn't be me.'

Bennett studied his reflection in the puddle again as if waiting to see if it had anything to add, then took a final drag and flicked his cigarette away, making the water hiss. Daniel stepped back, as if the water was alive, and Bennett noticed, but said nothing as he walked on.

'There's something you can do to help,' said Daniel.

Bennett's large brown eyes grew wider beneath his fringe of black hair. 'How do you mean?'

'Come with me now, to look for some answers.'

'Where?'

'Where do you think?'

'You mean climb down into the sinkhole?'

'No, I meant go and explore where I got out.'

Bennett coughed a bluish cloud and spat a gob of phlegm that landed on the wall beside them. He watched it scrambling down the bright red bricks like some green bug. 'Do you think there'll be any answers there?'

Daniel shrugged. 'It's a place to start.'

'You mean to help with the Mason situation? With finding someone to make the fit?'

'With anything.' Daniel wafted a toe over the gap between two paving stones as if wary of stepping on it and then put his foot down beyond it. 'It's OK. You don't have to come if you don't want to.'

Bennett stopped and just stared at him, and then he peered down at the black gap between the paving stones before planting both feet across it. 'I can see why you need to go back to the place you nearly died.' Daniel didn't say a word. 'But I wouldn't know what to do if it's all too much.'

'You'd know better than anyone else.'

Bennett's lips purred as he blew out a breath.

'I'm still the same Daniel you've always known. The one you met in nursery who tried to eat your socks. I'll be OK if you come with me.'

Bennett dipped his toe into the puddle beside them and as Daniel watched the ripples it was like he was back underground. He thought he heard running water and he clutched his arms around him as a cloud passed over the sun. And Bennett noticed that Daniel was suddenly somewhere else.

'Prove it then,' he said and stepped into the puddle. The water was barely five centimetres deep. He held out his hands to Daniel. 'It's just a puddle.'

'I know.'

'So come on in, the water's divine.'

Daniel propped his bike against the wall. Closed his eyes. He took a big step and felt the water sucking round his trainers as he stepped into the puddle. When he looked again, Bennett was staring back, holding on to his hands.

'I'm supposed to go home for some sort of family food "thing" in an hour or so. Lunch? You know it?'

'Yeah, sure,' said Daniel in a rush, feeling embarrassed to have asked at all. 'I understand. That's fine.'

'*So-o-o*, in a roundabout way, I guess what I'm asking is, will there be food on this expedition of yours?' Bennett grinned.

Daniel smiled back. 'There can be.'

'I like crisps. And would there be fizzy drinks?'

'Yeah, if you want.'

'Well then, I can't say no, can I?'

The longer they stood in the cold water, the more Daniel could feel it pressing round the edges of his feet, like the puddle was trying to suck him down somewhere deep. When Bennett let go of his hands, Daniel wobbled and his friend grabbed on to his shoulder until all the ripples around them had vanished.

'I'm sorry I wasn't here when it happened,' said Bennett, lighting another cigarette and taking a drag.

'That's OK,' said Daniel. 'You were on holiday. You weren't to know what was going to happen.'

'No one ever does, do they?' said Bennett and he glanced over at the traffic going past them as if waiting to be proved right. 'You're sure though? You're not upset with me?'

116

Daniel didn't know what to say, so he nodded. He looked down at the puddle. Saw his reflection smiling back. 'I'm just glad you're here now.'

'I prefer salt and vinegar by the way,' said Bennett. 'And Diet Coke. At least a couple of cans.'

Daniel frowned and then he grinned when he realized what Bennett was talking about and stuck his hands in the pockets of his shorts, making the change inside them clink. Bennett's lips lit up in a smile too, as if the two of them were connected by an invisible current to which only they were wired.

28

They rode to the train station on their bikes and over the concourse through unamused looks to the ticket machines where they each bought a return, which the barriers swallowed and spewed back out to let them through.

The platform for the local stops was tucked away from the mainline. A single track, with two rails smoothed syrupy and golden, and between them slender-necked weeds growing out of the grey ballast between the sleepers. Pigeons shuttled back and forth across the wooden struts in the eaves above them, cooing as they went. Wary of the smack of bird shit on the platform, they walked further down and found a bench and sat soaking up the sun, staring through orange lids.

'We could go anywhere we wanted,' said Bennett with a mouth full of salt and vinegar crisps.

'We could.'

*　　*　　*

The two boys stepped off the train with their ears ringing because all the windows had been open. Even so, the carriage had still felt like an oven.

The platform was made of plain concrete with its edge striped yellow. There wasn't even a bench. Daniel watched the two carriages disappear round the bend in the track, listening until he could hear nothing except for the birds and the breeze in the trees.

When he turned round, Bennett was waiting patiently. 'Are you OK?'

'Yeah,' said Daniel.

'It's just a day trip.' Bennett held up his ticket. 'We've already paid to go back.'

Daniel felt for his own ticket in his pocket too and then nodded.

The lane wound between high hedges. Daniel stopped every now and then to get his bearings, boosting himself up on to his tiptoes as he stood on gates and stiles. Each time he stopped and thought about going back, he looked at Bennett, saying nothing, until the moment passed.

Once, standing on a five-bar gate, he watched a blue car on the horizon wending its way along the road in the shimmering distance until it disappeared behind the curve of a hill. He was about to turn round when the car reappeared, beetling back the other way. Daniel watched it, sunbeams strobing off the wing mirrors, until it vanished again, as if swallowed into the ground.

He jumped down quickly, as hard as he could, to reassure himself how firm the lane felt beneath his trainers, before they continued cycling.

'Over there,' said Daniel, pointing across a sea of wheat to a meadow and the woods beside it. The boys heaved their bikes up and over the gate and walked down a bumpy tractor channel, the wheat hissing all around them, until they emerged from the field on to the grass.

Daniel remembered how the skyline had looked in the dark when he had crawled his way out of the ground, and wiped a film of sweat from his brow. Before he could turn round and say anything, Bennett was pedalling past him, waving him on, ringing his bell as loud as he could. And Daniel followed him, scared of being left on his own with his thoughts.

The opening to the tunnel was canted at an angle of about forty-five degrees, as if the ground had found a mouth to open in an 'O' and gawp in wonder at the sky. It was cool and filled with shadow as the sun beat down.

Wooden posts had been hammered into the ground in a rickety circle all round the tunnel entrance, and up over the grassy hump that rose behind it and down the sides, and were strung with bands of new barbed wire.

120

Lying on the ground were little bouquets of faded wild flowers with notes attached. Letters and cards had been tacked to the fence posts and some were hooked to the barbs on the wire.

'You've turned this place into a shrine,' said Bennett as he scanned a letter asking for someone's daughter to be cured of cancer. Before dumping his bike down, Bennett detached the headlight and then hitched himself up over the wire, ignoring the wooden sign telling him to KEEP OUT in red painted letters. He took the few steps across the grass on the other side and crouched by the entrance, staring into the tunnel.

'It's just a hole in the ground, Dan,' he said matter-of-factly. 'And you know what's down there anyway.' He crept on through, picking his way round the boulders and rocks scattered inside the opening, and vanished.

Daniel stood listening to Bennett's shoes slipping and sliding until there was just the grass prickling beneath his feet and the wind in the wire and the sign knocking gently. He raised his arms and waited for the goose-bumps to melt in the sun. Then he climbed over the fence and edged carefully towards the tunnel.

The sound of the waterfall was just audible above his breathing.

He remembered how cold the water had been.

He peered into the cool dark mouth of the tunnel, watching the crown of Bennett's head bobbing below him. His friend was already halfway down before Daniel started to follow.

29

The chamber was lighter than he had imagined it would be in the daytime, like a church lit by low winter sunshine. The grey walls were veined with marbled white lines and pocked with deep dark hollows.

When Daniel looked up at the tunnel mouth, it seemed smaller and brighter from below, an oculus filled with sky, and around it a corona of fuzzy blue daylight.

He and Bennett could have been worshippers of some kind as they picked their way round the shoreline, the cowls of their hoodies resting on the backs of their necks.

Sometimes the din of the waterfall amplified without warning, echoing louder round the chamber, forcing the boys to raise their voices, adding to the constant noise.

Ripples skittered across the green water.

Hoops of gold moved over the walls.

A chill blew off the pool.

When Bennett pointed to a low archway in the wall that Daniel could not remember seeing before, they made their way towards it, stooping through into a much smaller chamber where they could hear each other more easily.

It was darker though, and Bennett turned on his bike light and stood it upright between two rocks, opening up a fizzy white funnel to the ceiling. The cold was nipping at their bare legs and he drew out a hip flask from one of the pockets of his cargo shorts and spun off its silver top and took a swig before handing it to Daniel.

'Whisky,' said Bennett, 'and a drop of Diet Coke.' And he winked.

Daniel took a sip. It tasted like coarse, hot sherbet when he swallowed and it lit a fuse that burned down deep into his chest. For a moment, all he could think about was the fit and how it had felt.

'It's beautiful,' said Bennett, looking back through the archway at the waterfall, the spray coming off it like dust. All around the walls bejewelled webs shimmered in the updraught as the water fell.

'Yes it is,' said Daniel.

When Bennett pointed at something behind him, Daniel turned round to look. A circle of red handprints on the wall of the small chamber they were in, and inside it six red spokes, drawn wobbly over the rock, joined to one point at the centre, like the crude design of a cartwheel.

Daniel shook his head. 'I never saw any of this.' He bent closer to look. 'How old do you think they are?'

Bennett took out his phone and played the light from the screen over the red paint and then shrugged. 'Do you think they mean anything?'

'I don't know.'

They matched their palms to the echoes of ones that had gone before, understanding nothing except the rock against their skin and how it must have felt to whoever had made the pattern.

Further round the wall they found a set of square holes.

'Think they're man-made?' asked Bennett, feeling the edge of one.

'I don't think so.' But then Daniel shrugged. 'I don't know.' He pushed a hand into one of the holes up to his elbow and his fingers came out gritty and brown and shining.

A white snail shell, blobbed like cream in the topmost corner of another hole, shone amber when the light from Bennett's phone swept across it.

They stood for some time, looking around for anything else, but eventually all that was left to do was to kick through the stones and pebbles they were standing on. Bennett lit a cigarette he had rolled on the train and blew smoke into the beam from his bike light and watched it spiral round.

'Anything else?' he asked.

Daniel turned to the archway and pointed to the rock on the shoreline. 'That was where I ended up,' he said.

'Ready to take a look?' asked Bennett.

And Daniel took a deep breath and said he was.

They sat on the rock and watched the low light being spun into golden threads on the surface of the water.

'Well?' shouted Bennett above the noise of the waterfall.

But Daniel didn't hear. He was too busy staring at the water, remembering how cold it had been. He wondered whereabouts his iPhone was lying, lost forever beneath the surface.

When Bennett touched his shoulder, Daniel almost slid off the rock, gasping as the water kissed the soles of his trainers. He looked round into Bennett's smiling face and almost swore.

When Bennett saw the word H E L P scraped on to the rock, he picked up a stone and scrawled two more words beneath it . . .

THE WORLD

'Well,' he shouted, admiring his handiwork. 'It's worth a try if someone really did help you out of here.' And he noodled the stone between his fingers as if contemplating writing a request for something else. 'Have you tried asking if there's anyone else here? If they know anything about the fit too?'

Daniel nodded. 'But maybe I should ask more loudly?'

'Be my guest.'

'*HEL-LO?*' shouted Daniel. 'Can anybody tell me what's inside me? How it works? What was the point in saving me if I don't know how to help my dad? *ANY-BODY?*'

But nobody answered back.

They sat, watching for any sign, for any clue, passing the hip flask between them. Bennett took a big slug and his eyes shone. '*We* should try and make the fit.'

Daniel looked at him, cocking his head like a little bird. 'Bennett, seriously, you've drunk too much.'

Bennett stared at him, then smiled and slowly shook his head. 'Sorry,' he said. He picked up a stone and hurled it as hard as he could and watched it land in the water with a springy, hollow sound as if it had been dropped into a deep well.

'Let's just stick to being best friends,' said Daniel and Bennett nodded.

'Yep.'

'Thanks for coming,' said Daniel.

'You are very welcome, my friend.'

And the two of them smiled at each other.

Bennett spread his arms wide and flapped himself into a standing position like some lopsided chick on a ledge and grinned.

'Maybe we need to go in,' he shouted.

Daniel shook his head as he stared into the green water. 'It's cold, trust me.'

'It'll be good for you.'

'How'd you figure that?'

'How do you know it won't be?'

Daniel's fingers hooked even tighter into the little cracks and crevices on the surface of the rock. He kept looking at the water until he realized Bennett was still staring at him, waiting for an answer. It was the sort of thing he would normally have done without even thinking about it.

'I'll be here with you,' said Bennett.

They took off their trainers and socks and left them on the shoreline, wading in until their legs were eaten up to the bottoms of their shorts, the green and blue ripples coming at them. Greasy rocks moved beneath their feet, threatening to trip them up.

'See, it's not so bad, is it?' shouted Bennett and Daniel shook his head.

'No,' he shouted back.

Bennett scanned the surface like a lifeguard.

When Daniel saw something silver, he peered through the wobbly surface of the water and saw a tiny fish gawping, fanning its fins, until it seemed to sense him watching and vanished into a deeper part of the pool.

Bennett picked off a ruby crystal of blood where he had cut his finger coming down the tunnel and dipped it into the green water and watched a faint pink starburst appear, then untangle itself into nothing. When he raised his hand, he studied the cut, as if surprised to see it still there.

'There's definitely no magic here,' he announced, chopping the surface of the water with karate hands. 'I don't think you were saved. It was luck, that's all.'

Daniel was about to nod, the whisky woozy in his head, when a shadow moved over the entrance to the tunnel and the light dimmed for a moment, like a candle flame blown flat by a draught. Spooked, he looked up as Bennett scooped up water and drank, his chin dripping and shining.

'HELLO?' shouted Daniel, cupping his hands. 'Is someone there?' A blackbird landed at the mouth of the tunnel and looked down at them, before flapping away with a shriek. Daniel kept staring up at the entrance, his heart thumping. It was difficult to hear much of anything over the sound of the waterfall. By the time Bennett looked round, Daniel was already wading back to the shoreline.

'I think there's someone up there,' shouted Daniel, pointing at the tunnel as he emerged dripping from the water.

Bennett stood watching it like a hawk as Daniel picked up his socks and trainers and started back over the rocks, creeping as quickly as he could in his bare feet.

30

'Hello?' shouted Daniel again as he picked his way quickly over the rocks in the tunnel, hopping to put on his shoes one at a time.

But when he emerged, panting, into the daylight, with the fence all around him, there was no one there. He blinked in the bright sunshine, looking all about him. In the distance, a tractor the size of a toy suddenly breached the horizon and then turned and dipped below it again, into a green field half ploughed.

Daniel studied the ground around the edge of the hole.

'Well?' asked Bennett when he emerged, stamping his left foot down to make sure his shoe was on properly.

'I think there was someone here.'

'You think or you know?'

Daniel watched Bennett raise his eyebrows,

wondering what he meant, until Bennett waggled the half-empty hip flask. His friend plucked the topmost wire between two wooden posts, making it thrum.

'Well, if there *was* someone here, they've gone now,' said Bennett. 'Maybe it was just someone leaving another letter, worshipping at the shrine of Daniel.'

Daniel scanned the notes and offerings lying on the ground, and the ones hooked on to the wire and tacked to the posts, but he couldn't tell if there was anything new since the last time. He looked to his left and studied the dark fringe of the woods and then he heaved himself up over the fence and started walking towards the trees. He thought he heard Bennett muttering something, but he couldn't be sure as the breeze blew over his ears and he didn't turn to find out.

He lingered on the edge of the pines, looking into the cool, muffled dark, and then he walked on, beyond the first row of trunks.

The floor was a weave of soft brown needles, springy, like matting beneath his feet. He trod carefully as if it might give way any moment, listening for the sound of another person, his hearing seeming keener after spending so long near the waterfall.

The cracks of sky shone bluer between the tapering tops the deeper he went. But when he heard Bennett coughing behind him, the needles hissing as he kicked at them, Daniel stopped and picked at a nub of hard sap on the trunk beside him. 'Let's just say it was nobody then,' he said.

'Or a passing cloud,' said Bennett. He sighed. 'It hasn't been a waste of time though, has it?'

Daniel thought about that. 'No,' he said. 'Not at all.'

And Bennett smiled.

The boys pedalled back across the meadow, leaving two bright, winding trails in the grass. When they arrived at the wheat field, they started back through the lumpy tractor channel.

Daniel looked back over the bobbing, bearded heads of wheat towards the woods, imagining that someone was watching him. But there was just a wall of trees. And then he thought he saw something moving on the edge of the woods. It could have been a figure flitting between the trunks. Or it could have just been the sunlight and shadows falling through the branches of the trees.

'There's no one there,' said Bennett, 'however much you want there to be.'

Daniel kept watching for a few seconds more and then just turned round. 'Let's go or we'll miss the train,' he said.

31

Sitting on the warm platform, waiting for the train, they watched the shadows creeping across the concrete. Daniel moved his leg when one black finger touched his foot.

When the boys heard the rails begin to *twang*, the two of them stood up and picked up their bikes as two carriages came round the bend.

'We could just keep going, you know,' shouted Bennett above the noisy brakes of the train. When the carriage doors opened, Daniel propped his bike alongside Bennett's and imagined choosing a seat and riding the train until it terminated before catching another one going somewhere else, followed by another, and then another, never stopping anywhere and having to *be* someone. But, when the train lurched, the idea fell away inside him and he knew there was no point poking around in the jumble of daydreaming and pointless thoughts to find it, because he was never going to leave his dad.

The rest of the carriage was deserted. Bennett inspected the crescent moon of a burger and bap left in its tray on the seat opposite, but decided it wasn't for him. So he opened his hip flask and took a swig and offered it to Daniel who did the same.

As he handed the flask back to Bennett, a previously unseen figure rose up from the seats further down and tottered towards them along the aisle, like an ancient spirit of the carriage. He was a grimy, wiry man, with a matted beard the colour of rust, and he wore a tatty blue shirt, shorn of buttons to below his ribcage, which flapped beneath a tattered white mackintosh mapped with stains. His white, freckled chest was daubed with two nipples the colour of terracotta and, through the fuzz of cropped orange hair on his head, Daniel could see a pale scalp pocked and marked with scrapes and cuts.

The man stood swaying with the carriage, licking his blistered lips, then held out his hand for the flask.

When Bennett shook his head, the man sat down beside Daniel and reached into a pocket of his mackintosh and drew out a large darning needle and aimed its tip a couple of centimetres from Daniel's ribs.

'I'll burst his heart,' said the man.

135

Up close to him, Daniel could see muck in every pore. There was a hot, bitter tang around the man like a fox.

Bennett grunted something before handing over the flask and the man took it and wedged it between his knees.

'Pockets too,' he said.

The tip of the needle stayed close to Daniel as each of them handed over their loose change. When the carriage lurched, Daniel's fingers brushed the man's upturned palm as he dropped the coins into it, and when he drew back the man was staring at him, dropping the change into the pocket of his mackintosh. Suddenly, he moved across the seat to get closer, the needle flashing back the sunlight. Daniel shrank into the corner and felt the *click clack* of the wheels on the track up his spine.

'Leave him alone,' growled Bennett. But the man didn't seem to hear as he peered closer. Daniel could smell the reek from his clothes, like hot, wet cardboard. Teeth stained the colour of cork. But in his eyes a flicker of something bright. He grabbed Daniel's wrist, the fingers tightening like wire, the needle in his other hand drooping.

'Oh, you got the fizz, boy,' he said, smiling. 'You've got the voltage.' The man gasped. Whooped like a cowboy.

Daniel felt a sudden fluttering in his chest, but it was faint and feeble, a series of warm golden spots flitting inside him like fireflies.

'Can we make the fit?' asked Daniel. 'Do you know how to?'

'There was a time once I might have done, but now I'm not so sure.'

'But we need to try. See what we can do.'

'It'll cost you,' said the man, holding out a grimy palm.

'We already gave you everything,' said Bennett.

'No then. Cos a man's got to make a living, you know.'

'But I need to find someone who can help me,' said Daniel.

The man raised the needle like a single finger to make a point. 'It won't be me unless you pay for it.'

'I can get you money. I can.'

'No one knows the future,' laughed the man. 'No one knows that. So it's pay up now or never!'

'But it's important. I need to help someone.'

'The one in the bed or the bald man?'

Daniel's mouth opened, but he didn't know what to say.

The man just grinned. 'It's only flickers and sparks in me now. Flickers and sparks on a good day. Not the raging fire it used to be. But I can still see some things. So who is it? Who do you want to help most?'

137

'The one in the bed.'

'So what about the bald man? What about what he wants? How are you going to handle him?' The man smiled when Daniel said nothing. He shook his head as he picked out a blue loop of seat fabric with the needle. 'Find someone else to help you,' he said. 'That bald one's a problem that won't go away. He's like gum on your shoe.'

He laughed and lifted the hip flask from his knees and took a sip, watching Bennett as he did so with bright blue eyes in case he tried to snatch it back. After swallowing a mouthful and wiping his mouth on his sleeve, he said to them, 'There's something you should know though, and I'll tell you about it for free.'

'What's that?' asked Daniel edging forward to hear.

'That we all want lives we can understand. But the world doesn't work like that. It doesn't care what we want.' He wove the needle up and down, as if stitching an invisible thread through the air. 'So we sew in the bits that don't make sense, making up stories about ourselves we can believe in or at least pretend to.'

Suddenly, he stabbed the needle into the seat, making Daniel flinch and sending dust motes streaming into the sunlight. 'It's a curse being human.' He pulled out the needle and pointed the tip at Daniel. 'So make up

138

whatever stories you need to explain it. Make sense of that talent inside you however you want, especially if you find them.'

'Who?' asked Daniel.

'Someone else to make the fit with.'

'Where are they?'

The man laughed out loud. 'How should I know? Just make sure they fit you better than last time.' He pumped his hand open and shut and then balled it tight into a fist, making it shudder. 'Went off like a bomb, I bet?'

He smiled and stood up as the train started to slow.

'Wait,' said Daniel. 'I need to know where to look.'

'They'll be wherever you are because they'll need you as much as you need them. That's what making a good fit's all about, helping each other, but not in the way you're expecting. Don't ask me why. But that's how it was for me.'

He grinned and his smile was like a dirty crescent of moon. 'I ended up telling myself all sorts of stories to try and make sense of it, and now here I am.' He shook his head as the train pulled into the station and bade them good day with an elaborate bow, one arm twirling its hand and then sweeping aside the air.

They watched him get off the train, draining the last of the whisky and Diet Coke from Bennett's hip flask and beaming into the sun. Bennett picked up the burger in its tray and flung it at him before the carriage doors closed and the tramp waved them off as the train left the platform, a stripe of ketchup glistening on his mackintosh.

Before they lost sight of him, they saw him dancing down the platform as if accompanied by some ballroom music piped out of the sky for him alone.

32

Daniel's aunt was out and the windows seemed larger and more full of daylight, as though the house had taken a secret moment to relax without her. Daniel drifted from room to room, pausing to look in each one.

In the sitting room, his father was reading the paper with his feet up and the television turned down low.

In the kitchen, he was cooking pasta, a red sauce overheating in a pot, bubbles popping, freckling the worktop red. 'Where's the bloody colander?' he turned round to ask and then stood waiting until he faded like a ghost with Daniel still leaning against the door frame, shaking his head.

In the bathroom, his father was standing in front of the mirror, shoulders draped in a towel like a boxer, uprooting black hairs from his nostrils then suddenly tilting his head to one side and smoothing a hand through the thinning hair above his forehead. When he caught sight of Daniel watching in the mirror through the half-open door, he froze. 'Don't you dare say a word,' he grunted with a smile.

'I won't,' whispered Daniel to the empty bathroom and drummed his fingers on the wood in time to his heart. When he turned round, something swilled unexpectedly in his head and he paused, thinking he was still woozy from the whisky. But the sensation didn't pass. It filled out into something more, an inkling of a memory at first, and then it began spooling through him like a snippet of film and suddenly he was . . .

. . . running towards a door, along a landing laid with deep-pile white carpet, the fluffy threads bulging up over the rims of his brown lace-up shoes.

When he gripped the door handle, it slipped through his fingers and pinged back up because his hands were oily with blood.

After the moment vanished, Daniel stood trying to place it in his life. But he couldn't. He opened his bedroom cupboard and inspected all the shoes lined up along the floor, singling out a pair of brown lace-ups that might . . . or might not . . . have been the same ones. Frustrated, he began toying with the idea that the universe had taken so much from him recently it might want to give him something tiny back, allowing him at least to place one moment in his life. But he recalled

142

nothing else about the memory or when it had happened.

The whisky and sunshine felt heavy on him so he took a shower, inhaling the steam to try and rinse out his lungs. When he stepped out and wrapped a towel about his waist, he wiped the mirror clear and studied his flat, bony chest, trying to look through the wet skin and the stringy blue veins to see what might be deeper down. He stared harder at his reflection, fingers tightening round the edge of the basin, trying to invent an explanation that made sense of everything. It was only when he remembered the tramp on the train, and what he had said, that Daniel rocked back on his heels and let go.

Dressed and with his damp hair drying, Daniel stopped halfway down the stairs and watched through the balustrade as the front door opened then shut. His father stood in the hallway, hanging up his suit jacket on a peg, his work tie loosened and the top button of his white shirt undone. He plunged his hands in his trouser pockets and looked up. 'How's things, Dan?'

'Not great,' whispered Daniel and as he watched his father fade he spoke again. 'I'll help you, I will. I'll find out what to do.'

He flinched when the door suddenly opened for real, letting in the evening sunlight. But it was his aunt that looked up at him, her shadow stretching down the hall-way, pointed as a blade.

'How are things, Daniel?' she asked.

'Fine,' he replied.

33

After supper, Daniel went to bed. He lay blinking at the ceiling, unable to sleep, as he thought about his father and Lawson and what Mason had told him he must do. Through some cranky, twisted thinking, Daniel began to wonder if he had actually died underground and never found a way back to the surface at all, his body left stiff on the rock with the water lapping beside it, while the rest of him had slipped into some other place without realizing it until now. A hell maybe? Or some inbetween world?

But the bed felt real enough. And the long, uncomfortable silences during supper with his aunt had seemed authentic too.

The only other solution Daniel could imagine to explain what was happening to him was that he had dropped through a hole in the fabric of one universe into another where everything was familiar, but where his life was not quite the same. He sat up and looked round his bedroom, checking carefully for anything that might seem odd or out of place. But nothing was any different that he could see.

As he slumped back down, he remembered the strange memory that had come to him before his aunt had returned home. It was difficult to recall it entirely, but there were just enough details for him to ponder:

the deep pile of a white carpet on a landing . . .

brown lace-up shoes . . .

his hands covered in blood and a door handle slipping through them.

Daniel wondered if it could be a clue that might prove he had indeed fallen from one universe into another. Closing his eyes, he tried to picture everything he could about that moment and gradually it started coming back to him, and he was

. . . running towards a door, along a landing laid with deep-pile white carpet, the fluffy threads bulging up over the rims of his brown lace-up shoes.

When he gripped the door handle, it slipped through his fingers and pinged back up because his hands were oily with blood.

He got up and inspected the brown shoes in his cupboard again. They were definitely not the same. And then he looked at his hands. They weren't the ones

146

covered in blood that had reached for the door handle. His own fingers weren't as slender or as white.

Daniel tried to understand how he could have remembered something that hadn't even happened to him. Unnerved by the strangeness of it, he lay back on his bed and closed his eyes, replaying the moment over and over, trying to see if he could find out anything else . . .

. . . and then something clicked and he began remembering more . . .

. . . *his bloody hands grabbing hold of the door handle a second time and turning it to let himself through into a white tiled bathroom . . .*

. . . When he looked in the mirror above the white ceramic sink, he saw Lawson staring back, his bleeding nose cupped in his bloody hands . . .

. . . And then Mason appeared in the doorway behind him, looming like a storm cloud in the mirror over his shoulder . . .

. . . 'Don't try that again,' he grunted, 'or else I'll break more than your nose.'

34

Daniel and Bennett sat on the low wall outside King's College, eating chips for breakfast from yellow styrofoam trays, tourists glancing at them as they walked by.

'What do you mean it was Lawson?' asked Bennett.

'In the mirror, it was his face looking back at me.'

'But you just said it was like a memory. That you *were* him. How's that possible?' Bennett speared a chip and dipped it in ketchup. He moved his fork like a baton as if conducting his thoughts. 'Unless it's to do with the fit? That bits of Lawson got stuck inside you when things went wrong.'

A passer-by looked down at them; Bennett smiled at her with ketchup teeth until she looked away. 'Do you think you could remember anything else?'

'I'm not sure I want to.' Daniel cupped his hands round the styrofoam tray of chips, trying to warm them because even though the sun was out he felt cold.

'But you might remember something that helps. If Lawson knew other people like him, maybe there's somebody who could help you. You need to find someone to make this fit or who knows what Mason'll do?'

Daniel toe-poked a pebble as far as he could into the road. 'Lawson's dead, Bennett. It's creepy, thinking bits of him are stuck inside me.'

'Like starlight?'

'What?'

'When we look up at a star, we're seeing how it was in the past because of the time it takes light to travel across the universe. We're only watching a memory from an age ago.'

'I suppose.'

Bennett patted him on the shoulder. 'It'll burn out eventually.'

'If you say so.'

'I do.' Bennett speared another chip and watched it steaming in the sun.

He put the wooden fork down with the chip still attached when a woman with an American accent asked if she could take a picture of them sitting on the wall with the college behind them because it looked so *cute*. Bennett asked for a pound. 'I'm saving up for university,' he said. 'Thirty thousand pictures should do it. Or else I'm going to be trapped in my socio-demographic fishbowl for the rest of my life, looking out at what *could have been* for me.'

When three pound coins were placed in his outstretched palm, he lit up like a slot machine.

'Don't be stupid,' said Daniel as they walked away after the picture was taken. 'You can do anything you want whether you go to university or not.'

Bennett beamed for a moment like he had won the lottery. 'But I can't find your fit for you though, can I?' he said as they strolled among the tourists.

'No you can't.'

'And Mason doesn't sound like the kind of man to take kindly to bad news.' Bennett slung an arm round Daniel's shoulder and pulled him close. 'Why not try to see what else of Lawson is left inside you? It might help. Do you really think you're going to find someone just by walking round town? Mason only gave you three days and it's day two now.'

'Lawson was drawn to me when we met. Perhaps someone else will be too. The down-and-out on the train said the person I needed to make the fit will be wherever I am.'

'And you believe him?'

'There are people coming from all over the world to visit here,' said Daniel as groups of tourists bustled round them.

'Hello!' shouted Bennett at the crowds, pointing to

Daniel. 'Anyone here interested? He's someone you can make the fit with if you want?' But while some people glanced up at them, most just looked embarrassed and walked on.

Bennett raised his hands in surrender when Daniel scowled. 'OK,' he said. 'I can see it might be uncomfortable finding out what bits and pieces of a dead person are stuck inside you, so let's walk a bit more and see what happens, until we meet someone or we up come with another idea. I can multitask anyway. Work off the chips at the same time.' He belched and smiled at all the disapproving faces passing them by.

They wandered among the crowds of shoppers and tourists like two pilgrims searching for a hidden, sacred place. But the only time anyone noticed Daniel was when a young kid gawped at him, pointing him out to his mum, as if he had just stepped off the front page of the newspaper.

When a pack of girls from school recognized him too, they catcalled his name across the traffic, swigging from bottles of cider, their middle fingers raised, the sunlight flashing off their varnished nails.

'You've got to love 'em,' said Bennett, blowing them each a kiss.

When Bennett spotted the down-and-out they had met on the train, he chased after him down the street, shouting that he wanted his hip flask back. But the man ducked down an alley, his mackintosh flapping. When Daniel followed them, he found Bennett at the end of the alleyway, panting, his hands on his head as he stood pondering which of the three separate passageways to take.

'Vanished like a bloody cat,' he said and cursed.

Eventually, the two of them lay down in one of the parks on the sunburned grass. Bennett picked up a stick and turned it in his hands. 'So much for meeting someone. All we've done is go round and round this bloody town. People'll start talking, you know.' Bennett tossed the stick as high as he could and watched it cartwheel round and snap like a bone when it landed on the dry brown grass. He stared at the two broken pieces and clicked his tongue. When he looked round, ready to say something, Daniel was staring at him.

'OK,' he said. 'I'll try it.'

Bennett bought a notebook and pencil from a kiosk in the park and sat quietly beside Daniel, waiting to write anything down that might be useful.

Daniel lay silently for a few moments, thinking about Lawson, focusing on everything he could remember about the man. What he had been like in the hospital. How the house he had lived in was set out. Everything

152

he had mentioned to Daniel about the fit and what he hoped they could do together. Ever so gradually, Daniel began to sense they were having an effect as little flickers of the man's memories – things he could not have possibly known about – revealed themselves to him, flitting like sparks through the black of him as he kept his eyes tight shut.

They were mundane moments at first – Lawson brushing his teeth or eating a meal or driving a car. But they had a momentum of their own that carried Daniel into a deeper thinking and he started to remember other things in sequence from across the man's lifetime. Most of them were short, coming too quickly for Daniel to appreciate, but there was the odd more detailed one he saw clearly enough through Lawson's eyes to describe to Bennett:

As a toddler, playing with a black Labrador, pulling its ears.

Lawson on his first day at school, just a young boy in grey shorts with a satchel on his back.

Lawson the teenager sitting in his bedroom, focused on an HB pencil striped red and black which suddenly rolled a couple of centimetres or so of its own accord, making him whoop in delight.

In a cinema with a girl in the seat beside him, holding his hand in the dark.

As a young reverend, leading a church service, the pews containing just a few people.

Sobbing as he stood beside a new grave, the brown earth covered with wreaths of flowers, and swallows boomeranging round him.

Ripping out the pages of a Bible and letting them flutter to the floor.

As the older man Daniel had known him to be, standing in a dusty hallway of a stately home with a huge staircase winding upwards.

Being shouted at by Mason as they sat in a car.

Lawson, sitting in his living room, doodling a strange symbol on a piece of paper, practising it over and over on the page.

Standing in the hospital shop, looking at the photograph of Daniel in the newspaper.

Faster and faster the fresher, most recent memories started to come to Daniel.

Speaking to Daniel in the hospital . . . cooking supper . . . hearing a doorbell . . . walking with Daniel into his living room . . . the light bulb moving as it tied a knot in the cord . . . resting and talking to Daniel as the light bulb swayed above themandthenMason comingintotheroomandLawsonbeingsickandholdingthesilversignet ringandtellingDanieltoopenhisheartmoreandhishandexplodingfrom hisarmbloodspatteringacrossthewallsofthelivingroomandfeelingso littlepainitwasshockingandthenfallingforwardandexpectingtohitthe floorbutonlyplungingintoablackbottomlesshole—

Daniel opened his eyes, panting in the heat like a dog, and wiped his brow with a shuddering hand.

Bennett sat with him until he was calm, reassuring him gently that he was safe in the park.

Daniel looked through the notebook at everything Bennett had written down. He stopped when he saw a strange doodle, a figure of eight lying on its side. 'What's this?'

'You said Lawson was drawing a symbol, practising it again and again. It's the best I could come up with the way you described it. It sounded like the sign for infinity.'

Daniel studied it. Shook his head. 'No, it was more like . . .' Pausing, he tried to remember it and then he drew the crude shape of a cartoon bomb. Bennett looked at it and shrugged.

'It's not how you described it.'

Gradually, in the heat of the sun, Daniel fell asleep.

When he woke with a start, Bennett offered him a can of Coke, and Daniel could smell the whisky fumes drifting off it.

'You were having a bad dream,' said Bennett, waggling the can in front of Daniel's nose, making the Coke fizz inside the can. Daniel took a sip and handed it back. 'Do you get them a lot?'

'Sometimes.'

'About what? Being underground again?'

'Yeah. I'm back there, in the dark, with my phone, the rock shining back, the corners jutting out and catching the light so they look like teeth. Like the rock's about to eat me. And sometimes it does.' Daniel sat up and let the sunshine melt across his face. 'It's not just dreams. Sometimes a pothole widens when I'm crossing a road and I have to stop until it's shrunk back down. Or every so often a car goes by and I watch it, studying the road, hoping nothing happens. Even the water running through the pipes at home can set my heart pumping.'

Bennett offered him the can again. 'Maybe you should speak to someone.'

Daniel shrugged. 'It's not all the time.'

Bennett nodded. 'You can tell me anything whenever you need to.'

'Thanks.'

'I have another idea I've been waiting to spring on you. Maybe we should go to Lawson's house. Perhaps we can find something there that might help.'

Daniel tapped his fingers on the grass. 'Mason said not to go back.'

'He won't know as long as we're careful. We could just look around.'

Daniel drained the Coke can and squeezed it in the middle and tossed it into the bin beside them, the whisky buzzing in his head. 'OK,' he said.

They sped down the quiet lane towards Lawson's house, their bikes spinning grit on to the verge. But, as soon as they saw Mason's blue BMW pulled over on the grass, they had to brake hard, drawing black marker lines on the asphalt.

A mountain of rubbish had been built up in the front garden. There were suits still on their hangers. Stacks of newspapers tied with string. Carpets rolled into grey tubes.

Frank emerged with an armful of black curtains and threw them as high as he could on to the pile, like a thunderhead falling from the sky, until they landed and became an entrance into the mountain instead.

'Guess they've moved in,' whispered Bennett.

And all Daniel could think was how sad Lawson would have been to see everything going up in flames. But, as they cycled away, he wondered if it really had been him thinking that or whether it was the part of Lawson left inside him that felt that way.

35

The two of them went to the hospital and sat with Daniel's dad, listening to the machines keeping him alive. Daniel stroked his father's hand and then he washed his forearms gently and carefully as if they were made of fine china. He spoke to Bennett as he did so, explaining his father was still in an induced coma to give his brain time to heal which was why the ventilator was breathing for him and he was being fed through a tube into his stomach. Daniel stopped speaking when his voice started to crack and break apart, and the only sounds were the machines beeping and sucking and whooshing.

Daniel slumped into his chair after he had finished washing and drying his father's forearms. 'It's the not knowing that's the worst,' he said. 'Because none of the doctors or nurses can tell me if I'm never going to speak to him again or whether I'll be helping to nurse him back to health after he comes out of the coma. So that's why I need to make the fit, to try and help him. I don't want to leave it up to the world to decide what's going to happen. I want to make him better if I can. It's up to me. But what if I can't find anyone? What if I wasn't saved to help him at all? That all along I've just been hoping I was.'

Bennett sat in silence for a moment and then he stood up and went round to the other side of the bed and held Daniel until his friend had stopped crying.

36

His aunt had cooked supper by the time Daniel got home, but he wasn't hungry, despite not eating since his breakfast of chips.

When he picked up his plate, still heavy with most of the food, she rolled her eyes. 'You should eat more than that. You're a growing boy.'

Daniel ignored her and put the plate on the worktop beside the sink. He heard a little sigh as if she might be deflating. But when he turned round she was still there.

'What have you been doing with yourself today?' she asked.

'Nothing. Went to see Dad with Bennett.'

'I saw you walking around town with your friend earlier; it looked like you'd been drinking,' she said, scraping her fork round her plate, and the sound caught in Daniel's chest.

'No we weren't.'

She took a deep breath as if she was sniffing the air for clues. 'You were chasing some poor man down the street.'

'You don't have to be here if you don't want to be. If it's all too much.'

'Daniel, you're fifteen.'

'Like I said.'

She smiled as if he had told her a joke. 'And how do you know I don't want to be looking after you?'

'It's not like you've been interested in me before.'

'Maybe you should ask your father about that.'

'Well, that's a bit hard right now,' Daniel said and she bowed her head. 'Anyway, kids aren't your thing.'

'How would you know that?'

'It's obvious.' His aunt stared right back and something welled inside him and made him say it. 'Because you don't have any.'

She looked at her plate and then put down her knife and fork.

'Actually, I did have a son. He was called Michael. He died very young, before you were born. He would have been just a year older than you.' She wiped her mouth with her napkin. 'I never had the chance to have another child. Sometimes you realize that life gives you a blessing only after it's happened. That's what real heartbreak is. But I think you know that now more than most people.'

161

Daniel gripped the edge of the worktop because his legs seemed not to be there.

'I know what it's like to lose someone I loved very much, the same way it was with your mother, and that makes me the perfect person to be here helping you, don't you think?'

'Dad hasn't gone.'

'But he might, Daniel, because of how ill he is. And I'm sure you think about that from time to time. It's something you need to talk about and I'm here whenever you want to. I worry you're only telling your friend what you're feeling.'

She picked up her fork and started eating again.

Daniel walked back to the table with his plate and set it down in front of him and sat down. He began to eat too.

'I'm sorry,' he said after finishing a mouthful and swallowing. 'I'm sorry about Michael too.'

'Thank you. It was a long time ago.' His aunt smiled. Nodded. 'What do you tell him that you can't tell me?'

'Who?'

'Your friend.'

'Nothing.' But she gave him a look that told him she didn't believe him. 'We don't talk about anything important. That's the point.'

They finished the rest of the meal in silence, her eyes flicking up at him as if expecting him to tell her something private and balancing the world between them. But he couldn't tell her anything about Mason or Lawson. So instead he ate every grain of rice on his plate and tried to come up with something else.

'You're right,' he said finally. 'I have been drinking today. Just the odd sip with Bennett. Sorry.'

When his aunt smiled as he put down his knife and fork on his empty plate, he knew that was enough for her for now. She laid her hands flat on the table and took a breath.

'The consultant in charge of your father wants to speak to us tomorrow.'

'About what?'

'About what's happening next. They're going to start reducing his sedation in the morning because the swelling in his brain has gone down. They want to see if your father will wake up. If he starts to breathe on his own.'

'Do they think he will?'

'They don't know.'

'They don't know much at all, do they?'

His aunt's mouth fell open. But the words didn't come and all she did was close it and shake her head.

37

When Daniel woke with a start, it was still night and it seemed his bedroom was fast asleep around him, with no sign of anything that could have disturbed him. As he sat up, he tried to remember what he had been dreaming about, but there were only sad feelings left inside him, a black vapour trapped and swirling in his chest.

And then the silhouette of a large man suddenly moved, as if emerging out of the wall, making Daniel cower back, too scared to cry out.

'It's all right, Daniel,' said Mason calmly. He sat down on the bed, making the springs ping. He grinned and his teeth shone. 'This is just a dream, nothing but that.'

But Daniel knew it wasn't. He tried to move, but Mason's weight was pinning the duvet tight across his legs.

'Where's my aunt?' he asked. 'Have you done anything to her?'

Mason shook his head. 'Don't worry, it's only *your* dream, not your aunt's. Do you get me, Daniel?' Daniel nodded and stopped trying to move. Mason drummed his fingers on his thighs. 'And anything can happen in dreams, my son. Anything's possible. So I can be here, right now, sitting on your bed, having a perfectly ordinary conversation.'

Daniel said nothing. He could feel his heart thumping in the soles of his feet. His hands, planted behind him and holding him up, were sweating into the sheets.

'Now,' continued Mason, 'a little birdy told me you came round to Lawson's house earlier. You and a friend.' He hooked his thumbs together and his hands fluttered around like the silhouette of a bird. 'That birdy flew all the way and told me and I didn't believe it. I said there's no way Daniel would do a thing like that without asking me, not after I told him to stay away from the house. Am I right?'

Daniel nodded. 'Yes,' he whispered.

Mason slapped his thigh. 'Goddam that little birdy. I'll shoot him next time I see him. Roast him, shall I? Have him for my tea?'

'Yes.'

Mason sighed. 'But I like that little birdy. And we all make mistakes, don't we? Get things wrong. So I'll let

165

him off this time, shall I? People should get a second chance, shouldn't they?'

'Yes.'

'OK then.'

Mason got up and brushed the creases out of his trousers and fastened the middle button of his suit jacket. 'Just a dream, remember?' Mason clicked his fingers. 'It's just your brain working things out.' He bent in closer to Daniel, his hot breath sweet and sour and garlicky. 'Have you found anyone yet? Your fit?'

'No.'

'Well, you need to get a wiggle on.' He looked at his watch. 'We're into your last day.'

'I don't think there's anyone out there.'

'There has to be. You're just looking in the wrong places.' Mason made a popping sound with his lips. 'There has to be someone, otherwise none of what's happened to you makes sense. I mean, what was the point of you crawling out of the ground a week ago if today comes and goes and I have to mark your dad's name down in my little black notebook of things *to do*?'

'I was just lucky I got out. I went back to look. There was nothing there. No clues about anything.'

Mason shook his head. 'Everything happens for a reason.'

'How do you know?'

'Because life must have a design or what's the point?'

'Well, you need to prove it to me then.'

'No, Daniel,' growled Mason, 'I don't have to prove a thing. It's you who's going to have to show me it doesn't. I have no doubt you have a talent inside you that wasn't meant to go to waste. I don't believe it was luck you came out of the ground. You're part of some bigger plan, to help your father and get your life back, and to help me too, by getting me my money and the antique flask I asked Lawson to find.'

'If my dad wakes up and starts to get better without me helping him, that'll prove I wasn't rescued for a reason.'

Mason just grinned. 'What, you mean tomorrow? When the ward staff try to bring him out of the coma they've been keeping him in?'

Daniel opened his mouth, but didn't know what to say.

Mason shrugged. 'One of the nurses on the ward keeps me up to date on things. She says the smart money's on your father not waking up. That he's too damaged inside.' Mason tapped his forehead. 'If there's just mashed potato in your old dad's head then the doctors won't be able to do a thing to help him. It'll be all up to you to find a way of making him better if you want your life back the way it was.'

After Mason had ordered him to let him out of the

167

front door, Daniel went back to bed. When a car engine turned over and came to life, he peeked round the blinds and watched the blue BMW driving up the street, all the way, until it turned the corner and disappeared. He managed to breathe more easily then.

But it was difficult to sleep. Mason's aftershave left a sickly vapour that drifted round the room, making Daniel's head spin. The house felt fragile too, like something made of paper that Mason could tear down and ball up in a meaty fist and throw away whenever he pleased. As if he owned it now. As if he owned Daniel too and knew why everything in his life was happening to him the way it was.

Rosie

38

'Wake up, Dad. It's Dan. Can you hear me?'

Daniel let go of his father's hand and sat back in his chair and checked his watch. It was 10 a.m.

'How long has it been now?' asked his aunt who was sitting on the other side of the bed.

'Two hours since they started reducing the sedation and about fifty minutes since he's been taken off it completely.'

His aunt pursed her lips and then stood up. 'One of the nurses said she was coming back to help wake him up. Why don't I go see where she is?'

Daniel sat beside his father, listening to the ventilator, as he watched his aunt through the glass, talking to the nurse at her station. And then he sat forward on his chair.

'Wake up. You need to start getting better. I'm running out of time to find someone. It won't be my fault if Mason writes your name down in his little black notebook.' Daniel bunched his legs up to his chest and watched his father over the tops of his knees. 'You don't know what he's like.' And then he put his forehead against his legs. 'I won't watch,' he said quietly. 'I won't tell anyone you're faking it. It can be our secret. Tell me how to do it. Tell me how I can vanish like you and not care about anything.'

But not a word from the vanished.

When the nurse came to check on Daniel's father, she stood at the top of the bed.

'Mr Webb, can you open your eyes for me? *Daa-vid.* Can you open your eyes?' She prised one eyelid open with a thumb. 'David, I'm just going to have a look at your eyes. I'm just going to shine a light in them.'

She shone a penlight into the eye she was holding open, but there was no reaction in the pupil. She looked into the other one.

'David, your son Daniel's here for you. Can you feel him holding your hand? Can you squeeze his hand for me?'

But Daniel felt nothing: no pressure, no squeeze and no love. It made his heart tremble inside.

39

Later that morning, Daniel and his aunt sat down in two brown plastic chairs in the office of the consultant who had operated to save Daniel's father the day he had been brought to the hospital. She told them it would take twenty-four hours to be sure that all the sedatives had been flushed out and only then could the team be certain that Daniel's father was in his own coma. The consultant told them that some patients could remain comatose much longer than others, that each situation was unique.

'How long someone remains in their own coma depends on its cause, which in the case of your father, Daniel, is what we call a traumatic injury, and also the severity of any brain damage sustained from such an injury.'

'Do you know yet how much damage there might be?' asked Daniel.

The consultant was about to answer when the beeper on her belt went off, and she unhooked it to check the message, nodding at the junior doctor sitting with them in the consulting room to take over.

He nodded nervously and cleared his throat. 'There are various ways of measuring how much damage there might be,' he said. 'We use brain scans and there are also certain scales we use to ascertain the level of a person's consciousness, the depth of their coma and the degree of their brain function.'

He stopped when he realized the consultant was listening closely, hands clasped together, and then he went on, aware that he was now being assessed. 'Your father scores lower on one of the key scales we use which suggests a higher degree of brain injury.'

'What does that mean?' asked Daniel.

The junior doctor pursed his lips, flashed a look at his superior.

'It suggests your father has a poorer outcome,' replied the consultant. 'That he might not wake up or, if he does, that he might be very different to the person you remember him to be. That physically and mentally he might be very changed.'

'How different?' asked Daniel.

The consultant took a sip of water from her plastic cup and set it back down on the table beside her. She looked at the junior doctor who seemed reluctant to say anything.

'James, can you suggest anything here?'

'At the moment we don't know anything for certain,' said the junior doctor. 'We have to wait and see. Although you need to know the reality of your father's situation, time is really only the best way we have of predicting what sort of recovery he might make.'

'But how long till you start to worry?' asked Daniel. 'How long is it till you're going to say that he's definitely not going to be my dad any more when he wakes up?'

The consultant perched forward on the chair, listening to what the junior doctor might say next.

'No one can say for sure—'

'How long?' asked Daniel's aunt, ignoring him and looking straight at the consultant.

She nodded as if the anxiety in Aunt Jane's voice had clicked something 'on' inside her. 'The majority of patients like Mr Webb who score low on the scales are more likely to die or remain in a vegetative state.'

The junior doctor stared at the floor. When he looked up, the consultant was watching, waiting to see if he had anything to add, and he cleared his throat again and turned to Daniel.

'More scans will give us a better view of what's going on inside your father's brain. We need to consider all the evidence before we start thinking about what might happen next. About what's in the best interests of your father, what he would want to happen.'

'That's something for the future,' added the consultant. 'For all of us to discuss at a later date. Daniel, for the time being, we need to watch and wait and see how well your father does over the next few days.'

'You haven't told us everything.' Daniel shifted in his chair and sat up straight as the three adults all looked directly at him. 'You haven't said *why* it's happened.'

The consultant studied her fingernails and thought about that. James tapped his pencil on his pad.

'I don't think anyone can, Daniel,' said his aunt.

'So you're saying none of you can tell me then?' He waited for someone to speak. 'I need to know because somebody told me everything happens for a reason and I want to tell them they're wrong.'

'Oh, Daniel,' said his aunt, squeezing his arm. 'Who said that?'

But Daniel just shrugged. When he felt his eyes warming up, he rubbed his fingers across them to wipe away the wet.

James leant forward and looked at Daniel. 'Life may or may not have a purpose, but one thing it definitely has is love and you're proof of that. It's why you're here in this room now, listening to everything we can tell you about your father. And all that love you have might be the most important thing to him right now. After they've

176

woken up, patients in comas have talked about hearing loved ones around their beds. I read about one patient who said he felt his wife's hand in his and heard everything she was telling him about their children and their life together as she sat beside him. That he had found her presence reassuring. So you let other people argue about why things happen in life, especially the bad things, because I'm not sure there are any answers to questions like that, at least not any good ones. You just focus on what you do best, which is to love your father like you've always done.'

Daniel nodded. Said nothing more.

The consultant folded her arms and stared at something on the floor and then she nodded too as she looked up at the junior doctor in the chair beside her. 'Thank you, James,' she said.

40

After the meeting with the consultant, Daniel and his aunt went back to see his father. When they opened the door, it was like cracking off the top of a bottle as the ventilator hissed. It was only the second time his aunt had been in his father's room and Daniel could sense her discomfort. They sat down in the plastic chairs either side of the bed and Daniel watched her looking around the room, not seeming to see his father at all until she folded her arms and dropped her chin on to her chest like a tiny bird getting ready to roost.

'Daniel,' she said in a whisper. 'Your father and I haven't spoken in a very long time, at least not what people would call a normal conversation.'

'Dad? I'm here with Aunt Jane. She's staying at home, looking after me. She's here now with me.' He stopped to see if his aunt might say something, but she didn't. And then he took hold of his father's hand. 'I'm not sure how long she's going to be staying or whether you even approve, but she's helping to keep things ticking over till you wake up. It's the summer holidays now. I don't know if you remember that or whether the part of you that cares is even listening.' He sat forward in the chair. 'Because it's only the machines that tell us you're still up and running. But we're here just in case you can hear. In case it makes a difference to you. And because it must be fucking boring lying there.'

There was a little cough from his aunt. Something disapproving muttered into a cupped hand.

But Daniel kept staring at his dad, waiting for a smile, until he gave up and looked at his aunt, his eyes fixed on her until she cleared her throat and leant forward in her chair.

'Hello, David, Jane calling.' She smoothed her hands down the trousers of her suit. 'David, I've come to stay like Daniel said. I'm looking after him so there's no need to worry. You just work on getting yourself better. I'm sleeping in the spare room. Which is nice. The bed's fine. Springy.'

'Tell him how you're feeling,' Daniel urged.

She folded her arms and leant back in the plastic chair. She smiled as if remembering some past remark. 'Oh, your father won't care about that.'

179

'But I do,' said Daniel, and he perched further forward on his chair.

'Well.' She paused. 'Well, I feel sad. Your accident was a terrible thing—'

'Tell him you've come to say sorry,' hissed Daniel. 'That you're putting an end to whatever went bad between you.'

Her eyes shone as if she had been slapped. 'Daniel, it's more complicated than you think.'

'Then tell me what happened and I'll tell you what to say.'

She rubbed at a spot on the moulded plastic arm of the chair. 'No. It's between me and your father.'

'But it might help. He might hear. It might *do* something.'

'I'm sorry. But I'm not able to do what you want.'

'You don't want him to get better.'

'Of course I do, Daniel, but—'

'But what?'

'But however much you want him to wake up there's nothing you or I can do to make that happen. We're just going to have to wait. Daniel, you need to accept how things are. I know it's hard. That none of it makes sense.'

When she reached out, Daniel thought she might touch his father's arm. But her hand stopped short and landed on the bedspread and smoothed out the wrinkles that had gathered there.

'He can't just be lying there with nothing going on,' said Daniel. 'Where's the rest of him? Where's Dad?'

But his aunt shook her head. 'I don't know, Daniel, really I don't.'

41

After a while his aunt said she had to go home and do some work, so Daniel sat by his father on his own into the afternoon, watching for any sign that he might be awake.

Nursing staff came and went, wanting to know if he had seen anything, but each time they asked he shook his head.

When a nurse came to open his father's eyes again and look into them with a penlight, Daniel asked if his father could really hear them speaking as the junior doctor had suggested earlier in their meeting.

'I don't know is the honest answer,' she said. 'But some people do think speaking helps, that patients like your father can hear, and are aware of, things going on around them. Sometimes patients have woken up here in this unit and said exactly that as they've slowly got better.'

Although there was no way of knowing if his father could really hear, Daniel decided he was going to keep believing he could, that talking to him would make a difference and help him weave a little magic all of his own.

So after the nurse had left he started to describe the little things at first.

The room they were in.

The nurse sitting at her central station.

What the hospital was really like because, even though it was on the outskirts of Cambridge, the city in which they had always lived, until now they hadn't paid it much notice.

On and on, until he found the words he wanted most.

'I didn't mean what I said in the car.'

To prove it, Daniel told his father about the camping trip they were going to take as soon as he was better, describing how they would pitch their tent in a clearing of soft brown needles, with a stream nearby into which boulders had tumbled an age ago.

'At night, we'll make a fire inside a ring of stones,' said Daniel. 'And when the logs have burned down to red-hot bricks we'll put tins of beans round the sides, and we'll cook sausages and bacon in a black pan, and fry eggs. We'll sit by the fire with the trees around us, eating and talking about whatever we want to, watching moths shine above the coals and listening to bats

183

clicking in the dark, the cold at our backs, imagining the rest of the world has been shorn off into space.'

But his father didn't move, as if the future meant nothing at all.

Daniel didn't give up. He kept talking, describing things that had already happened in their lives as clearly and as truthfully as he could remember them, like the yew tree they had cut up after it had fallen on the greenhouse two years ago. About the evening they had come back from the cinema to find the back door wrenched open and the television gone, a bright rectangle left in the dust on the cabinet. Even the weekend in a cottage with his father's friends where the four men had drunk themselves to sleep in the living room, leaving Daniel to wake them in the morning with heads sore enough to make them swear never to drink again.

'Wake up,' urged Daniel. 'Please. I don't know what's going to happen if you don't.' The longer he sat beside his father, waiting for something to happen, the more the frustration built up inside him as he thought about Mason. By the time two nurses came to give his father a bed bath, Daniel had already decided what he was going to do. As he left the room, the nurses told him the ward would be in contact if anything happened and he nodded and said thank you for all their hard work and kind words before he left to find Mason and tell the man that he should leave him and his father alone.

42

The lift was busy with patients and hospital staff leaving work and Rosie was stressed. There were elbows close to her face and bad breath coming in bursts. She began to realize that somebody had just farted too as she glared at all the innocent faces around her, trying not to breathe too deeply. When she met her mother's gaze, they raised their eyebrows at each other.

Rosie felt a scream floating up from her guts towards her mouth like a bubble about to pop.

The lift rumbled down the inside of the hospital building like some missile being lowered into its silo, and she willed it to speed up and reach the ground floor more quickly so she could step out and breathe clean air. It was a sort of test for her to try. The amazing things she had learnt to do in the past few weeks, since just before her diagnosis, like moving things a few centimetres across her bedroom floor and catching glimpses of what people were thinking, had been exciting, but she wanted to do more. However, it was difficult to know how, even with the advice of her grandmother, the only person Rosie had dared tell about what she could do.

The lift kept to its slow, rumbling pace however much she wished for it to go faster. Frustrated, she tried looking into the heads of the people standing beside her, searching for secrets to distract her from the intolerably slow journey. But all she sensed were snippets of things, swirling round her, and she could not tell who was thinking what or which pieces of information belonged to whom. It was like being submerged in some sort of private psychic soup of which no one else was aware. Like seeing into the Cloud, she thought.

When the lift stopped and the doors opened, Rosie silently gave thanks for the fresh air and then immediately cursed whoever had stepped inside and added to the crush.

It was a boy. Mousey-coloured. Plain-looking. Ordinarily, she wouldn't have given him a second glance. But as the doors closed she kept staring at him, her eyes like magnets she could not pull away.

She knew, somehow, that there was something special about him as he turned round to face the doors as they clicked shut.

Her brain ticked over until she suddenly recognized him. That was it. He was the boy who had fallen into the sinkhole and survived. She had seen a picture of him on someone's Facebook page, on lots of pages in fact. Even from her brief look at him before he had turned round, it struck her now how different people could look in real life, less real somehow than on a screen.

But Rosie's curiosity wasn't satisfied. There was something else about him. Without even thinking it might be rude or too forward, she reached out and touched him on the shoulder and her fingers seemed to stick to him as if nailed there. As the boy tried to turn round to see her, struggling with her arm locked tight to him, Rosie heard voices instantly all around her and it shocked her for a heartbeat until she realized what they were: the thoughts of each person in the lift. They were so loud a switch seemed to have been flicked on in her head. The boy appeared to hear them too, pausing to listen for a moment, before he managed to turn right round and look directly at Rosie as her arm dropped away.

But Rosie still felt a connection to this mousey-haired, plain-looking boy. As if the air between them was charged. It made her feel invigorated somehow, open to the idea that she could do whatever she wanted if she put her mind to it.

When the lights flickered and the lift lurched downwards for a second, everyone gasped as their stomachs hit their throats and Rosie blinked and told it to slow again. She felt excited and afraid by what she had done while people all around her exchanged relieved looks as the lift continued to rumble on at its stately pace.

But the boy was still looking right at her as if he knew exactly what she had done. A thought occurred to her – that they had done it *together*. Somehow, he had made her gift more powerful.

43

'Go, Mum, I'll be fine. Just let me hang out and be a normal teenager, will you?' Rosie squeezed her mum's hand as they stood in the foyer of the hospital. 'Honestly, you don't need to worry about me every second of every day.'

'But what about getting home?'

'I'll get the bus. I have change. Exactly the right amount, so there's no need to worry.' When her mother rolled her eyes at that, Rosie looked round at Daniel who was waiting for her beside the rows of blue plastic seats. 'I know him from school. I just want to hang out.'

'I recognise him.'

'Yeah, the sinkhole, you know? With his dad.'

Her mum nodded. 'You never said he was at your school, Rosie.'

'No? Well, I'm sure I never said he wasn't either.' Her mum kept looking at her, as if trying to figure out if

Rosie was really telling the truth or not with just her eyes. 'I'm a big girl, Mum.'

'You're a sick girl, Rosie.'

'I know. But life doesn't stop because of it, remember? We agreed that.'

'But you've got an important day tomorrow.'

Rosie rolled her eyes. Nodded. 'Yeah, I know and I'd like to forget about it, just for a little while.'

Her mum took a deep breath. 'You promise you won't overdo it. That you'll be sensible?'

Rosie held up her hand. 'I do humbly swear to uphold the law according to my mum.'

When Daniel said hello and they introduced themselves, he noticed the girl was as pale as the pink on a rose. It made all her other features come alive. Her green eyes and black hair. Cheekbones as sharp as razors. The delicate veins in her hands were so blue they were like tiny underground streams.

She was the sort of girl he would have glanced at, but would have been too embarrassed ever to speak to.

His mouth slapped shut when he realized he had been staring and saying nothing. All the questions in his head were logjammed somehow.

Rosie laughed and nodded. 'I know, right,' she said. 'I'm blown away too. It was really something in the lift. Our . . . connection?'

'It's called the fit,' replied Daniel. He dug at the rubber floor with the toe of a trainer. 'So I'm guessing you don't know anything about it?'

Rosie shook her head.

'I don't know much. A bit, I guess. It lets people like you with particular gifts do more than you could before. That you plug into me somehow. But I don't know how it works. All I can tell you is how it feels for me.'

'And how's that?'

'I get a sensation in my chest, a good one. Warm and golden. Like something good is happening.'

'Can we try it again now? Do I need to touch you first to get some kind of—' But when Rosie took a step towards him, and held out her arm to touch his shoulder like before, Daniel stepped back, his hands closing into tiny fists.

'Wait!' His shout was so loud that people looked up as they passed him by. 'We have to be careful,' he said more quietly, 'before we try anything.'

'Why? Daniel, what's the matter? Whatever we did in the lift was great. Fantastic!'

'When I tried making the fit with someone else, things went wrong.'

'How do you mean? Daniel, what happened?'

'I think it can be dangerous if you push too hard. I don't know why. Because I don't know much about how it really works. I want to try with you, I do. Because

191

I have to find out if we can make something very important happen, something really good. But we need to know how it works first to make sure nothing goes wrong.'

A thought bubbled into Rosie's head almost immediately. 'You want to help your dad, don't you? He's here in the hospital, right? You want to find someone to make this fit with so you can help him?' When Daniel nodded, Rosie felt something exciting rising inside her. 'And what about helping other people, not just your dad?'

Daniel looked at her, through all her beauty, and beneath it he saw how pale and fragile she really was. 'You're ill, aren't you?'

'Tumour.' And Rosie tapped her head. 'Up here. A couple of weeks before my diagnosis I started doing things, making stuff happen that ordinary people aren't supposed to be able to do.' She rubbed her hands because there were goosebumps all over her fingers as she remembered. 'I know someone who might be able to help. I trust them more than anyone else in the world. They're the only person who knows about my secret.'

As Rosie continued talking, Daniel realized he wasn't listening to her any more. He was watching the lift doors open, letting people spill out into the foyer. Suddenly, he wanted to rush for them before they closed and take Rosie straight to his father's bedside to see if

192

they might be able to help him. *Mason would never know*, he thought. But his feet stayed stuck to the floor because there was so much he didn't understand yet about the fit.

When Rosie touched him on the shoulder, he flinched.

'Daniel, did you hear me? I said my gran will know what we need to do. She can help us. She's only a bus ride away.'

'Can you trust her?'

'Yes, of course! She's my gran.' Rosie frowned as she looked at him.

Daniel watched the lift doors closing and when they clicked shut it seemed that the world had decided for him what he should do.

'OK, let's go and see her. I'll tell you everything that's happened to me since the sinkhole on the way. Then you'll understand why I'm being so careful about who I can trust.'

44

When Agatha heard the doorbell, she thought it might be a salesperson or somebody canvassing for votes. No one she knew pushed the button as hard or for so long.

She crept to the spyhole and saw a bald man, his face globed like a fishbowl, waiting on the step. He was smartly dressed in a blue suit with an electric sheen, all three single-breasted buttons done up, and a black tie and white shirt. No clipboard or folder. Some instinct told her not to open the door. But when he rang the bell again, even longer and louder than before, she wondered if he might be a potential client.

He rang again, his face bulging as he moved closer to the spyhole, as if he knew she was watching him. His suit moved with him like some reptilian skin and Agatha thought it must be tailor-made. His tie and shirt looked expensive too. She smoothed down her grey hair and turned the Chubb lock.

The man beamed at her when she opened the door, holding out a large manicured slab of a hand, a silver cufflink emerging from his sleeve jacket and winking in the early evening sunlight. So big and solid, he was like a statue come alive. He kept staring, his thumb cocked back like a trigger and his fingers fused and ready to fire, grinning, as though Agatha was expected to do him the honour of shaking his hand.

She could still feel his grip after it was gone.

Suddenly, she wanted to shut the door, but before she could—

'I'm Mason,' he boomed, stepping up on to the white marble step, nostrils flared like a bull ready to charge. 'A little birdy told me you help people.'

Agatha looked beyond him. A blue BMW was parked on the other side of the road, the windows too dark to see if there was anyone else inside. The colour clashed with Mason's blue suit and it made her feel dizzy and she coughed and cleared her throat.

'Can I ask where you heard that?'

'A friend of a friend,' said Mason, and his hands made a bird shape and fluttered all around. 'A little birdy, like I said.'

Agatha was cold in his shadow. She moved to one side, into the rays of low sun coming past him, and Mason stepped inside the house, like an old friend for whom it was the most natural thing in the world. The soles of his black leather shoes hissed on the carpet as he took a few paces and then turned round. He put his arms behind his back and studied her.

'I'm afraid I only see clients in the mornings unless they're regulars,' she said.

'I just need five minutes of your time,' said Mason and folded his arms.

They sat in the study, at the small card table Agatha used for readings.

She took a breath and then smiled. 'So how can I help you, Mr Mason?'

He reached into the inside pocket of his jacket and placed a silver signet ring on the green felt between them. 'I need to know more about this ring. I found it and want to return it to its rightful owner.'

Agatha licked her lips. 'Why don't you tell me why you're really here?'

Mason grinned. 'So you are psychic then.'

'People tend to be economical with the truth their first time. I need to know your real motive for coming. To help with my sight.'

'So you think it's my first time seeing a psychic?'

When Agatha swallowed, her throat seemed lined with tiny shards of glass. 'I'm presuming it is, going by what most new clients tell me.'

Mason nodded, picking up the ring, which was far too small for any of his fingers. 'It belonged to a man I knew. I'd like to know more about him.'

'So you didn't know him that well?'

Mason's eyes flicked up at her and something swelled in his jaw, but then it disappeared and he smiled, holding out the ring in the flat of his palm, as though there was no more time to discuss it.

It was lighter than she had imagined. And colder. She half expected it to melt in the warmth of her hand like a snowflake.

'I'm looking for a good psychic to help a friend of mine,' continued Mason. 'He's having trouble finding the right person he needs so I thought I'd rally round and help him out. He doesn't think there's anyone out there for him, but I believe there is. Fate always lends a hand when it's required. So this . . .' and he nodded at the ring, '. . . this is a kind of test to find someone. That's why I looked you up.' He plucked a black notebook from the inside pocket of his suit and flipped it open. 'See? You're number one on my list,' he said, pointing to her name at the top of a column.

She was aware of Mason's heavy breathing. The velvet sounds as his nostrils flared. He was wearing a woody cologne, but there was something else beneath it, something she couldn't quite place. Like blood or the coppery smell of an old coin.

Closing her eyes, she tried to forget the man in front of her. Instead, she found a space and drifted into it as her fist closed round the ring.

When she looked again, Mason was still staring back. She shook her head and a tiny ticking started in his jaw then stopped and his right leg began tapping immediately.

'I'm afraid I'm not getting anything,' said Agatha.

'There's no need to be afraid.' Mason leant back in the chair and the joints creaked. 'We all have our off days, don't we? Doesn't look like you have that many though.'

'I'm sorry?'

Mason looked around. 'This is a nice gaff. Business can't be too bad.'

'My husband was a lawyer.'

'But he's not now.'

When Agatha forced herself not to look away, Mason grinned as though everything was working out perfectly.

'I'm sorry, Mr Mason, but sometimes I just don't get the right feeling.' She placed the ring on the desk between them. 'The connection doesn't work like a switch. I can't turn it on and off like a light.'

'Sometimes I wish I was psychic. It would make things a whole lot easier in my line of work. I'd know who was lying to me.'

'And what work is that?'

'You tell me.' He stared at Agatha. Eyes like marbles. His foot stopping mid-tap. And, for a moment, there was just the ticking of the grandfather clock in the hall. Then Mason blinked, shook his head and smiled. 'I've run a few scams in my time too.' And his eyebrows moved up and down like they were on strings.

Mason picked up the ring and put it in his pocket and stood up. He took a wad of money from inside his suit jacket, licked his finger and drew out a fifty-pound note and slapped it on the table like a bet.

'That's not necessary. I only accept payment from satisfied clients,' Agatha said, keen to get rid of him.

'Oh, I'm satisfied.' And Mason grinned and drew a line through her name in the notebook with a pencil he had found in his suit pocket.

He pushed the note further across the table, pinning it with a forefinger, and turning the tip of his fingernail white. 'I know what certain people in my line of work would think if they ever knew I was here.'

Agatha opened her mouth. Then closed it. She slid the note out from underneath Mason's large finger and put it in her cardigan pocket.

After closing the front door, she listened to him crunching over the gravel and then she slid the chain across the door. Looking through the spyhole, she watched him go, bulge-backed in the glass like a troll as he lumbered away. On the far side of the road a door of the blue BMW opened. By the time Agatha had walked into the living room and nudged back the curtain with a finger to get a better look, the door had already shut and Mason had vanished.

The BMW remained parked there and Agatha kept wishing it would drive away. But it didn't. The faint smell of Mason's cologne wouldn't leave either and she opened the back door to flush it out of the house.

She hid the red fifty-pound note deep in a drawer full of odd buttons and offcuts of material, the nubs of pencils and little nests of string.

When she peered out of the window again, keeping close to the wall so as not to be seen, she saw the BMW's bonnet was up and two large men were standing beside it. One of the men had a hump on his back, which grew as he leant over the engine and started tinkering with the hoses.

Both of them looked up suddenly when one of the rear passenger doors opened and Mason appeared and pointed at something back down the street. When the two men turned round, Agatha pressed her face closer to the window to see what Mason was pointing at.

It was Rosie.

And she was walking up the street towards the house with a boy.

45

The three of them sat in a row on the sofa in the living room with their hands in their laps. Mason was perched on a chair opposite, grinning, and when he slapped his thigh it was like a gunshot.

He swore excitedly under his breath. 'Another five minutes and I'd have missed you.' He grinned at Daniel. 'You think the world's just chaos now? You know it can't be. Not with you meeting this lovely girl in the hospital and the two of you coming here to ask her gran about this connection of yours, and me being here too. You've got to believe it's all down to fate now, that it always lends a hand when needed. That life's playing out according to some plan.'

Daniel shifted in his seat and cleared his throat, but no words came out. Yet Rosie seemed to know exactly what to do as she took his hand in hers and held on tight, her fingers cool and strong.

'If that's what you want to believe, Mr Mason,' she said, tucking a curl of black hair behind her ear.

'Oh, it's more than that,' said Mason, shaking his head. 'I *know* it. Go on, Daniel, tell her all about you, how life's worked out to bring you here, right up to this moment.'

Daniel shifted his feet. Took a breath. But, before he could say anything, Rosie was speaking.

'Daniel told me everything on the way over here. You're a bully and you've threatened to hurt his father unless he helps you find your briefcase of money and this other thing you want, this flask. And you've told him that you think what's happened to him is all down to some cosmic plan in which you happen to be involved.'

'And *now* I think that you, you pretty thing, are the one Daniel's been looking for to prove it, to make the fit,' said Mason, waggling a big finger at her.

'Maybe,' she said. 'Or maybe not. If you're the expert on making the fit then do tell me more because I'm new to all this.' Mason's leg pumped harder, as though he was charging his voice to shout something loud, but Rosie carried on slowly and quietly. 'My grandmother's the one who's psychic. We came to see her, not you, to find out more about the fit and how it works.' She leant forward until she could see herself in Mason's eyes. 'Daniel told me what happened to Lawson and I'm not about to let the same thing happen to me.'

202

Mason grinned as she sat back. 'You're as pretty as a wasp, Rosie, you know that?' And then he pointed at Agatha without looking at her. 'I'm not sure your gran's going to be much use, to be honest. I'm pretty sure she's a fake, fleecing punters for a few nuggets of made-up comfort to make them feel better about taking their money. So I've got a better idea.' He took the silver signet ring from his pocket and held it out for Rosie. 'Let's just get things moving ourselves. I want to kno—'

But Rosie shook her head, cutting Mason dead, making him frown as if his brain was curdling. 'Not until I know more.' When Mason kept his hand stretched out, she shook her head again. 'You don't scare me.'

'Really? Why not?' He tapped a big finger against his lips, as if mulling this over. And then he smiled. 'You were at the hospital, so what's wrong with you? Touch of death, is it? Heart? Cancer?' He nodded when Rosie's throat moved. 'Cancer it is. Chemo not going too well? Not got long? Or maybe you've only just been diagnosed and you're still feeling angry at the world.' When Daniel squeezed Rosie's hand, Mason noticed. 'Bingo,' he said quietly.

'Leave her alone,' said Daniel, his voice steely and sure. 'It's not her fault she's ill.'

Mason beamed. 'There he is! There's the boy who survived being swallowed by the ground.' He folded his arms and observed them. 'You two were born to make the fit. Look at you. Only met an hour ago and now you're inseparable.' He cricked his neck and grunted like a dog that's found its itch. 'Well, you might not be scared of me, Rosie, but you'll learn to be.'

Mason perched right on the edge of his seat, one hand splayed over his thigh like a giant starfish. 'You see,' he whispered as if they were in church. 'I've got a way with people that makes them do what I want. So pretty please. Go on. With cherries and cream on top. Or else Gran here might meet with an accident if you know what I mean.' He held out his other hand again, the ring in the centre of his palm and winked at Rosie.

Rosie kept watching as if expecting him to laugh and say it was all a joke. But he didn't. When she couldn't bear to look at him any longer, she turned to Agatha. 'What are we supposed to do, Gran? How does all this work?'

'I'm sorry, Rosie,' she said. 'I don't know anything about this.'

Mason grinned and raised his eyebrows as if he had known what she would say all along. When Agatha noticed that, she thought for a moment and sat up straighter and squared her shoulders until something defiant shone in her eyes. 'But Rosie darling, if you think there's something between you and this boy, some sort of connection, then trust in it if you think it's good. Because there's so little good in the world it must count for something against all the bad.' When Agatha looked straight at Mason, he stared right back.

'Get you, Granny,' he said, nodding as if he approved of everything she had said.

Rosie squeezed her grandmother's hand and then she turned and took the ring from Mason's palm and clenched her fist round it. 'Tell me what Lawson did, Daniel,' she said, ignoring Mason's excited gasps.

As she stared at him, waiting to hear what he had to say, Daniel wondered how this delicate and beautiful girl would ever be strong enough to make the fit when it seemed she would break apart in his arms if he simply hugged her. But when the fingers of her other hand gripped his wrist he felt a strength in them. Like wire. It strengthened something inside him too and he turned and looked at Mason.

'Whatever we're going to try isn't for you. It's to see if we can make the fit that's going to let us do something really good with it, like helping my dad and Rosie too.'

Mason drummed his fingers on his great big knees. 'Of course it is, Daniel. Whatever you say. Now let's get on with it, shall we?' And he took out his little black notebook from his jacket pocket and opened it, ready to write everything down with his pencil.

'Focus on the ring,' said Daniel, turning to Rosie. 'Then do whatever you did in the lift earlier. I'm going to focus on you, Rosie. I'm going to open my heart to you and let you do your best to use what's inside me. I'll warn you if anything feels wrong. I'll keep you safe.'

Rosie nodded and closed her eyes and Daniel did his best to focus on her, trying to forget about Mason as he watched. Then, in the next moment, he felt the familiar flutter in his chest and a warmth coursing through him, as if his blood was turning golden.

He began to see moments playing out around him, like little snippets of film, just as he had done when Lawson had made the fit with him . . .

A dead man's face, his eyes staring at nothing . . .

. . . the silver signet ring on his little finger . . .

. . . he was lying in a pool of blood on a road bordered by shops shuttered up for the night, under the glare of a street light . . .

. . . as a white car idled further on down the street.

And then the driver's door opened.

A pair of silver boot tips stopped beside the dead man's head and a hand picked up a leather briefcase that was lying in the road.

And then the white car began to drive away . . .

. . . A right indicator flashed as the white car reached a junction at the top of the street and then disappeared, leaving the dead man under the light.

Rosie described these things to Mason and he leant forward and asked for more. 'Tell me who took my money, Rosie. Tell me,' he growled.

There was not the slightest fear inside Daniel of anything feeling wrong as the warmth increased in his chest, and he knew that Rosie was trying harder to make their fit stronger. He kept focused on her as more moments spun out of nowhere and played out around him . . .

The face of a man, thickset, with a black moustache and a scar across one side of his cheek, opening the briefcase and looking inside at bricks of money, then snapping it shut and walking away from the body in the street . . .

. . . the leather briefcase lying on the passenger seat of the white car . . .

. . . the man with the black moustache sitting in the driver's seat, pumping the clutch with a silver-tipped boot as he drove away from the dead man, just a dark hump on the road in the rear-view mirror.

A letter lying crumpled in the well of the passenger seat below the briefcase. A tax demand for a Mr Gates. Address: 31 Highfield Crescent, Cambridge CB2 9BT.

Over and over Rosie repeated what she was seeing until she opened her eyes, and she was blinking in the early evening sunlight coming low through the window in front of her, her face red and glistening with sweat.

You could have popped a marble through the 'O' of Mason's mouth as he stared at them, his pencil poised above the notebook, apparently surprised neither of them had come to any harm. When he seemed to accept it, he looked at the name and address he had written down and then flipped the notebook shut and stood up.

'You two come with me,' he said. When neither Daniel nor Rosie moved, Mason clicked his fingers and motioned for them to stand up. 'It's important. You need to see what happens next. So you both know how serious I am about everything.'

As they stood up, he winked at Agatha. 'Your grand-daughter's a real peach, you know that?' He blew a kiss across the room at her. 'See you later, Granny-gator.'

46

The man with the black moustache and the scar was lying on the floor of the bedsit, bloodied and beaten, his nose a nub of red putty. One of his wrists was broken, misshapen like an overripe fruit about to burst. Frank and Jiff stood impassively in one corner, looking on as Mason showed Daniel and Rosie into the room. He clicked the door shut behind them, then turned to survey the room, tutting disapprovingly. A cheap desk splintered and thrown on its side. The bed upturned and the stripy mattress ripped down its centre with a knife. A lamp on the floor, its white shade askew and the bulb peeking out.

Mason picked up the leather briefcase, which stood beside Frank, and scowled as he judged its weight.

'How light?'

'A couple of hundred quid,' said Jiff.

'He's just a chancer, boss,' said Frank. 'Thought he'd won the lottery when he found it.'

'Not stupid though,' said Mason. 'Didn't blow it all in one go. Or else we would have heard about that.' He pursed his lips. Then trod slowly down on the man's broken wrist, making him cry out.

'I'll go easy on you, Mr Gates. You've had a bad day already by the looks of things. Ten per cent interest. Daily. That's what you owe me now. It's my money, you see.'

He picked up a chair and positioned it squarely in the centre of the room and sat down. He flicked open the locks on the briefcase and stared at the money. Thin bricks of notes, each one with a yellow rubber band around it. There were two spaces.

He felt underneath the money and found a slim black box. He flicked the small silver switch in its top right corner back and forth and then gave it a shake and listened to something rattling.

'Did you break the transponder?'

The man lying on the floor gurgled something. Coughed. Spat a string of blood. And then he shook his head because even such a small word seemed to be beyond him.

'No, I expect you didn't,' said Mason, looking round the room. He lobbed the broken transponder at Frank. 'Buy British next time.'

Snapping the briefcase shut, he smiled to himself as he drummed his fingers on the leather top. When he

210

looked up at Daniel and Rosie, he stared at them for some time. Neither of them knew where to look. Not at Mason. Or at the man gasping on the carpet or the gloved black hands of Frank and Jiff standing still as rocks.

'You see what I can do when people disappoint me?' said Mason.

Daniel nodded slowly. So did Rosie.

'Well then,' said Mason. He stood up and plucked a small brown teddy bear off a shelf with a red ribbon around its neck on which a tiny bell was attached and shook it close to his ear. When he lobbed it at Rosie, the bell rattled when she caught it. 'A memento. So neither of you forget.'

When they came back out into the alley where Mason's BMW was parked, there was no longer any evening sun because a mist was curdling in the street, blocking out the sky and slowly deleting the buildings around them.

In the car, Mason laughed and joked with Frank and Jiff who were sitting in the front seats. The BMW smelt of white leather and cologne and beer because Mason was sipping from a bottle of Bud, which frothed against the glass every time he took a sip.

Daniel let down the window and smelt the mist and the wind funnelling down the street. He pushed his head out until all the men's voices had disappeared in the roar so he could be alone with his thoughts . . .

. . . the hope he had for what he and Rosie might be able to do to help his father . . .

. . . the man lying on the floor in the bedsit . . .

. . . Lawson.

He thought he heard Rosie's voice above the drone of the wind and looked back. But she was facing straight ahead, beside him, with her eyes closed. She looked older, as if time had played a trick on his memory of her. When she opened her eyes, Daniel smiled, but her lips stayed fixed, like two pink rods. So he took her hand in his and held it.

Mason popped the lid off two more bottles of Bud and thrust one under Daniel's nose and waggled it, making the beer fizz white as it rose in the neck.

'You're one of the gang now.'

He held the bottle out until Daniel grabbed hold and took a fizzy swig and all three men cheered. And then Mason made Rosie drink from the other one too.

When they pulled up, they could barely see Rosie's house through the mist. But they could all tell it was big and white, with a gravel drive that set it back from the road.

'Looks nice,' said Mason. 'What does your dad do?'

'He's a doctor,' she said quietly.

Mason nodded as he thought about that. Gave her a nudge with one of his big arms. 'But not a cancer doctor?' And he laughed out loud like it was the punchline to a joke.

Rosie kept blinking at him, something ticking in her jaw, until she looked away, tucking a curl of hair behind her ear.

Mason grinned. 'I said you'd learn to be scared of me, Rosie, didn't I? Didn't I say that, boys?' Frank and Jiff grunted and nodded. 'Maybe I'm a psychic too. Come to think of it . . .' Mason tapped his great bald head, his brow furrowed, then raised his hands like some TV evangelist about to preach a great truth. 'Yes, I can see it. I can see the future for both of you. Now you've found my money, you're going to get me what I *really* want. The antique flask that Lawson promised he was going to track down. And you're both coming with me tomorrow to look for it.'

'I can't,' mumbled Rosie.

Mason grunted. He plucked the brown teddy bear from Rosie's lap and waggled it, making the bell around its neck jingle.

But Rosie shook her head. 'I have my first chemotherapy treatment tomorrow.'

'What time?'

213

'All day. They have to do blood tests and then they make up the drugs the same day, which takes time, and then I'm given the infusion. It's non-negotiable.'

Mason cricked his neck. Sighed. Looked at the teddy bear and shook his head. 'No, I don't think she'd lie. Naughty bear for thinking such a thing.' He cuffed the teddy's head. 'You wouldn't lie, Rosie, would you? Not now we have an understanding?'

He paused when Rosie reached across Daniel and clicked open the door. Quickly, she took Daniel's head in her hands and kissed him. He tasted apricots and peppermint. Her hair smelt of ginger. When she hugged him hard, she whispered something quietly so no one else would hear.

'Ten o'clock tomorrow with your dad.'

All four of them watched her blurring at the edges as the mist rolled round her until she was drifting towards the house like a ghost.

Mason pinged his electric window down and shouted, 'You forgot teddy!' They heard the front door slam shut. 'They're touchy, these psychic types,' said Mason as he rolled the window up. 'Or maybe it's just the tumour.' He patted Frank's shoulder and they pulled out on to the road, and drove through the mist in silence until they pulled up in Daniel's street.

'She in, do you think?' asked Mason.

'Who?' Daniel felt something in his throat and couldn't swallow it down.

'Your aunt.'

Daniel looked at his feet and tried to think of something else.

'Maybe.'

'I should meet her.'

'Not sure you'd want to.'

'Beat your balls, does she?'

'Yeah.'

'Well then.' And Mason drummed his fingers on the leather seat beside him as if it helped him to think. Eventually, he produced a mobile phone from the inside of his jacket pocket. 'Give me a shout if you need anything. I'm under M. For Mason.'

'I'm not sure I will.'

But Mason kept the mobile in his palm, and Daniel took it and put it in his pocket.

'Anything,' repeated Mason. 'Remember, you're one of us now.' And Frank and Jiff in the front seats growled as if in agreement. 'Keep the phone with you,' said Mason as Daniel opened the door and got out of the car. 'I'll be in touch about the flask.' And then he leant across and slammed the door shut and the BMW drove away into the mist.

As Daniel walked in the direction of his house, he heard the shriek of an animal. A metal bin crashed to the pavement and a lid rolled somewhere like a giant penny and clattered to a stop. In the silence afterwards, Daniel waited in the mist, his breath soundless and white, wondering what was happening until a fox appeared suddenly on the pavement in front of him, its damp fur bejewelled and the white of its throat roughed with the damp.

The creature sniffed the air and blinked and then trotted away, its shoulders like pistons under its pelt. Its brush twitched before it disappeared into the mist as if adding the finishing touches to a brand-new world in which everything had been painted out except for Daniel himself.

47

When Daniel's aunt woke in the middle of the night, she wondered why until she heard Daniel crying out again, his muffled voice coming through the walls. She got up and padded out of her room and down the landing and opened his bedroom door.

Daniel was asleep, curled up like a dormouse in his duvet. His aunt listened when he started crying out again, burbling words and names she did not know, and then, before she knew what she was doing, she went and crouched beside him and started stroking his hair, shushing him.

When he moved sharply in his sleep, the duvet swilling like sea foam around him, her hand froze. Then, without warning, his eyes fluttered open and he blinked up at her.

'Mum?' His voice was full of sleep and his eyes were dreamy.

'Yes,' she whispered back immediately before she knew what she was saying, instantly regretting it, and holding her breath to see what he might say when he realized it was not a dream. But all he did was blink and nod and seem to decide through some sleepy mechanics of his brain to close his eyes and settle seamlessly into sleep again. She watched him for some time, as if guarding him from the world, listening to him breathing peacefully, the nightmares inside him gone.

After closing the door, she stood on the landing until her hands had stopped shaking in the dim orangey light coming from the street lights outside. When she felt ready, she went downstairs and picked up the photograph of her twin sister off the dresser in the hallway.

'You don't need to worry,' she said. 'I'll look after him, I promise. I'll do the best I can, just as if he was Michael. I won't let you down. Either of you. I won't.'

The Man Who Came
Up Out of the Floor

48

Bennett checked his watch to stop his foot tapping. It was 10.05. He was about to ask Daniel if he had remembered to tell the ward staff that Rosie was coming when the door opened and she stood there, blinking at them. She looked so willowy and tall, Bennett expected her to sway back and forth in the draught from the door as it shut behind her.

'It took me a while to get rid of Mum,' she said. 'I sent her off shopping.' She held up a bleeper. 'They're going to let me know when they want me back for my chemo so we've got a little bit of time.'

Bennett stood up and introduced himself and offered her his chair and then leant against the wall with his arms folded.

'I don't want to get in the way,' he said. 'I'm just here in case it doesn't work, for moral support.' And he raised a thumb at Daniel who nodded back.

Rosie sat herself down beside Daniel and looked at the man lying in front of her. 'He looks so calm.'

'All the sedatives are out of his system,' said Daniel. 'That's what the nursing staff told us. He's definitely in his own coma now.'

'We're going to do everything we can,' said Rosie. 'We're going to help your dad. We're going to find out what we can really do with these gifts of ours.'

Daniel watched her sit up straight in her chair as if preparing herself for some testing question. 'What happens to you when we make the fit?' he asked. 'What do you see?'

'A light,' she said, staring at Daniel's father. 'I see a ball of bright white light inside me. And I know it's there to help with whatever I'm trying to do. It's there like some battery for me to draw on. It's strange and yesterday is the first time I've felt it. It's when I'm with you, Daniel. It's only there when we make the fit.'

She took hold of Daniel's father's limp hand and closed her eyes. A moment later, Daniel felt little golden sparks flitting in his chest. 'Can you see that ball of bright light?' he asked anxiously. 'Is it there?'

'Yes,' said Rosie. 'It's right inside me, just like it was yesterday.'

Daniel felt the golden warmth in his chest increasing as Rosie made the fit between them stronger.

'I can feel how much your father loves you,' she whispered. 'I can sense it through all the things you've done together. All his memories are there inside him. His whole life is there for me to see.' She was smiling. 'You've done so many things together. Oh, Daniel, he loves you so much.'

'Can he hear us? Does he know we're here?' Daniel sat further forward on his chair and touched his father's arm. 'Dad, if you can hear us then let Rosie know; please tell her so we know you're there.'

Daniel's chest was full of a golden heat now and he was beginning to sweat. Rosie's white face was twitching and flickering as she made the fit stronger, trying to look deeper into the man in the bed beside her.

'He's very hidden,' she said. 'I can't find *him*, the thinking part of him, the dad that you know.'

'Keep looking,' said Daniel. 'Please, Rosie. Please don't stop. There's got to be more than just memories inside him. There can't just be the past. He's got to be there too.'

Rosie was flinching now and her arms were twitching. Her lips were trembling and peeling back to show her perfect white teeth. Little currents raced up and down the muscles of her throat.

Daniel put his hand to his chest when he felt the heat in it starting to become painful, just like it had done with Lawson. But when he saw his father's face beginning to flicker he told himself to ignore it.

223

'You're doing something, Rosie,' he told her. 'Something's happening!' Daniel heard Bennett's voice muttering in astonishment behind him, but he was too excited to turn round. His father's whole body was twitching now and his mouth was moving as if the man was trying to speak. One of his eyelids rolled slowly back and Daniel ignored the pain in his chest and leant over.

'Dad! Dad! Can you see me? It's Dan! Can you hear me?'

He heard one of the machines chiming a warning sound and he looked up at Rosie, her face shining with sweat. Before he could tell her to keep going, he felt the pain rising rapidly in his chest. It was so harsh it took his breath away and for a moment it was impossible to speak.

'*St-op!*' he shouted as his breath came back to him. '*St-op!*'

But Rosie shook her head. 'Just a little more,' she managed to say. When she wiped her nose, a tiny smear of blood striped the back of her hand and Daniel remembered that Lawson had done exactly the same, before everything had gone wrong.

'Stop, Rosie! Please!' But she didn't seem able to hear him now. He put out his arms to try and shake her, but the pain in his chest had taken all his strength away.

A sound started up inside him, a clicking noise. Steady and regular like a metronome beating time.

Daniel remembered the sound and what had happened to Lawson's hand after it had stopped. He shouted to Rosie again, but his words were slurred now. It was like chewing toffee as he tried to speak. The clicking grew faster and faster. Louder and louder. It seemed like a wasp had flown deep into his skull and was lost there, becoming angrier and angrier as it tried to get out.

Suddenly, he was dimly aware of Bennett standing beside them, drawing back his hand and striking Rosie hard across her face, the crack of his palm like a whip on her cheek.

It brought her back from whatever place she was in and her eyes snapped open and she sat back in the chair, breathing heavily, a red stripe forming on her face, sweat strung in beads across her brow.

The buzzing in Daniel's head was already fading and the pain in his chest was softening, melting away.

'Oh, Daniel,' whispered Rosie. 'I couldn't see anything. I couldn't see your dad. There was nothing there.'

When the door opened, the nurse came rushing in, but the machine had stopped chiming and Daniel's father was lying there peacefully as if nothing had happened at all.

Bennett brought them plastic cups of cold water filled from the reservoir beside the ward door. He said sorry to Rosie again for slapping her and told them that he had been scared and hadn't known what else to do.

She nodded and said it was OK. But when she rubbed her face again Bennett wasn't sure if he believed her.

'I thought if I just pushed a bit harder I could find him,' said Rosie. She shook her head. 'I'm sorry, Daniel.'

'It's not your fault.'

'It is. It's me. I need to learn more about what I'm doing. We need to practise and then we can try again.'

Before Rosie could say anything else, the bleeper went off and she knew her chemotherapy infusion was ready.

'We'll try again. We will,' said Rosie as she clicked the bleeper off and then she hugged Daniel and left to go back to the unit where her mother was fretting, waiting for her, asking where in the hell she had been.

After she had gone, Bennett sat down beside Daniel. 'Do you think you can really do it? That you can really help your dad?'

'I do in my heart, Bennett.'

'But in your head?'

Daniel tapped his foot.

'Daniel, do you believe it in your head?'

He looked up at Bennett. 'Of course I do. How can I think anything else?'

49

When Rosie looked again, the cannula was already pricked into the vein on the back of her hand, secure with a dressing, and the nurse was walking away.

She watched the *drip drip drip* of the vincristine drug in its solution inside the transparent bag, hanging from its stand, and tried not to think about how bad the side effects of the chemotherapy might be. Whatever worries she had didn't come close to matching the fears that constantly bubbled up inside her about her tumour and what the cancer might do to her.

She had googled survival rates for low-grade gliomas like hers constantly, after her diagnosis, trying to decipher her future from the numbers and graphs. When she had started reading about the experiences of other patients like her, everybody had seemed to have their own story to tell. It had all seemed so random to Rosie that she eventually gave up using them to search for clues to the truth about how her own story was going to turn out. Despite being told by doctors that having chemotherapy before surgery might be very effective in her particular circumstances it was hard not to daydream about the worst of it now that she was here finally embarking on her treatment.

Seeing Daniel's father made all her fears seem more real too. The man had seemed so empty inside, like something hollowed out. It reminded her of the eggs she and her mum used to paint at Easter when she was younger, the shells pricked through with pins so the yolks and the whites could be blown out into a Pyrex bowl and kept for cooking. Rosie wished she had been able to do more to help him, and to help Daniel too. But she hadn't seemed close to being able to make anything happen, not even right up to the moment she had felt the sting of Bennett's slap and her eyes had snapped open.

Her hands balled into white-hot fists the more she thought about it, refusing to believe that she and Daniel had made the best fit they could. It felt like everything was up to her to try harder because Daniel was only the battery who increased her power.

She began to watch the two other teenagers in the room who were also receiving their chemotherapy, both of them lying on beds and wearing headphones, plugged into screens. Rosie knew a little bit about the girl because they had met on the ward before. Her name was Sophie. She was a year older and had been diagnosed with a medulloblastoma. Rosie focused on her first, trying to use her talents to find out something personal about the girl, about what her life was like outside the ward.

But the *drip drip drip* of the vincristine in the bag hanging above her seemed to get in the way of Rosie's thinking. She found it impossible to get a hold on Sophie and find out anything. She kept trying, but her brain felt useless and heavy. She could have been holding hot coals in her hands as she clenched her fists to try harder. The coil of tubing on the pillow beside her moved when she did and kept breaking her concentration.

Frustrated, she turned her attention to the patient sitting on the other side of her, a boy called Mike who was the same age as her. He had been diagnosed with a rare form of leukaemia and his bare scalp shone in the daylight like a wet rock. But when she tried to look inside him nothing happened, as if a valve had been switched off inside her to stop her using her gift. The harder she tried, the more the *drip drip drip* of the drug in the bag above her seemed to grow louder until it was all she could hear, like something was dripping inside her.

When Rosie gave up trying, she decided the efforts with Daniel's father must have tired her out. Maybe she needed to recharge somehow. So she sat back and wished the drugs into her system and deep into the tumour that had grown mysteriously and silently in her brain.

The infusion only took ten minutes after which the cannula was removed. Rosie was given two different coloured tablets – one blue and one ivory. She was asked to repeat the strict instructions about when to take the tablets in the upcoming days because the nurse wanted to make sure she understood.

'How will I feel?' asked Rosie. 'How long will any side effects last?'

'Do you feel ill now?' asked the nurse, concerned.

'No . . . but . . .' She paused and wondered what to say. 'No, I'm OK,' she said and bit the inside of her cheek as her mother pushed open the doors and came back through into the unit, ready to whisk her home.

50

Daniel and Bennett decided to wait and see if Rosie came back. But the longer they sat there talking, trying to involve Daniel's father in their conversation, the more certain they became that she wouldn't.

Bennett suggested they watch YouTube clips from Daniel's father's favourite films on his phone, saying he had been reading up on coma patients and what might help. So they played scenes from classic movies like *Jaws* and *Star Wars* that Daniel's dad was always quoting lines from and they joined in loudly when the most famous lines came up. They went through clips from *Alien* and *Blade Runner* and comedies like *Ghostbusters* and *Beverly Hills Cop* and *The Breakfast Club*.

They tried playing songs that Daniel knew his father liked, singing along to rock tunes and dancing to house music and banging their heads to grunge.

Eventually, the battery on the phone was too low to play any more and Bennett said he had to go and he told Daniel that he should go home too.

'I can't,' Daniel replied. 'My feet feel like they're stuck to the floor.'

'Why don't you think of one memory then?' suggested Bennett. 'A really special one your dad might like to hear. Then you'll know that you've tried your best for today.'

Daniel rubbed his head as if trying to summon a personal genie to tell him the very best memory he had. 'We went fishing once,' he said eventually. 'Fly-fishing. It feels stupid now, talking about it.' He shrugged like it was a bad idea. 'Maybe—'

'Go on,' said Bennett.

'But nothing really happened.'

'Tell me what it was like. I want to hear.'

So Daniel told him everything he could remember about it. How it had been an early August morning last summer when they had been staying in a holiday cottage in Devon. His father had found two fly rods in the attic and had knocked on Daniel's bedroom door as the world was breaking open for the day.

'They were two-piece canes as light as bones,' said Daniel. 'Each one had a cork handle, and they were so dainty you could balance them on a finger. There was a river a mile from where we were staying. After we walked there, we found a spot clear of trees and started to cast. I'd never tried fishing before.'

He described to Bennett how the cane rods whipped and the wet lines hissed as they peeled up off the water, unfurling behind them, then hurtling forward with a flick of the wrist to land soft on the face of the river.

'We aimed the flies for spots that looked likely. Dark holes in the water or pools or beneath an overhanging branch. The first tug of a trout I felt, I struck too hard and yanked the fly out of the water in a coil of line. Three times I missed a fish. And after the third time, as I was pulling back to cast again, I saw a tiny fish hooked to the end, a parr Dad called it. It was so small I hadn't felt it. I was so shocked I lost control and shanked the line and it caught in a branch, leaving the tiny fish hanging like a Christmas decoration, flipping and spar-kling, gasping in the air. We cut it down and I slid it off my hand back into the water, watching it swim safely back into the deep.'

He told Bennett how they spent three hours fishing in the sharp morning light with the blue sky hardening above them and the air starting to bake as the sun burned off the mist. And they barely spoke. Somehow, the silence made them one with each other and at one with everything around them. It was a memory to cherish.

233

'I remember it all, Dad,' said Daniel. 'It'll stay with me forever.'

As they left through the ward security door, Bennett immediately recognised the junior doctor, James, coming the other way along the corridor. They said hello and Bennett told Daniel that James had been at university at the same time as Bennett's brother where they had been best friends.

'We drank a lot together,' said James ruefully. 'And did some silly things along the way to getting a degree. Just.' He tapped his lips and then asked if he could speak to Daniel alone for a moment.

'You can speak to both of us. Bennett's *my* best friend. That's why he's here.'

James nodded. Tucked the folder of notes he was holding tighter under his arm. 'I've been thinking a lot about what you were asking yesterday, about why things happen and how to explain them. It reminded me of a book I read a few years ago by a man called Viktor Frankl. I thumbed through it again last night.' James cupped his chin in his hand and thought for a moment. 'How about we say it doesn't matter *why* things happen, but only *what* they can do for you.'

'I don't understand what you mean,' said Daniel.

James drummed his fingers on the folder of notes he was holding.

'Imagine you switch your brain from trying to figure out *why* something happens to you to thinking about how to respond to it. If you do that then the power's with you to decide *who* you want to be, *what* sort of person you want to become. The most important thing isn't about trying to work out why things occur, or how the world works, it's about discovering who you are in the face of everything that happens to you, the good as well as the bad, and even the somewhere in between.' He smiled at Daniel. 'I thought it might help in some tiny way, to have something positive to ponder rather than all the dark inside you. Daniel, if there's anything you want to talk about, anything at all, then please ask and I'll do whatever I can to help. The ward staff know how to get hold of me.' He bade them goodbye and then went on his way.

Bennett leant in close to Daniel as they walked towards the lift. 'James was like you, you know.'

'What do you mean?'

'He was in the papers as well, about ten years ago. My brother told me what happened. He was a bit younger than you when he ran away and got kidnapped by travellers. My brother said James told him there was some weird stuff that happened. Black magic stuff, the sort that people would never believe if they knew about it.'

'Like what?'

'Maybe you should ask him. Maybe he can help you and Rosie with the fit. He might know something?'

Daniel shrugged as he punched the call button for the lift. 'He's a doctor, Bennett. I bet he wouldn't know anything about how it works.'

On the bus ride home, Daniel thought about everything James had told him. But it was hard to stop wishing for answers about the sinkhole and what had happened to his father, and how he had found a way out of the ground. He didn't want to think about who he was supposed to be now, he wanted to be the same person he had always been, the boy his dad had always known and would recognise when he woke up.

A buzzing in his pocket made him flinch, scattering his thoughts, because he knew what it was immediately. But he didn't look at Mason's text straightaway. He sat there, pretending that Mason lived in a different world to the one he was in. But when the phone started to buzz again and again he checked the messages. They all said the same thing:

Will pick u up tomorrow. Hospital. 12pm. Bring Rosie. Mxx

Seeing 'M xx' at the end of every message made Daniel so angry that when he stepped off the bus at his stop he only managed to walk a few steps before he hurled the phone against the wall and heard the screen crack.

51

Foxton was a small village seven miles outside Cambridge. The cemetery there was separated from the churchyard by a narrow lane banked on either side by a drystone wall decorated with green ferns the size of ostrich feathers. A wooden gate was hung on spring-loaded hinges, powdered with rust, and Daniel watched it click shut as Mason and Rosie walked on ahead down the grassy path between the gravestones. Jiff was ambling behind them, the hump on his back like a tiny burial mound of his own.

All the gravestones around them were crooked and slanted askew in the ground. Daniel wanted to turn round and run away rather than walk between them. Looking back, he saw how easy it would be to sprint across the lane and disappear into the hedge and hide there. But Frank was leaning against the blue BMW parked up the lane, and he looked up suddenly from his phone as if a text had pinged in to tell him what Daniel had been thinking about doing. When he stood up and started walking, Daniel just turned round and pushed the gate open and went on through.

He tried not to look at the gravestones as he walked down the path, letting them bob at the edges of his eyes, his fists turning damp on the inside.

Mason stopped at a round-topped headstone made of sandstone that had been dulled by the wind and the rain, with lichen smeared over it like gum. A plain stone. A plain inscription. Mason rubbed it over with the flat of his hand:

HERE LIETH THE BODY
OF FRANCIS GREEN
BORN
FEBRUARY 17TH 1718
DIED
AUGUST 26TH 1779

Carved above it was an ornate oil lamp with a tiny flame protruding from the spout. Mason crouched down beside Rosie and Daniel, a thick, hot smell coming off him.

'Know what an oil lamp means on a gravestone?' They shook their heads. 'Immortality. Legend has it Mr

Green was an alchemist who discovered the secrets of eternal life. Didn't do him much good though, did it, boys?' shouted Mason, and Frank and Jiff both laughed, nodding as they lit up cigarettes.

Mason grinned as he patted the grass beneath him. 'We dug up the bones a few weeks back and Lawson looked them over. Said they were Green's all right because Lawson saw things. Moments. Like Green making a beautiful golden flask. *Like something made from sunshine*, Lawson said. And he said Green gave it to his wife as a present and it stayed in their family for years. Lawson only found out bits and bobs about the flask. But you two, well, you two might be different; you might see a whole lot more than he did. You might be able to see where it is now and that's got me very excited.'

'Mason wants to live forever,' said Frank, puffing on his cigarette. 'Don't you, boss?' He raised his arms. 'Not like all these poor buggers.'

'In this world?' grunted Mason. 'You must be joking, Frank.' He grinned at Rosie and Daniel. 'So don't worry, I won't be around forever. I don't believe the legend. I want the flask for another reason. So I need you to tell me what Lawson couldn't. To find out what other secrets are lurking in those bones below us and tell me where the flask is now. For you to have a look around in the places I can't get to.'

'You want us to do that right here?' asked Daniel.

Mason nodded. He looked up into the sky and screwed up his face at a big black cloud. 'Looks like rain so we should hurry up,' he growled. 'This is an expensive suit. Savile Row, don't you know,' he said, rhyming it like it was a line of verse. And then he folded his arms. 'Come on, I'm all ears.'

When Rosie closed her eyes, Daniel expected something to happen, but it didn't. There was no golden warmth in his chest. No sensation at all. When he saw Rosie's face tensing more and more, he knew that something was wrong. Before he could say anything, she opened her eyes and stood blinking in the sunlight. Then she reeled back suddenly and grabbed hold of the gravestone for balance. In one sweeping bow, she leant forward and vomited on to the grass.

The first drops of rain hissed as they landed. They looked like wet thumbprints on the gravestones, but Mason just stood there, more raindrops popping on his shoulders and his chest as he watched Rosie wiping her mouth with the back of her hand. 'Well?'

'I didn't see anything.' Rosie took a breath and spat something white and foamy as far as she could.

'What? Nothing?' asked Mason. And Rosie shook her head. 'But even Lawson got something.'

'Well, why don't you try asking him?' hissed Rosie, crouching down, pulling something stringy and white from her lips and wiping her hands on the grass.

'Because he's dead, Rosie. Daniel popped his hand off like a champagne cork. Which means you two are filling in now.'

The rain was pattering harder and Mason's bald head was starting to glisten. A droplet rolled down his brow, making him frown even more.

'I need to go home,' said Rosie.

'What?' replied Mason, blinking like a baby bird.

'I'm not feeling well.' When Rosie wiped her eyes, the green in them glistened. 'It's the chemotherapy. It's done something.'

Mason dug a divot in the grass and stared at the moist, muddy earth. Then he looked up at the grey sky, into the drops of rain, as if weighing up whether it was just a shower that would pass.

'We could dig up the coffin like we did for Lawson, see if that helps. Give you something more to work with. But we'd have to wait till tonight to do that.'

'Didn't you hear me?' replied Rosie. 'The chemo's done something. I can't make the fit with Daniel.'

'Well, what would you like me to do?' Mason wiped his face and his eyes shone as though a fire had been lit inside him. 'This isn't exactly what I was expecting.'

'I don't know.'

241

Daniel folded his arms and stood as tall as he could. 'We should go. Try again another time.'

Mason clicked his tongue against the roof of his mouth. Then he pointed at the church. 'No, we're not going anywhere. Let's sort this out in the dry.'

52

Inside the church, the rain sounded like tacks falling out of a box on to the roof. Rosie and Daniel stood, hot and prickly with damp, on the flagstone floor as Mason clunked the big oak door shut behind them, the echo ringing round the stone walls as if all three of them had entered the belly of some ancient, fossilized beast. He walked past Daniel and Rosie and stopped on a red carpet running the length of the aisle.

'Dearly beloved,' he quipped. 'We are gathered here today to ask you, God, and baby Jesus too, to help Rosie get over whatever problem she's got so she and Daniel can make the fit. Because I need them to. Amen. Bless you and all that.' He bowed comically and tried to make the sign of the cross and then he turned to Rosie and Daniel.

'I told you. It's the chemotherapy. It's done something. I can't see anything,' said Rosie.

'What do you think, Daniel? I thought you were supposed to be the battery, the power. Maybe you just need to bump up the charge to help Rosie, is that it?'

'I don't know how it works,' replied Daniel. 'If Rosie can't do anything then I think we need to wait until she feels better. Try again—'

'BUT ... I ... DON'T ... WANT ... TO ... WAIT!' shouted Mason and his voice rolled like thunder round and round the vaulted ceiling, forcing a trio of pigeons, roosting outside the stained-glass windows, to flap noisily away. He smoothed a hand over his bare head and glared at the two of them as the silence settled again. The air was bitter with Brasso and wood and cold stone as Daniel struggled to breathe.

'Francis Green may or may not have been an alchemist,' continued Mason more calmly, 'but he was most definitely one of the finest goldsmiths of his time. In fact, his contemporaries said he struck a deal with the devil his work was so unique, so *ex-quis-ite*. You can look in any auction catalogue or museum guide to see why.

'Now a couple of months ago, I got talking to a collector about Green at a function, one of those hoity-toity affairs with pearls and bow ties and drinks bubbling in glasses on silver trays, that people like me are always desperate to get invited to. And this collector told me he was very keen to find a particular piece of Green's work. A flask made of gold. The Headington Flask. Rumoured

244

to be somewhere near Cambridge, buried in the Fens perhaps or maybe hidden in a church or one of the colleges in Cambridge. And I promised to find it for him because this collector is willing to pay a lot of money. *A lot* of money. And, as you know, I like money.

'I thought to myself, *Lawson can help me out here. Lawson's my go-to guy for that kind of stuff.* But now Lawson's gone and if I can't locate the flask I promised to deliver then I've got a problem. So I don't need you, Rosie, to be a problem on top of another problem. That just would not do. Because I don't have time for problems. Not even at the best of times.' Mason glared at her. Clicked his fingers and raised a large forefinger. 'You're my go-to girl now Lawson's gone.'

'I don't want to try anything now,' said Rosie as she raised a trembling hand to her brow. 'Please, I don't feel well. I have a headache. I don't want to do this.'

Mason shook his head. 'You're going to have to try harder. Work through the problem. What you need, Rosie, is some gentle encouragement.'

Mason took a deep breath and strode down the aisle, raising his arms as he looked about him. 'We've got lots of dead people here. Names on plaques. Tombs. Even a person on a cross. We'll work through this chemotherapy problem with you or else I'm going to start cracking a skull or two and I'll begin with your gran's.'

Mason tripped back down the aisle like an over-weight Fred Astaire and dug around in the change in his pocket and popped a pound coin into the donations box beside the door. When it hit the bottom with a *thunk*, he picked up a small pamphlet entitled: 'A History of St Barnabas's Church'.

Mason dabbed a finger with his tongue, parted the thin pages and started reading out the names of people.

'Francis Levant. Josephus Dunn. Charles Lavelle.' He paused and tapped the page. 'John Bannister's the one!' Mason beamed. 'It says here he's buried down in the crypt.'

They stood in the semi-dark, with a lit candle and the tomb of John Bannister in front of them. Mason was using his phone to see the page of the pamphlet clearly, the light setting his face in relief like some gargoyle.

'Come on, Rosie,' whispered Mason. 'Get that talent of yours up and running. Make the fit with Daniel. I know you can.' He tapped the page. 'Tell me something about Mr Bannister to prove it or else I'll break your granny's fingers one by one ... *snap* ... *snap* ... *snap* ... like little sticks of kindling.'

Rosie's face was all bone and shadows in the candle-light. When Mason grinned even more, motioning at her to go ahead, she closed her eyes, swaying until she put her hand against the wall to steady herself.

There was nothing at all inside Daniel. No golden glow. He watched Rosie's face tensing up. Her hand was pressing harder against the wall and then the fingers started to clench up into a claw.

'Rosie,' whispered Daniel. 'You don't have to do anything. You don't—'

'Daniel,' said Mason, 'you're not helping. Be a good boy and let Rosie concentrate.'

Rosie's hand was a fist now. Her arm was juddering and the knuckles were chafing against the wall. In the candlelight, Daniel could see that she was rubbing them raw.

When he started to feel something in his chest, it was not a golden warmth. There were painful spots all over it, so electric and sharp it was like his skin was being stippled with a needle.

Daniel shuddered as the pain became more intense, the stabbing sensation faster and harder. Rosie's face twitched and danced as the candle puffed and skittered, catching the draught coming down the steps into the crypt. She started to talk about John Bannister and who he had been and what he had done. Her fist rubbed frantically over the wall, making the skin start to bleed. When Daniel felt more pain, like nails being tapped into his chest, he cried out.

'Something's wrong, Rosie. This doesn't feel right. Rosie, stop!'

But she gritted her teeth and spat out a few more words and phrases from the pamphlet that Mason was holding until he held up his hand and announced that she could stop.

She fell back against the wall, clutching her raw, bloody hand to her chest. Daniel crouched down, breathing hard, as the pain in his chest slowly began to fade.

'I knew I could trust you, Rosie,' said Mason and gave her the thumbs up. 'You just needed a bit of encouragement, that's all. Now you two find that golden flask for me. Tell me where it is and I'll forget today ever happened. I'll even give you a clue: The last place Lawson had been looking for the flask was an old stately home called Ashwell Lodge. I know the spot. It's a few miles outside Cambridge. Lawson said he'd read something about Francis Green possibly staying there when he was an old man, and wanted to look around more, that he was on to something after making a few visits. So you two scoot along there tomorrow. I want to know straightaway if there's anything there that might help or whether it's just a dead end. Or else we're digging up Green's bones again.'

Mason walked across the crypt and stopped before he reached the steps. 'The collector who wants this flask is going to pay me a lot of money for it, enough so I can retire and go live somewhere hot and lie like a hippo by

248

a pool.' He smiled for a moment and cupped a hand to his ear. 'I can hear the clink of ice in the glasses now. The sun on my face. And those insects. The grasshoppery ones, what are they?'

'Cicadas,' whispered Daniel.

'*Seeec-ahhhh-daaas*,' repeated Mason in some mock foreign accent and then he beamed. 'You could come and visit once I'm settled.' He shifted his feet on the dirty stone floor, the dust and the grit crackling beneath his leather soles. 'You see what I'm saying here? Find this flask and I'll be gone, out of your lives forever. It'll be like I was never here.'

He turned and started walking up the steps, whistling as he went until his voice came ringing back down, telling them to hurry up or else there wouldn't be a lift back to town.

53

Ashwell Lodge was set back from the road down a narrow lane with silver birch trees jammed branch to branch on either side, their trunks like dim lanterns in the shade beneath the canopy.

Daniel and Rosie steered their bicycles over the pocked asphalt, slaloming round the potholes. As they emerged out of the copse, they caught sight of the big house in the distance. It looked decrepit and grey like an old shoebox left out in the rain.

They pedalled over a cattle grid, buzzing their bones, and went on down the driveway. Two rabbits pricked their ears, crouching low on the warm tarmac, watching them coming closer until some alarm sounded and they scattered into the knee-high grass, sending the feathery tops winking in the sun.

* * *

They left their bicycles lying on the driveway and walked up a set of stone steps worn thin in the middle from years of comings and goings. The front door was set back from the circular driveway in a porch framed by two white Doric columns pocked and chipped and tinged with green.

But, when they discovered it was wedged shut with something heavy jammed behind it, they waded through weeds to the nearest bay window and jumped up on to the broad stone ledge, then clambered through the rectangle of clean air above it, their hands hidden inside the sleeves of their sweaters.

Inside the house, the air was still and musty, and the floor crackled as they walked over more pieces of glass.

Rosie went into the hallway and struggled to pull away two pieces of timber wedged against the door until Daniel helped her, sending each piece spinning to the floor. They lifted the latch and dragged the door open, letting in the sunlight. It looked like the floor was steaming with all the dust that rose from it.

When Rosie wiped her hands on the wall to try and clean them, plaster spilled from tiny cracks. 'So?' she asked, standing in the doorway with the sun warming the back of her neck. 'Anything?'

Daniel took out the notebook that Bennett had bought from the kiosk in the park a few days before and scanned what his friend had written down.

251

'One of Lawson's memories was about being in a stately home with a big, winding staircase when I tried with Bennett.'

'Was that about this place?' asked Rosie, pointing at the large staircase.

'Maybe. I don't know. It was just a jumble of stuff that came out.' He held open the notebook for Rosie to see what Bennett had written down. She scanned Bennett's scribbled notes and descriptions. When she saw the symbol he had tried to draw and then Daniel's attempts to redraw it more accurately, she put her finger against the page and traced the shape because it looked so odd, like a small child's crude sketch of a bomb or maybe a goldfish with a triangle for a tail.

'Do you want to try again now?' she asked. 'See if you remember anything else?'

'OK.' Daniel closed the notebook and took a deep breath and closed his eyes. He thought, first, about the house, picturing how it had looked when they had ridden up the driveway. He listened to the creak of the door on its hinges, the sunlight ticking in the walls around them. He inhaled the dusty air and smelt the damp and the mildew. He stood silently for some time to see if anything came to him. But nothing did. Eventually, he opened his eyes. Shook his head.

'It's like Lawson's memories have already burned themselves out,' he said.

252

He stood beside Rosie in the sunshine, looking out at the driveway, scanning it for any clue that might help him remember something. But nothing came to him. 'Let's have a scout around,' he said eventually. 'It might help me. We might find something useful.'

Rosie kicked out at a ball of hair and dust being sucked out of the front door and on to the steps in a draught. 'Daniel, I'm worried about what the chemo's done to me. That the gift I had . . . that now it's broken somehow.'

'Is that how it feels?'

Rosie nodded. 'And what if it's not temporary? What if I don't know how to fix it?'

'All your other side effects are supposed to be, aren't they? The nausea? The tiredness?'

'Yes.'

'So we have to assume this one is too.' Rosie looked so drawn and tired he kept staring at her, wishing for her to feel better. Her pale cheeks glowed green and yellow in the bright sunshine.

'Tell me I don't look *that* bad?' she asked.

'OK. "I don't look *that* bad."'

Rosie smiled and punched him gently in the chest. 'You're a funny guy. I've taken my anti-emetics. I'll be fine. The bike ride took a bit out of me, that's all.'

'So do you feel like walking around, to see if we can find anything?'

253

'Sure.'

Rosie grabbed his arm to stop him marching off. 'Daniel? About what happened with your dad before my chemo.'

He looked at the floor. Drew a wobbly line in the dust with his trainer, even though he was trying to draw it true and straight.

'What about it?'

'Do you think we can really help him?'

'Yes. I don't want to think anything else.'

Rosie nodded. 'Good. Because I didn't want to think I'd let you both down.'

'You didn't, Rosie. Not one bit. As soon as the effects of your chemo wear off, we'll try again.'

They wandered around the ground floor, moving from room to room as silent as thieves, planting footprints in the dust, which rose in little twisters, worrying their ankles.

There was a grand fireplace in the living room, with the carcass of a dead pigeon arranged in a nest of its own feathers in the hearth. Daniel studied a line of graffiti spray-painted in red on the wall above the mantelpiece. But they were random letters that he could not make any sense of at all. A white enamel pot full of grey water sat in one corner. The wallpaper above it had peeled away from the damp plaster into tiny curls as tight as wood shavings. When he kicked the pot, it made a dull chime.

'Daniel!' shouted Rosie from another room, and he turned and ran without even thinking.

'Someone's been living here,' she said, placing a foot on the mattress and testing the springs.

Daniel kicked out at some empty biscuit wrappers and trod down on a spent carton of orange juice, sending the blue plastic top skittering across the floor like a tiny puck.

'I'm not sure there's anyone here now,' he said. He went to the white sink where a large rust stain had spread from the plughole. He tried the taps and the pipes groaned. The odd red drop of water fell and that was all. 'Can you imagine living here?'

'Yeah, it could be a brilliant house.'

'I mean with it like this.'

'Things would have to be pretty bad, I guess.' She kicked the mattress and sent up a cloud of dust. 'I wonder how *that* feels.' And only when she grinned at Daniel did he smile back.

When Rosie started to cough, she put her hand against the wall to steady herself and waved him back. 'Dust. It's just the dust.' But she went on coughing for some time, her face turning whiter and her green eyes shining even more electric. 'I guess the bike ride took a bit more out of me than I thought,' she said.

*   *   *

255

While Rosie rested in the sun, Daniel drifted from room to room, waiting to see if any glimmer of one of Lawson's memories came to him. He lingered on the large staircase, keen to see if he remembered anything about it, but nothing came back to him.

When he found a small room on the first floor with a desk and a swivel chair on casters, the seat made from cracked red leather, he sat down and looked out of the window in front of him, which overlooked a large, overgrown garden. He placed his hand in the dust on the desktop as though trying to locate some connection with the place. When he lifted up his arm, his palm was blue and furry and the print in front of him was perfect. It started him thinking how big a handprint his father's hand would have made, but he stood up before he fell too far into himself and slapped his hands together to clean them.

Daniel examined the kitchen like a potential house buyer, scrutinizing the state of things. In the musty light, he saw cupboard doors sagging on their hinges, a stack of newspapers swollen by the damp, tarnished knives and forks scattered over the floor. A headless wine glass stood on the worktop, the bowl beside the broken stem, lying on its side like some diaphanous bloom shed an age ago.

He twisted a brass doorknob and discovered a pantry, lined with empty shelves furred with cobwebs. Nothing else.

But as he turned to leave he noticed a black mark low down on the wall just above the skirting. He thought it was mildew at first. But it was a symbol no larger than a thumbprint drawn on the grubby wall in black marker pen:

ঙ

He drew out the notebook and opened it. The symbols he and Bennett had drawn were similar enough to the one on the wall to make him too interested to leave. Daniel kept quite still, imagining how Lawson might have crouched down in exactly the same spot and drawn it. He kept looking at the strange black mark on the wall, trying to find anything inside him that might make sense of it. But not a second of any of Lawson's memories came back to him to explain if the man had drawn it or why.

Daniel started tracing the symbol on the wall with a finger, copying it over and over until he had the hang of it and could draw it with his eyes shut.

Eventually, he stood back from the wall and stared at it for a moment longer, and then he turned round to fetch Rosie.

54

'It can't be coincidence,' said Daniel, holding up the open notebook against the symbol on the wall. Rosie looked from the pages to the wall and back again and nodded.

'We need to find out for sure though. And what it means.' She cleared her throat. 'Let's try again. Make the fit. See what happens.'

Daniel shook his head. 'It didn't feel right yesterday,' he said. 'I don't know what might happen if we push too hard.'

'You mean I'll end up like Lawson?'

'Or something just as bad maybe.' Daniel shifted his feet in the dust on the floor. 'You'll get it all back, I'm sure you will. We'll help my dad. And we'll help you too.'

Rosie looked at him. But she didn't say a word.

They inspected the walls in the pantry for more clues, but there were no other symbols or marks anywhere.

'So? How else are we going to find out what it means?' asked Rosie eventually, tapping the symbol on the wall with a finger.

Daniel looked at Rosie for some time, thinking everything through.

'OK,' he said. 'But we stop if we feel it's not right. Before anything can go wrong.'

But, as soon as they tried to make the fit, Rosie coughed and spluttered and Daniel felt needle pricks in his chest almost immediately. They became so painful he thought they might be drawing blood.

'Stop, Rosie! It's not right. It's not working.'

'No,' she hissed through gritted teeth, her face tensing until it seemed to be twisting out of shape as if her skin was made of rubber. But when Daniel felt the pain in his chest become harsher he yelled at Rosie, grabbing her by the shoulders and shaking her until her green eyes popped open.

'It's too dangerous,' he said, panting. 'I can sense it. We can't use the fit, not like this.'

She nodded and leant against the wall, gulping in great shuddering breaths as she tried to speak. A single drop of blood appeared at one nostril and splashed on to her chest before she had time to wipe it away.

'I can't . . . it's me . . . something inside me's definitely not working like it should.' She drew another shaking breath. 'But I saw something.'

'What, Rosie? What did you see?'

'Lawson was here. He definitely drew this symbol. There are more in the house. They're important. Hiding things . . .' she hesitated, '. . . no, protecting them . . .' But then she shook her head. 'No, that's not right either.' She brushed her fingers over the wall as if trying to feel for a clue. 'It's like . . .' She paused, struggling to find the right words. 'It's like each one is an X that marks the spot or something like that.'

'Are they anything to do with the flask?'

'I don't know.' Rosie wiped her face. Another drop of blood appeared out of her nose and she caught it on a finger and sucked it away. Daniel watched her, saying nothing. She was calmer now, her breathing more even. She slid down the wall and crouched down and waved Daniel away. 'I just need a minute to get my strength back.'

Daniel stared at the symbol on the wall. Touched it again with a finger. He went so close to it he could see the dirt caught in the dimples in the plaster.

'If it means something's here, maybe we can find out what it is.'

He put his hands on the wall and pushed as if expecting it to roll back. He knocked on it, listening for any off-key sounds that might alert him to something out of the ordinary. He knelt down and felt along the skirting board, trying to discover if it lifted away. Defeated, he

260

sat back on his haunches for a moment and then he knelt forward to inspect the black rubber doorstopper in front of him. It had been screwed down through its rubber centre into an old floorboard secured by nails that had clearly been hammered into each corner decades ago. He gripped the stopper and tried to twist it round. But it didn't turn.

He sat back and looked at the symbol again and then stood up and disappeared into the kitchen. Rosie watched him pick up an old silver knife from the floor and return to the pantry and kneel back down. The tip of the knife fitted the head of the screw and Daniel pushed down hard as he tried to turn it between his hands as if preparing to make a fire with a spindle. With a yelp, the screw turned and he spun it looser until the doorstop came free from the floor.

But there was nothing beneath it except for the screw disappearing into the floorboard. He was about to twist the rubber doorstop back when Rosie stopped him.

'There's something odd about it.' She ran her finger over the wood the doorstop had been covering. 'The doorstopper must be new, otherwise the wood beneath it would be a lot brighter and cleaner, wouldn't it? And look at the screw: it's shiny. Not like those,' she said, pointing at the old brown nail heads, one in each corner of the floorboard. 'Perhaps Lawson put it on?'

'Why?' But Rosie shook her head. Daniel bit the inside of his check as he tried to figure it out and then he screwed the doorstop back in and stood up and brushed himself down. 'Let's see if we can find another of those,' he said, pointing at the symbol. 'You said there were more. It might help.'

They went from room to room, inspecting the walls, window frames, the ceiling. They kicked away the dust from the floorboards where it had drifted into piles.

Rosie found it eventually, the same symbol as the one in the pantry, drawn in black marker pen on the skirting board in a room that might once have been a library or a study, with bare shelves lining the walls. Daniel knelt beside it, knocking on the skirting and making a hollow sound. There were old nails hammered into the wood, but he worked his fingers all the way down the top edge, trying to see if it would come away. When he felt a small section move, he pulled harder, his finger-nails trying to find some purchase. He pulled again, his nails turning white, until suddenly a small section of skirting came free with a clunk, disengaging from two round magnets stuck to the wall behind it. He ran his fingers over the two other magnets fixed to the piece of skirting in his hand, observing how the old nails hammered into the front of it had been sheared off flush to the wood on the other side.

262

He rubbed their clean silver ends. 'It's supposed to look like you can't take it off.'

'Look! Daniel, there's something behind it.' Rosie reached into a nook lined with cotton wool that had been gouged into the plaster behind the piece of skirting and drew out a gold wedding band. A piece of black twine was knotted round it with a loop tied at the free end, just like a Christmas tree decoration ready to hang. Inside the ring was an inscription that read:

David and Helen Forever

'We should go back to the pantry,' said Daniel.

When he knelt down again, Daniel gripped the black rubber doorstop and pulled as hard as he could. The piece of floorboard came away cleanly, popping free from four magnets attached to the joists below. On its underside were four more magnets with the old brown nails sheared flush to the wood, just as they had been on the piece of skirting board that had been hiding the wedding ring.

Lying in the cavity below, between the joists on a bed of cotton wool, was a silver–plated, rectangular box.

'It looks like something my mum would keep her jewellery in,' said Rosie as Daniel lifted it out. When he opened the lid, Rosie gasped and put her hand to her mouth, muffling a string of swear words. There were four wooden compartments, each of equal size, and lying in the furthest one to the left was a man's severed finger. The nail was long and yellow and pointing at them. A tangle of black hairs covered the knuckles. Black twine was wound round the finger and a loop had been tied at its other end and hooked through a small metal clasp fixed to the underside of the lid.

Daniel placed the ring in the compartment next to the finger and hooked the piece of black twine around it through the clasp after pinching it open. Nothing happened after he shut the clasp. But Daniel wasn't sure if anything should and he shrugged at Rosie.

'Perhaps there are two other things to go in the box,' she said.

'So two more symbols, you think?'

Rosie nodded.

'And then what? What do you think it does?'

'I don't know.'

55

They searched the house for more symbols, rubbing walls free of grime, pulling apart cobwebs, looking in nooks and alcoves and under the mildewed corpses of cushions and behind curtains.

Eventually, they found another one, drawn on a yellowed window cornice in a large bedroom. Daniel stood on the wooden sill of the big bay window, pressing and pulling with his fingers until he worked a piece of dirty plaster free from the magnets fixed behind it. Hidden in a hollow was a lock of blonde hair with a slim red ribbon tied round the middle in a bow, the top half of the hair above it braided carefully like a corn dolly and its bottom half left flared.

'Lawson made all these hiding places very carefully,' whispered Rosie as she opened the box and Daniel placed the hair inside, hooking the piece of black twine that was attached to it through the clasp on the under-side of the lid.

'There must be one more to find,' he said. But, when Rosie started coughing, Daniel took hold of her greasy white fingers and held them until she had stopped. 'Let's take a break,' he said and led her downstairs.

He dragged the mattress they had found into a room that was full of the most sunshine.

They sat for some time – in what might have once been a dining room – watching the golden spokes of sunlight drop lower through the windows as the day drew on. The house seemed to grow colder little by little, like some newly dead creature with the heat fading from it. Daniel dozed and when he woke up a shaft of sunlight had lanced the wall beside him, like a spear just dodged.

Rosie slept too, on the mattress, stretching her legs out in front of her when she woke up. It seemed to Daniel that she was disintegrating when she moved, sending up little streamers of dust all around her.

'What are you thinking about?'

'Nothing,' he replied, trying to flush the thought about her from his mind.

'Liar. You're going red.'

'I was thinking about my dad. That I haven't been to see him today.'

Rosie picked out a tiny green burr from her hair and studied it, rolling it between her finger and thumb, wishing she had found the seed for her tumour. 'Would talking about him help?'

Daniel sighed. 'I'm not sure it would.'

Rosie flicked the green burr away and nodded. 'You're right.' She drew up her legs and hugged her knees, resting her chin in the groove between them. 'Tell me something funny instead.'

Daniel looked at her to see if she was serious. And she was. Nodding at him to go ahead.

'You know what people say behind my back at school? That I'm the person in the year least likely to succeed, that I won't be anybody at all. Ever.'

'That's not true.'

'Ask Bennett. It's written on the wall of the ground-floor bogs if you don't believe me. Last cubicle down. On the left-hand wall. Someone took a crap and thought of me.'

'Daniel,' deadpanned Rosie. 'That's hila-*rious*.'

'It's the best I could do.'

'OK then, get this. My dad is officially an asshole. We're in debt up to here.' And she put her hand above her head, 'mortgaged to the hilt because of some cowboy investment that went wrong. So now, even though he's a doctor, my mum works three jobs to pay the bills and put enough food on the table. It means I feel guilty every time I need something new to wear, which is every few months because it seems like somebody's still putting Miracle-Gro in my socks or shoes or my bra. All our family manages to do is get by. We survive.'

'So do lots of people, Rosie.'

'Yeah, but the point is we never used to have to.'

Daniel nodded. 'Well that, Rosie . . . is . . . hyst-*eri-cal*.'

Rosie stared at him. Her eyes blazed as she tried to keep a straight face, but she couldn't and ended up punching the mattress to let it all out. 'Do you think it's supposed to be this hard?' she asked.

'What do you mean?'

'Do you think we've been doing something wrong?'

Daniel shrugged. 'I don't think it's us.'

'Then *why's* it so damn tough?'

Daniel picked at a blackened knot in the floorboard beside him. 'Maybe that's not the right question.' He looked up at Rosie and shrugged. 'One of the doctors told me I should only be thinking about the "what" not the "why" when we were talking about dad. He said I should focus on figuring out who I want to be, whatever happens, because it's impossible to know why things turn out the way they do.'

And Rosie thought about that.

'So who do you want to be, Daniel?' she asked eventually.

He shook his head. 'I don't know. I think I'm still figuring it out. I guess I'm waiting to see what happens next.' He rubbed his face because he didn't want to cry. But he missed wiping away a tear and it splashed down on to the front of his hoodie, darkening over his heart. 'But I do know I don't want to be left on my own. That I don't want Dad to leave me here all by myself.'

'You won't be alone,' said Rosie. 'There's Bennett. There's your aunt. And I'll be here too. I promise.' He watched her stand up and then slump down beside him, laying her head on his shoulder.

When she looked up at him, he felt goosebumps flicker on his arms and legs. Her eyes were shining like wet pebbles. She smelt of apples and sunshine and talc and dust. In the gloaming, her face seemed to be moving and breaking apart and he gripped her harder, fearful she might fade away. 'You can't make a promise like that, can you? That you'll be here.'

She kissed him on his cheek and snuggled in close. 'No, you're right, I can't. But I promise I'll stay with you for as long as the world lets me.'

'It's more than that, Rosie. You need to make sure you stay here to do all the things you want to in your life.'

They held on tight to each other in silence for some time, as the grainy evening fell around them like a curtain being lowered.

56

Gradually, the walls and the floor turned paper-white in the moonlight. The window frames looked like they were made from bone.

Tiny scutterings inside the walls set their eyes wandering, but they saw nothing out of the ordinary and they sat musing on what the noises might be, trying not to let their imaginations catch fire. The night brought out something ancient in them, and they heard it in their breathing and felt it on their skin, like electricity, making them charged and alert.

'Are you scared?' whispered Rosie eventually.

'Yes,' said Daniel, staring into the dark places hiding from the moon to try and see if anything was there.

'More scared than you are of Mason?'

'No. I want to stay. We need to find that flask. Give Mason what he wants and get him out of our lives for good.'

'Yes,' said Rosie. 'We certainly both want that.'

He opened the silver-plated box lying on the floor beside them and stared at the gold wedding band and the finger and the lock of hair in their separate compartments, all hooked to the clasp on the underside of the lid with black, woolly twine. Daniel kept looking at them for some time in the moonlight. But he shut the lid eventually.

'Nothing,' he said. 'I don't remember anything.'

Rosie sat up and looked at him and smiled. And then she closed her eyes.

When Daniel started to feel little pricks of pain in his chest, he knew that Rosie was trying to make the fit again. 'Rosie, be careful,' he said. 'Please. Let's try looking for the last symbol instead.'

But her face twitched and jerked and he wasn't sure she could hear him.

When the pain rang clean in his chest like a bell, he gasped and tried to move his arms to shake Rosie out of her trance. But they were turning numb. There was no strength in them at all. 'Rosie!' But his voice was so pitiful that he could barely hear it himself.

He started to hear the ticking sound inside his head. Like an alarm clock about to go off. Or a bomb about to explode. He remembered how Lawson's hand had detonated in a red mist and it scared him so much that he managed to summon all his strength and raised his arms towards Rosie as well as he could.

271

'Rosie! Stop!'

When she collapsed forward, he had no strength to catch her and her head cannoned on to the floorboards with a crack.

The pain was gone from him immediately and, as the strength flowed back into his arms, he lifted up her limp body gently. 'Rosie! Rosie! Wake up! What have you done?'

There was blood coming from her nose and it was thick and dark and velvety. It fell in drops to the floor, splashing into the dust. He checked her hands. Inspected her for any signs of damage. But there were none that he could see.

'You said you wouldn't leave,' said Daniel, rocking her gently. 'You promised.'

He felt her tense in his arms and then shudder, her eyes popping wide open as if waking from a terrible dream.

'Oh, Daniel!' she gasped as more blood came out of her nose, making her sputter and cough. 'I saw Lawson. He was here in this room. He was kneeling.' And she waved a hand towards the hearth.

'Rosie, what did you do? What's happened?'

She put her hands to her mouth as the blood ran down into it from her nose and she wiped it away. 'I'm OK. I'm still here. I pushed as far as I dared. I stopped when I heard your voice. I'm OK. Go and look over there.' She pointed at the hearth again. 'Lawson was there. I'm sure of it.'

Daniel stood up and knelt down in front of the fireplace, searching for anything that might seem odd or out of place. The moon was shining in through the window behind him and he inspected everything in the hearth by its silvery light. Written beneath the grate on one of the tiles in black pen was another symbol, shining like wet paint in the moonlight. Quickly, he started testing each tile until he found a loose one, which he prised up with his fingernails. A tooth beneath it, a molar with a long tendril of root, attached to a black piece of twine. After plucking it out, he crouched down beside Rosie as she opened the silver box and he placed the tooth into the last empty compartment, hooking it to the clasp on the underside of the lid. When Rosie closed the box, Daniel heard something and looked round, trying to see what was there in the room with them.

'What?' asked Rosie.

'A scratching sound, can't you hear it?'

Rosie shook her head, her tongue wiggling in the corner of her mouth as she listened harder.

And then they both saw it, a grey column of fine mist rising from a section of the floor. It coalesced slowly into the blurry shape of a head and torso and arms. It was a man of sorts, up to his waist in the floorboards, until he drifted free of them to reveal his whole body. He was hazy. Indistinct. As if fashioned from a delicate silk that was constantly catching in a draught. He stood taller than either Daniel or Rosie, his cloudy grey feet hovering above the floor. The features of his face were blurred, but the eyes were bright blue and watched them keenly.

'Who are you? Where's Lawson?' asked the man in a voice that sounded like dry leaves rattling in the wind. When he moved nearer to Daniel, the boy took a step back.

'Dead,' he said quickly.

'Then what about the flask? Who has it now?' The man drifted even closer. 'You should tell me the truth. I can see a lot of things about a person if I want to, much more than when I was alive.' The blue eyes burned bright in the blurred face. 'So I already know you didn't mean to kill Lawson.' Closer and closer the man came. 'What else is there, hiding deep down inside you?'

Daniel felt Rosie behind him, her hand clutching hold of his, the fingers clenching tighter.

'Stay away from us,' he shouted at the man. But the creature swept forward as if blown by a sharp gust of wind and plunged a blurry arm deep into Daniel's chest, making the boy gasp.

'I can't hurt you,' the man whispered. 'There's no need to be scared of me. Not like Mason.'

Daniel tried to step back, but he seemed fixed to the man, a chill burning steadily colder inside him.

'Now I see everything.' And the man laughed and pulled out his arm. 'If you think Mason's going to retire when you give him that flask, you're wrong. He told Lawson the same thing, but he didn't believe it. Mason uses people then tosses them away like dirty rags. Nobody rats on him because they don't get the chance. He doesn't trust anyone. But it keeps him alive, at the top of the pile. He killed me on a whim a few months ago just because I'd done a job for him. Lawson knew better than to trust him. That's why he put me here to make a deal with me.' He pointed at the silver box. 'Lawson knew how to keep a person in the world even after they'd died.'

'What sort of a deal did he make with you?' asked Daniel.

'To draw Mason into a trap you have to be clever. He's paranoid. Alert to any trick. Lawson knew he'd need me to help him. He's been waiting for weeks to tell Mason about the flask, winding him tighter and tighter until he wants it so much he's ready to burst. And I bet he is now. So tell him the flask he so desperately wants is hidden here, that the ghost of Ashwell Lodge is the only one who can reveal it to him. Use the charms that Lawson made. Put them back where they were. Let Mason find them so he can see me. I'll lead him to a place from which he'll never return. But bring the flask with you too. I want what Lawson promised me. I'll only help you if I know you can give me what I want.'

275

'Where is it? Where's the flask?' asked Daniel.

'Lawson kept it here. But the last time he came he took it away with him. When he didn't come back, I thought he'd left me here forever, trapped in this place.' The man began to drift down into the floor, disappearing from view. 'If you can find the flask and bring it with you then you can get rid of Mason. It's the only way to save yourselves from him now.'

57

They pedalled as hard as they could down the driveway, not looking back until the house had vanished
round the bend in the road behind them.

Daniel gripped the handlebars, the air whooshing
electric around him.

'Hey!' shouted Rosie and, when he glanced round
and realized she was struggling to keep up, he slowed
and waited for her. Eventually, he looked back to see
her standing in the road, her hands on the handlebars
as if the bike was the only thing keeping her up.

'I don't feel so good,' she said as he pulled up beside
her. When he touched her, she was trembling like a
baby bird. Blood was coming from her nose again,
splashing in three big drops on to the road.

Daniel held her until she had stopped shaking.

'I'll walk if you can steer,' he said, and he made her
sit on her bike as he gripped the handlebars and pulled

her, his own bike ticking beside him, and her coughing and shaking as the wheels turned.

There were stars in every puddle that they passed.

'I hate being like this,' she said.

'It's fine.'

'No it's not. Nothing is.'

They kept going for some time, not speaking, until Rosie summoned enough strength to say something. 'He's not like your father,' she said. 'They're not the same at all. That man was dead. He said so.'

'Not all of him was.' When she opened her mouth to say something, Daniel got there first. 'Do you feel ready to ride a bit more? It's late and we need to get you home.' He pointed at Cambridge in front of them, glowing in the distance like some fairy forest. 'We've still got a way to go.'

Rosie nodded. 'Yes, in a moment. I think I might be able to.'

'Perfect.'

When Rosie decided she had enough strength to start peddling for herself, they speeded up a little, Daniel keeping close to her, watching her as she wobbled, his heart lurching whenever she did. But they managed to keep going.

'Daniel, how are we going to find the flask?' asked Rosie as they cycled down the street towards her house.

'I don't know.'

'Are all of Lawson's memories really burned out?'

'I think they are, yes. I can't find anything inside me at all.'

Rosie braked. Slipped her feet off the pedals on to the road to keep her steady.

'I can't make the fit again. Not now. That last time . . . something happened. I'm too scared to try.'

'We'll find the flask another way.'

'What way?'

'I'll figure it out. There's someone I know who might be able to help.'

'Who?'

'You don't know them.'

'But—'

She stopped when the front door to her house opened and they both realized how loud their voices must have been in the still night.

'ROSIE?' It was her mother, backlit by the light in the hallway until she started trotting down the steps to the driveway. 'Rosie, where have you been?' Her voice rang out as Rosie hissed at Daniel to go.

'I'll find the flask. I will,' he said and started to peddle.

He heard them arguing in the street. Her mother's worried voice ringing shrill and excited round the houses. Daniel found it strangely comforting. The love that Rosie's mother had for her, coming out in all its anger, seemed so clean and pure and undiluted. He stopped and hid in an alley and listened in secret to them arguing until they went inside.

As he cycled slowly, wending through the streets, he pretended that his father was waiting at home for him, ready to be angry too. But he knew there was only his aunt, and however angry she might be it would not feel the same at all because it wouldn't be his father's love ringing out at him the way he craved.

When he did reach home, all the lights were off and it shocked him for a moment. He wondered if his aunt was even there. He crept upstairs and saw the line of white light beneath her bedroom door disappear with a tiny click.

Daniel stood there, waiting to see if she might appear. But she didn't. Suddenly, he wanted her to. He wanted to go and bang on her door and demand it. But after the red surge in him had disappeared he found himself thinking that it was just enough for now that she was there, that the light had been on and then gone off with a simple-sounding click as soon as he had come home. For the first time since she had arrived in his life, he was glad that she was here. It was like a lens had been put in front of his eyes and he was seeing everything more clearly, imagining the world from her point of view and not just his own. He wondered why it had happened. Where it was coming from. He tried to trace his thinking back to its source, stopping when he remembered how Rosie had hugged him and told him he wouldn't be alone. Somehow, she had unlocked his heart to a love in the world that he hadn't been able to see before.

But, as he got himself ready for bed, he soon got to thinking about his dad again, feeling guilty for even thinking about his aunt in a way his father wouldn't have ever wanted him to. So he buried the good thoughts about her deep down inside him until being in the house without his dad felt wrong, just like it had done for the last few days. Not standing in the bathroom brushing his teeth. Not sitting on the loo. Not even standing in his bedroom about to undress.

'We're not staying here,' Daniel said to his reflection in the mirror on his bedside table.

He went to the shed in the garden and sat in the armchair he and his father had carried there some months ago when the snow had been thick on the ground, which seemed like an age ago.

The seat was lumpy. The broken springs creaked as Daniel tried to get comfortable until he was looking up past his grasshopper-sized thighs at the wall in front of him.

A line of empty bottles was webbed together on a rickety shelf.

There were magazines fat with damp piled on the floor.

A pair of shears was hanging from a nail, like the skeleton of some ancient bird.

The shed was a place full of forgotten, meaningless things, bereft of purpose and left to rot.

And it was here that Daniel managed to fall asleep.

When he opened his eyes, it was still dark and he knew he had dozed off, the crick in his neck driven in deep like a nail. His hands were cold and he hid them under his sweatshirt in the warm beside his stomach. He noodled the springs in the chair to try and get more comfortable and then stopped when a light played across the window, drawing a white stripe across the inside of the shed.

At first he thought it must be his aunt, with a torch. He held his breath, trying to listen. Nothing. Not a sound. He crept to the window and pulled apart the cobwebs. The glass was milky with moonlit dirt, but he could see the shape of a man standing in the garden, the light flashing as he moved, looking for something.

Suddenly, the figure stopped and turned to look right at him, the light from the torch shining into his face. But Daniel knew who it was immediately and flung open the door, running into the white tunnel of light.

But then the torch suddenly flipped up and pointed at the sky because his father was off balance, falling backwards into a deep dark sinkhole that was opening in the lawn behind him. Daniel rushed across the grass until he was teetering on the edge of the hole. He could see his father and the torch falling into the black bottomless pit so he jumped in too, feet first, falling straight and true like an arrow being fired downwards. As he looked up, the wind rushing in his ears, he saw people standing around the edge of the hole. His aunt. Bennett. Rosie. James. They were looking down and shouting at him to come back. But Daniel couldn't stop as their voices rang round and round the dark black walls of the sinkhole . . .

Daniel woke up, blinking in the early morning sunlight coming through the window of the shed.

The phone Mason had given him was ringing in his trouser pocket, working still despite its cracked screen. His finger hovered over the answer button. But he didn't press it.

When the ringtone stopped, he sighed with relief, but a moment later the phone started up again. He turned it to mute and hid it back in a pocket.

When he closed the shed door behind him, Daniel's hands were shaking as they lifted the latch, then clinked it down. He turned round to stare at the lawn where the sinkhole had opened in his dream and then he started walking across the green springy turf towards the house.

As he got closer to the back door, he realized his aunt was watching him through the kitchen window, her forearms up to their elbows in a thick crust of foam as she did the washing-up.

She didn't say a word as he opened the back door and walked through the kitchen and went upstairs.

The PK Party

58

Daniel spent the morning with Bennett, determined to find the tramp from the train. They walked the main streets where people often sat and begged for money, gradually venturing into the smaller alleys and cut-throughs like two explorers mapping the tributaries of some dried-out river system.

Eventually, they reached Jesus Green and saw a group of them sitting underneath an oak tree, the sun dappling their shoulders. Despite the heat, they were wearing thick coats and jumpers, passing a bottle of vodka between them, taking swigs as if it was only spring water catching the light.

Their talking was babble and burble and burps and laughter.

It was like walking up to the sixth-formers at school.

'I'm looking for someone,' said Daniel as they all looked up at him and Bennett through red, rheumy eyes.

One of them, a woman with rickety teeth and a boil on the side of her neck, laughed and shook her head.

'I'm trying to find a man. He's got red hair,' said Daniel again. 'And a red beard too.' But they just kept passing round the bottle of vodka, laughing loudly as one when something landed with a *splat* between the shoulders of a raggedy man wearing an old blue donkey jacket, the rising laughter scaring the wood pigeons out of the tree above them.

'He carries a big darning needle with him,' said Bennett.

'Bobby,' said one of the men absently, shading his face as he looked up at the two boys, and the others nodded. 'Bobby carries a needle.'

'Thinks he's the fourth bloody musketeer,' said one of the women and the others laughed, some of them slapping the ground because it seemed so funny.

'Do you know where we can find him?' asked Daniel.

'Is it important?'

Daniel nodded. But they all blinked at him as if they didn't believe it. 'I think he can help me with something.'

'We can help, can't we?' said the woman with the boil on her neck and the others agreed.

'I think it's just him.'

They looked at Daniel and Bennett, the lines in their

faces inked with grime, their teeth marbled with brown streaks.

'Try the canal,' said a thin man wearing a dirty baseball cap and then he took a swig from the bottle. 'He likes it there, says it reminds him of where he grew up.'

'Thanks.'

Daniel reached into his pocket and dug out some pound coins and held them out, but the man shook his head and the others all started laughing as Daniel turned red and walked away with Bennett.

The path beside the canal was brown and dusty, cracked into hexagons by the heat. The water was the colour of milky coffee. When Daniel bent down to try and see through it, he saw it was swirling with tiny yellow grains, like dots of pollen. Bennett kicked a stone off the path and it disappeared through the murk with a plop, a single ripple vanishing quickly, swept away in the flow.

They walked for some time, passing people coming the other way, overtaking others loaded with shopping bags or marshalling toddlers away from the water. When they reached the edge of town, they sat on a lock gate and looked at the buildings around them. Old warehouses three or four stories high, with the windows blown out, and weeds with bright yellow heads growing out of the walls, bouncing on their green stems in the breeze.

'Have you been checking Mason's phone?' asked Bennett.

'No.'

'Maybe you should.'

Daniel saw there were ten missed calls from Mason, but no messages.

'You'll have to speak to him eventually,' said Bennett.

Daniel didn't know what to say.

The sound of coughing made him look up and he saw Bobby emerging from one of the warehouses, his dirty mackintosh wrapped about him with his hands in the pockets. When the man stopped and took a swig of something, Daniel saw the sunlight glinting off the top of Bennett's hip flask as he screwed it back on.

'Grubby bastard,' grunted Bennett.

'Stay here,' said Daniel. 'You might scare him off.'

When Daniel walked up to the man, he smelt of the sea, but there was something sweet-smelling too. Like warm popcorn in a bucket.

'Ahhhh,' said Bobby and gave a bow. 'The young gentleman from the train.' He clicked his tongue against his teeth, making the *clackety* sound of a train. 'I believe your travelling companion was kind enough to furnish me with a drink.' He waved the flask and laughed at Bennett who raised a finger in reply. When Bobby shuffled on past Daniel, the boy put out his arm.

'Stop.' But Bobby didn't, the dirty mackintosh creaking like a sail as he went. So Daniel walked on after him. 'I need your help. I want to make the fit with you. I need you to try and help me find something.'

The man stopped and licked his blistered lips. Played with a wisp of his ginger beard, rolling it between his fingers. 'Make the fit? With me?' And something caught fire in his eyes as if the sun had lit something deep inside him.

Daniel nodded. 'As much as you dare. Please.' He took out the twenty-pound note he had been keeping in his pocket and all the change he had too. 'This is all I have. I don't know anyone else who can help me.'

Bobby peered at the boy's face as if staring through a magnifying glass that had cracked. 'What do you want to know? What can I work with?'

'I have something that can help,' said Daniel and he held up the two pieces of Lawson's business card.

Bobby's tongue wiggled out of the corner of his mouth, like a leech looking for a spot to clamp down. 'I'm keeping the hip flask; he can't have it back.' And he gave a little wave at Bennett.

'OK,' said Daniel. 'I'll sort it.'

Bobby nodded and took the twenty pounds and the coins, dropping it all in a mackintosh pocket. 'It's a beautiful day,' he said. 'So let's not screw it up.' He began shuffling through the knee-high weeds and grasses towards one of the warehouses, sending bees and butterflies swirling round his shins.

They sat on a bare patch of concrete with broken glass catching the sunlight all around them, like three people shipwrecked on a tiny desert island.

A bird flapped up through a large blue crack in the ceiling, and it took a while for the quiet to creep in again.

Bobby took the two pieces of the business card and looked at Lawson's name. He eyed Bennett for a moment and then smiled. Bennett just grunted and shook his head.

'Lawson found a flask,' said Daniel. 'It's very special. He put it somewhere and I need to know where.'

'Well, that depends on whether we can make the fit.' Bobby closed his eyes. 'Can you feel it?'

'Yes.' Daniel saw tiny golden sparks popping behind his eyes when he blinked, as if someone was holding a sparkler out in the dark of him. There was a familiar warm sensation in his chest.

'Tell me about this man you want to know more about.'

'His name was Lawson. He was a vicar once. He lived in a house just outside Cambridge.'

'And what did he look like, this Lawson?'

'He was dark. Tall. Neat and tidy. He—' Daniel stopped when Bobby's hand reached out for his wrist and grabbed hold.

'I see somebody.' Bobby started to breathe more deeply, his breath oaty and sour as he leant closer to Daniel. 'I can see a man in a bed. Machines blipping round him.'

'No, not him,' said Daniel. 'It's Lawson I need to know about. He had a flask and I need to find it.'

'I've got to work harder to see it,' said Bobby. 'I'm not as strong as I used to be. I'm all rusted up. Ginger on the inside too.' He spluttered a laugh and held on tighter to the boy's wrist.

'What can you see?' asked Daniel.

'The man in the bed is very ill.'

'Not hi—' Daniel paused as he thought about something. 'What about this man in the bed?' Daniel glanced at Bennett who was about to say something and then thought better of it.

Bobby muttered sounds that didn't make sense. 'Open your heart,' he said finally. 'Open it as big as you can. As wide as a barn door pushed back. I can almost see it.'

'See what, Bobby?'

'What's going to happen to him.'

Daniel tried keeping his mind pure and clean and simple, his breath a knife that cut apart any thought as it came to him, good or bad or hopeful. But something was welling up inside him. Bloating him. Something red and hot and angry.

'I see him!' shouted Bobby. 'I see the blighter.'

'Be careful,' whispered Daniel. Bobby's teeth were shiny with spit. He wobbled and held on tight to Daniel.

'You found a good fit with that girl, Daniel. It gave you what you weren't expecting, just like I said it would. It didn't help your daddy though, did it? It didn't do that. It was telling you to let go of him.' Bobby was juddering. His shoulders were jerking. 'He's going to die, your daddy. He's going to die and there's nothing you can do to stop it.'

Daniel tried to shake off Bobby's hand.

'Let me go!' he shouted. He felt Bennett's hand trying to pull Bobby away. But the man was hooked on tight.

'It's the *what* not the *why*,' screamed Bobby. 'Tell me, Daniel. Tell me: who are you going to be when your daddy's gone? Who's the girl going to be with this tumour in her head?'

Bennett yelled and swiped Bobby across the head and the man's hand fell away and Daniel felt the connection between them cut off, like a plug had been pulled from its socket.

Bobby fell back and lay gasping on his side, his eyes flickering open and his head resting on the broken pieces of glass lying around them.

'That's all I can see,' he wheezed. 'Not Lawson. Not this flask you want. My mind's a muscle. It's out of shape. It doesn't do what I want it to any more.' He found the hip flask in his pocket and took a long sip before holding it out to Daniel who shook his head. When Bobby managed to sit up, there were red spots of blood on his head. Splinters of glass sparkled in his hair like the remnants of a frost.

'Come on, Daniel,' said Bennett. 'Let's go. He's no good. He's a nobody.'

'Least I still got both hands,' shouted Bobby and he roared with laughter as they crunched their way out of the building over the broken glass.

59

Something kept tightening in Daniel's stomach as he walked quickly back down the towpath, like a screw was being turned deeper and deeper.

He took a bus to the hospital with Bennett to see his father. But when they got there they were told they couldn't see him because the doctors were examining him.

'What's wrong?' asked Daniel. 'What's happened?'

Two of the ward nurses took him aside into a room and told him that his father had pneumonia. They told him that it was one of the risks of being on a ventilator and of being fed through a tube.

'But he'll get better from that, won't he?' asked Daniel.

'We're treating the infection, doing all we can,' said one of the nurses. The other one just nodded and smiled to back her colleague up.

'We'll come back later,' said Bennett and he led Daniel away.

As they walked out of the hospital doors into the daylight, Bennett took his friend by the shoulders. 'That Bobby's a drunk, a tramp with an old rag for a brain. That stuff he said wasn't true.' But Daniel wasn't sure what to think. 'You should go home to your aunt. Tell her about your dad. Talk about him with her and tell her how you feel.'

'I'd prefer to hang out with you.'

'Daniel, she's come all this way to look after you. She didn't have to, did she? She could have said no and stayed in California. I think she must love you very much. Remember, it's hard for her too, being with you, being with a person she doesn't know. She needs you to tell her how to be with you or else she's just guessing. And people make mistakes when they guess at things. That's just the way it is.'

When Mason's phone went off in Daniel's pocket, he checked it again. 'I can't tell her about Mason. She won't be able to help with that.'

Bennett frowned. He scuffed the ground with a shoe. 'My brother's having a party tonight. He has some friends who are into trying out "stuff".'

'What do you mean?'

'They're "alternative".' And he made two rabbit ears with his fingers. 'New Age. At least some of them are.

297

Last time he had a party some wacky things happened.'

'What sort of things?'

'I wasn't there. I think they got pretty drunk though and high. My brother said it was like a dream. I'm just telling you in case it might be useful. You can't make the fit with Rosie, and trying with Bobby was a waste of time, so why don't you come along?'

Daniel nodded. 'Thanks.'

'But only if you go home now and see your aunt.'

Daniel shifted from one foot to the other like he was standing on hot coals.

'James might be there too tonight. You can always speak to him.'

Daniel thought about that. 'OK,' he said.

When Daniel got home his aunt was out. She had left him a short note saying she would be back later, not mentioning where she had gone or what she was doing.

The words felt like little daggers on his tongue as he read them out loud the second time around to the pot plant on the kitchen windowsill. But he remembered what Bennett had told him and it was like holding up a lens to the note that made him see it differently. When he read the words out loud again, they didn't hurt any more. In fact, they sounded sad and upset, not curt at all.

He wrote a message beneath hers, telling her about his dad's pneumonia and saying he would be out tonight at a party at Bennett's house. He signed it with an initial, D. Someone moved his hand for him and put a couple of kisses next to it and he immediately wished they hadn't. But there was nothing he could do once it had happened.

60

By the time Daniel had cycled to Rosie's house, Mason had called fifteen times. But left no messages. He watched the streets warily as he pedalled, expecting the blue BMW to turn out of one and start following him or for Mason to walk out of a shop and shout at him to stop.

Rosie's house was Georgian, with plump red bricks separated by clean beige lines of cement. The white sash windows were full of sky. A bronze knocker hung from a black varnished door. The house was set back from the road and Daniel wheeled his bike up the gravel drive, dotted with weeds and covered in tiny slicks of bird shit.

He waited, studying the glossy black door, and adjusting his head to see what small bits of him he could find in the shiny paint.

But no one came to answer so he rapped the knocker again.

He tried the wooden gate at the side of the house, but that was locked.

He stood in the driveway, watching a Frisbee riding the breeze in the street as two kids spun it between them, and then he got back on his bike.

When Agatha opened the door, she nodded, as if satisfied it was him she had seen through the spyhole, and held out a hand to welcome him in.

But, as he stepped over the threshold into the hallway, she clutched his arm. 'Rosie's here but she's not well. The chemotherapy is making her feel very sick.'

'Is it just that?'

'I think so, yes.' Agatha held on to his arm. 'She told me what happened last night. She's in no state to do anything if that's why you're here. I wouldn't allow it.'

'I didn't come for that. I just want to see her.'

Agatha nodded and then let go of Daniel and shut the door behind him.

Rosie was lying with a red bedspread pulled up to her chin. Her eyes opened when Daniel sat down on the bed and the grey in her face seemed to fade as she smiled.

'Did you find the person you said might be able to help?' Daniel nodded. But when he said nothing more, the grey rushed back into Rosie's cheeks. He watched her eyes contracting in their dark cups. When she

301

sighed, something rattled in her chest. 'I've got a splitting headache. Like I'm going to throw up. The tablets the hospital gave me don't seem to work that well.'

'I went round to your house.'

'Mum and Dad had an argument about money again. Dad stormed out. Packed a case and said he was leaving. I couldn't stand it so I came round to Gran's. I'm going to stay here for now. I think the poison the hospital is putting in me is seeping into them. I'm making it worse between them.'

'You can't be.'

'I'm their little girl. But they can't do anything to help me.' She coughed and her fingers felt for his hand, gripping it like the feet of a tiny bird. 'Daniel, what's going to happen? If we don't find the flask, what's Mason going to do?'

Daniel picked at a thread in the bedspread. 'I don't want to think about it now.' He lay down beside her and they held each other close. 'Dad's more ill than ever. He's got pneumonia.'

She stroked his hair.

He closed his eyes and shut out the world.

After falling asleep, he dreamt of Bobby sitting on his father's bed, holding the darning needle and swishing it back and forth as if sewing a thread into the air in front of him.

'What are you doing?' asked Daniel.

'Sewing in a bit that doesn't make sense. Making up a story about your dad you can believe in.'

'What are you sewing in, Bobby?'

'He's dead, Daniel, and you've got to accept it somehow because there's nothing you can do to help him. I've almost sewn it in. I almost have—'

When Daniel woke, it was warm and dark and there was a film of sweat under his shirt. Rosie was asleep. He stood up and let himself out of her bedroom without waking her.

Agatha was drinking tea and when he came in to say goodbye she turned the TV to mute and clinked her teacup down in its saucer.

'It's up to you to look after my granddaughter,' she said. 'Protect her from Mason. You're the one who brought him into her life.'

'I will,' he replied.

But Agatha just turned on the volume again and started watching what was on the screen.

Daniel let himself out of the door and took his bike off the wall.

He cycled a little way down the street until he saw a nail on the path under a street lamp, and he braked and stooped to pick it up. He leant over, juggling his bike between his legs, and scratched a word on the pavement in white, wiry letters.

303

HELP

He tossed the nail and waited.

But nothing happened this time.

He saw no way out from this new dark place he was in.

61

No one answered when Daniel rang the doorbell. He could hear the gentle thump of music inside and the murmur of voices, like the sea in his ears. He rolled a rhombus of stone with the toe of his trainer, wondering whether to leave. And then a sash window lifted on the first floor of the house and Bennett stuck out his head and smiled, waving him round the back, the music rolling out into the night air.

'The back gate's open!' he shouted down, and before Daniel could give a reply he was gone.

The kitchen was full of warm bodies and smoke and conversation so earnest that nobody really noticed Daniel. He slipped through the noise like a ghost as people parted for him and then closed ranks again without quite seeming to know why as they went on talking and laughing.

The kitchen island was sticky and covered with green bottles of beer like stalagmites sprouted out of the wood.

Swollen cigarette butts were floating inside some of them like the ends of fingers snipped off. Daniel picked up a giant pretzel from a bowl full of them and bit into it and suddenly felt like a five-year-old as the crumbs sprayed everywhere and he tried to catch them with his hand.

He thought he heard someone laughing as he brushed them off his chest and he remembered what was written about him on the toilet wall at school.

When a hand squeezed his shoulder, he knew it belonged to Bennett so he didn't say anything and just looked up and smiled as the pretzel churned into a dry, doughy ball in his mouth.

Bennett's eyes were browner than normal. And the flecks in them seemed to be on fire. Daniel wondered what he had been taking as he swallowed hard to clear the pretzel.

'More people came than my brother thought,' said Bennett and he swigged from his bottle, his lips popping off the rim and the beer washing like surf against the glass. 'I'm glad you made it. I thought maybe your aunt might not let you come. Did you talk to her?'

'No. She wasn't in. But I thought about what you said. I left her a note.'

'A note! What did it say?'

'Nothing.' Daniel was already regretting mentioning it. When Bennett smiled, it was too big. His eyes seemed to pop. He reached for a beer and hoiked off the cap and handed it to Daniel, the brown rim still smoking.

'Where's your mum?' asked Daniel.

'She took "little sister" away for some horsey thing.'

'Point-to-point?'

'What?'

'Right.' And Daniel just nodded and looked away.

'So? This note?'

'I'll tell you about it later.'

'Tell me about it now.'

'It's not really the time.'

'Sure it is.'

'There's too many people.'

'Well, let's go somewhere else.'

'No, it's fine.' Daniel took a big swig of beer and then another when he saw Bennett still staring. 'It's a party. I probably just need to relax.' He clinked his bottle against Bennett's and it made an awkward off-key sound as Bennett swayed and his bottle moved with him. 'You said there might be something going on tonight that could help.'

Bennett brightened. 'Absolutely. There's a girl you need to meet. A friend of my brother's. She was in charge of stuff at his last party. I've already told her about you.'

Her name was Amanda. Her black bob had an edge as sharp as the blade of a kitchen knife. She was way older than Daniel. Early twenties. It was as though she was made from a different sort of material from him. Her dress was black and clung to her like it had been painted on. Her plastic see-through shoes were strappy and sunset-coloured with laces that wound round her shins almost to her knees.

'Bennett's a dick when he's drunk,' said Daniel after he had left them and they had smiled and said hello and listened to the conversations around them for long enough to make the silence between them uncomfortably loud.

Amanda laughed. 'I don't really know him so I'll take your word for it. He's very fond of you though. Told me all about your troubles. About your accident and your dad.'

Daniel nodded. 'Life hasn't been great lately.' He figured that would be the end of the conversation. But, instead of wandering off or looking round the room for somebody more interesting to talk to, she cocked her head to one side.

'Bennett said you've been doing some weird stuff.'

'Like what?'

'Like psychic stuff.'

'What else did he say?'

'He said I should ask you about it. I'm into that kind of thing.' She tapped her nails against the wine glass she was holding and Daniel noticed they were as black as space.

308

'I think Bennett's making stuff up to make me sound more interesting than I am.'

But Amanda didn't smile.

'I get a feeling about people, you know. I can't get a read on you though. Like you're hiding something.' She reached out a hand and then stopped. 'Can I?'

Before Daniel could reply, Amanda had placed her hand on his shoulder and closed her eyes. Daniel checked to see if anyone was watching, but no one was. The beer made everything warm around the edges. He felt Amanda squeeze harder and then she opened her eyes and shook her head.

'Damn!'

'What?'

'I must have drunk too much.' Her laugh was harsh and sparkling, like a frost. She raked a set of fingers through her hair and it fell back into place exactly like a curtain. 'You're staying for a while, right?'

'Yeah.'

'Good.'

And then she turned round and left him standing on his own as she pushed a path between the crowd in the room.

Daniel kept looking for her from time to time, intrigued by whatever she had in mind, and by what Bennett had mentioned had happened at the last party. But he gave up believing she might come back after he had drunk another beer. Someone offered him a puff on a joint because he was standing in a ring and he took a sweet lungful and held it as long as he could, then breathed out through his nostrils like a dragon and handed it on.

When someone asked about his dad, he just shrugged and said it would all be fine. It wasn't his voice, but he was happy to let someone else inside him do the talking for a change and he watched the joint go round and licked his lips as it came close again.

A hand slipped into his.

The cold fingers shocked him.

When he looked up, Amanda was already turning round and pulling him away from the others. The soles of his feet were like suckers for a moment as he opened his mouth and then closed it, and then he peeled them up off the floor and went with her, walking in the wake of her perfume. Faces swam as he passed them and he thought he heard someone shouting his name, but the voice seemed to come from nowhere.

She led him upstairs into a master bedroom where other people sitting on the floor looked up as if they'd been waiting for him.

Bennett was sitting on the bed, grinning, toasting him with a half-empty bottle of vodka. The arm holding him up was wobbly and drunk, the elbow clicking out every now and then as if he was on a waterbed, threatening to make him collapse. Amanda shut the door. Daniel nodded at Bennett's brother who was sitting in the corner with a pretty-looking woman, not paying much attention to anyone else.

'Let's get this PK party started,' announced Amanda.

As Daniel looked around, he realized that everyone else had a piece of cutlery beside them. Spoons. Forks. Knives. The light flared in spots, catching the different metal stems as people picked them up.

Amanda handed him a fork, folding his fingers round the elegant silver handle. He held on tight because a thought was blipping in his head, telling him he would fall over otherwise. He knew it was the joint. The smoke he had inhaled earlier still seemed to be inside him, wafting round his head and making him unsteady.

'We all need to make an emotional peak,' said Amanda. 'That's how it happens.'

'What?' Daniel found himself asking.

'The freaky stuff!' shouted Bennett's brother. Bennett cheered and swigged from his bottle of vodka, then passed it to the girl next to him on the bed.

'Psychokinetic events for those of you who haven't done this before,' said Amanda and she smiled at Daniel. 'People got together for parties in the eighties to prove that we all have psychic energy. They called them PK parties and did all this whacked-out stuff, bending spoons, metal objects. All with the power of the mind.'

'So that means we all have psychic energy,' said Bennett and Daniel could see he was speaking directly to him. 'We're all the same. Some people just tap into it better than others.'

'Precisely.' Amanda held out the spoon in her hand and stared at it. 'All of us have to be focused on making something happen. Anyone who doesn't want to be here, who doesn't believe that anything out of what we call the ordinary is possible, should leave.'

Everyone looked at everyone else, daring them to get up and go. Bennett was grinning, his lips loaded with a comment for anyone who might leave, but no one seemed to want to. Not even Daniel. He gripped the fork harder.

'Everyone's got to think positively,' said Amanda. 'We don't want negative energy. It's not about bending the spoon or the fork in your hand, it's about harnessing the energy inside you and seeing what it can do. It's called a kindergarten experience. If the metal bends, it's just a way of showing you how powerful your mind really is.'

When the giggling died away, the thump of the music downstairs seemed to hit Daniel harder in the soles of his feet. He was the only one standing up. He licked his lips and remembered what Amanda had said, that no one should be negative. So he closed his eyes to try and concentrate, and saw Amanda's face in the dark of him, smiling at how hard he was trying. He knew he was smiling too, a goofy one, because he wanted Amanda to like him, so he tried being as positive as he could.

He heard a gasp somewhere outside of him and it broke his eyelids open. He saw a girl sitting on the floor with a spoon in her outstretched hand, the bowl starting to soften as if someone was pushing it inside out.

Amanda was beaming. 'Everyone keep positive. Shout. Holler. Make some noise!'

Bennett was staring at the spoon and then his eyes flickered to Daniel and he nodded and then he whooped. Other people in the room started making noises too. Daniel whooped as well. He shouted, feeling invigorated by the energy in the room. He opened himself up and the energy centred itself in his chest where it sat, warm and golden. As he looked around, he watched things starting to happen . . .

. . . a boy was sat against the wall with a spoon, its bowl crimped . . .

. . . on the bed, Bennett was crushing his fork into a tiny ball . . .

. . . some girl yelled as she tied a knot in the floppy stem of her spoon.

Everyone was shouting, like some ancient sect in a glorious act of worship. Somebody pointed and Daniel saw that the fork in his hand was droopy like a parched flower. He smiled at the apparent magic of it all. He wished he could bottle whatever was in this room and take it to his father and administer it to him like a medicine.

He reached out to Amanda and drew her close.

'Tell everyone to think about my dad,' he whispered. 'Please. Let's see if they can help him too. He's very ill. I need their help.'

Amanda nodded and announced it to the room, pointing at Daniel as she spoke. 'This is Daniel. He's had a terrible time. Some of you might have heard about it. His dad's very ill. In a coma. If we try and visualize him, maybe we can help him. Do something good and bend more than just spoons and forks.'

Bennett cheered and so did his brother. Others applauded.

When Daniel felt the energy building in the room again he opened himself up to it as much as he could and he felt a surge through his body. It was so strong and sudden it made him gasp and arch his back. The noise in the bedroom became mangled and distorted. There was no golden warmth in his chest, but an immediate burning sensation. He heard a ticking sound in his head.

He started shouting at people to stop, but everyone was looking up and grinning and nodding as his voice came out distorted, in a long, low moan.

'Concentrate!' shouted Amanda. 'No sceptics. We all have to believe and help Daniel's dad.' She started chanting Daniel's name and other people joined in.

The panic in Daniel's chest was something distinct now, like fingers scrabbling to get at his heart, scraping through the skin and grating at the ribs. The ticking in his head was louder than he remembered it being when Lawson had tried to take the fit too far. Daniel was scared. He knew what was going to happen even before it did.

Suddenly, the ticking stopped and he was full of something pure and cold.

He heard a snap like someone stepping on a twig, so loud he thought something had broken inside him until he saw a girl sitting on the floor, screaming and holding her broken forearm to her chest.

Other arms started snapping too. Like someone had thrown firecrackers into the room. All the shouting and noise gave way to screams and crying.

Amanda was moaning, her arms held aloft, moving them around like two flippers as she looked at the faces staring back. The broken tips of the bones in her right forearm had penetrated the skin. Her other forearm was lumpen below the elbow, swollen and misshapen where the bone was broken.

Daniel leant back against the wall. The pain in his chest was gone, but there was an empty, sore feeling.

He took a sip from someone's bottle of beer and rinsed his mouth around to try and flush out the bad taste in his mouth.

Bennett was white-faced. He was glancing over at Daniel as he and his older brother ushered people out of the room.

Daniel heard clicking sounds as someone took a photo on their phone.

Bennett's brother crouched beside Amanda, speaking to her, stroking her hair, and Daniel realized there must be something between them. And he felt a fool for some reason he could not pin down.

And then Bennett's brother was standing up and holding Daniel tight by the arm.

'What did you do?'

'Nothing. I didn't—'

'Look what you did to her, you *freak*!' Flecks of spit flew off his lips as Bennett tried to drag his brother away. 'If your dad dies then I reckon you deserve it.'

Daniel ripped his arm free and pounded down the stairs as he heard Bennett calling after him.

Once he was outside, he walked quickly away from the house, gulping in the night air to cool him down. He passed a fence overgrown with clematis, the yellow flowers like a collection of tiny, faded stars. He stopped to breathe their perfume and tried to let it wash away what had just happened. But Daniel's mind was sharp and quick now as the night air nipped at his neck. It began to play tricks, telling him people had known what he'd done. He heard the click of a camera phone and saw a picture of him shouting as everyone stared back. He heard Bennett's brother again: '. . . *you freak.*'

Daniel sat down on the low wall bordering a garden with the dark against his back and the street lights throwing down an orange haze. He thought long and hard about Amanda and the others, telling himself over and over again that he couldn't have known what would happen. That he had not done anything on purpose.

The Men Who Died
Twice

62

Daniel tried to sleep, but all he managed was to slip into some hazy state when he closed his eyes. He could see the bedroom again and he could hear the arms snapping over and over.

Eventually, he padded down the landing, past his aunt's snoring, and went downstairs to sit in the dark of the living room with the curtains open, watching the street. When a blue BMW pulled up outside the house, he hoped he was dreaming it, but knew he wasn't. Mason heaved himself out and stood up, looking around. Fastening the middle button of his jacket, he walked purposefully over the road.

Daniel listened to his footsteps echoing down the path at the side of the house and then they stopped.

When they started again, he knew that Mason had climbed the fence.

And then Daniel got up and went and picked up the landline phone from its station in the hall.

By the time he reached the kitchen, Mason was already clicking the back door shut behind him. There was a lock pick in his other hand. He didn't seem surprised to see Daniel.

'It isn't a dream this time,' said Mason.

'I know.'

'Where's the phone I gave you?'

'I lost it.'

Mason took out an iPhone and scrolled through it for a number and hit the dial button and waited. Upstairs the faint sound of a ringtone started. Mason clicked off his iPhone.

'My aunt's upstairs.'

'Don't worry about that, she won't hear a thing. I promise.'

Daniel took the landline phone out of his dressing-gown pocket, his thumb raised over the call button.

'What are you going to do, call for backup?' Mason pulled out a chair from the small round table and sat down. 'How are you getting on with finding the flask?'

'Not so good.'

'Really? But it's your top priority.'

'There was nothing at Ashwell Lodge.'

Mason took a deep breath and let it out and the room seemed to swell. He dialled the number for Daniel's phone again and they heard the ringtone upstairs once more.

'It's the truth.'

Mason clicked off his iPhone again.

'But you see my dilemma? Now that I know you'll lie to me, how do I know I can trust you?' He rubbed the back of his neck. 'Maybe you want the flask for yourself.'

'Why would I want it?'

'For the same reason I do. It's very valuable. And because I always think the worst of people.'

Mason spread a big hand on the table and seemed to be counting that all his fingers were there. 'Why didn't you answer your phone, Daniel?'

'I was scared.'

'Of what?'

Daniel felt his brain firing. He could hear it sparking. Something glittered on his tongue. 'We went to Ashwell Lodge, but we didn't find anything. We tried making the fit, but we couldn't make anything happen.'

'So you were avoiding me because of that? Because you were scared of what I might say.' Mason was completely focused on him, like a tiger about to spring on to its prey.

'Yes. Something's broken inside Rosie. It's too dangerous for her to make the fit. I don't know if it's her chemotherapy. But we need to wait and see.'

'But I can't wait. I want that flask.' Mason sighed. Folded his arms. 'I know your father's got pneumonia. One of my little birdies told me. You need Rosie. I need Rosie. Time's a-ticking. Where is she? I went round to her house, but there was no one there.'

Daniel hesitated, wondering what to say.

'Where is she, Daniel?' growled Mason.

'At her gran's.'

Mason drummed his fingers on the table and then he nodded and stood up, and Daniel took a step back.

When Mason came closer, Daniel raised the phone and pressed his thumb lightly on the call button, but the man just put his arm round the boy's shoulders and hugged him. 'Come round to Lawson's house in the morning. I've got an idea that might work. That we need to test out.'

He rubbed Daniel's head as if the boy was a dog. 'Don't look so glum! You're important to me, Daniel. You're special. Rare. You were saved, brought back from the brink of death for a reason, like I've always said. There are bigger things at work here than either of us can comprehend, and who am I to jeopardize that?' He grinned. 'Now let me out of the front door, will you? I'm not climbing over that bloody fence again in this suit.'

63

Mason was sitting in a brand-new armchair in Lawson's living room, the sunlight dappling his black-suited legs as the green tops of the trees moved outside. Daniel was standing in front of him like a naughty schoolboy. The beige carpet beneath his socked feet was brand new.

Mason pointed at Daniel's socks. 'I don't want muck on it, you see.' He rubbed a set of black-socked toes up and down the pile. 'I wasn't sure about the colour. What do you think?' And Daniel just nodded. Mason wafted his hands around him as if trying to touch the sunshine as it came through the window. 'Done the whole lot. Lick of paint. Curtains. Freshened the place up. I might rent it out again. Or I might not. I can do what I want.'

Mason took out a silver Colt 45 from his jacket pocket and placed it on the arm of the chair, with the muzzle pointing directly at Daniel, and the boy held his breath. Mason said nothing for a while and then rubbed at a spot on the barrel with his thumb.

'What did you call those insects again, the grasshoppery ones?'

'Cicadas.'

'*Seeec-ahhhh-daaas*,' repeated Mason. His fingers began tiptoeing backward and forward over the gun. 'I told you I'd retire if you got me the flask. The deal's still on. If you find me the flask, you get to dodge the bullet, Daniel. Rosie too.'

He picked up the gun and pointed it at Daniel and pulled the trigger and there was just a dry click. But Daniel heard a *bang* and flinched anyway and clasped his hands to his stomach and looked down, half expecting to see blood bubbling through his fingers. And then he blinked and he was staring at Mason again, the sweat on his back as prickly as hair.

Mason grinned. 'We won't have to see each other ever again, unless you want to come out and visit on your holidays of course.'

They heard a car pull up outside in the lane and the engine being turned off. Car doors opened and clunked shut.

'Perfect timing!' Mason slapped his thigh. He stood up and straightened his suit and locked the gun away in a drawer as Daniel heard footsteps coming down the path towards the house. Two pairs of feet, he thought.

The front door opened and slammed shut and Daniel heard footsteps walking down a set of stairs.

'Why don't you make yourself a cup of tea?' said Mason. 'Give us five minutes and then we'll get started.'

'Started doing what?'

Mason grinned and walked out of the room and then he stopped, beckoning Daniel to follow.

'I'll have one too. Milk and two sugars. Sorry about the mess in the kitchen – give me a shout if you can't find what you need. We had a break-in last night. Some vagrant. Didn't steal anything as far as I can tell. Just trashed the pantry, looking for grub even though there was hardly anything there. He was high. Drunk. I don't know. Nasty business.' He raised his eyebrows. 'Nastier for him though.'

Mason opened a door beneath the stairs and disappeared down a set of concrete steps to what Daniel presumed was a cellar.

He walked on down the hallway and opened the kitchen door. Tupperware boxes were stacked on the work surfaces. Cardboard boxes too. He filled the kettle and flicked the switch and stood looking for a teabag until he plucked one from a white ceramic pot.

As he dropped it into a mug, Daniel stared at a hip flask sitting on the worktop near the sink. He recognized it immediately because it was Bennett's.

He stood watching it, as if it was a bird about to flit

away. He could hear Mason's muffled voice talking in the cellar as he crept quietly to the pantry door and looked inside. The blond pine shelves had been pulled down and were stacked loosely on the floor. The new paintwork on the walls had been scratched and scraped and thumped with something hard and black leaving dints in the plaster.

Daniel stood looking around him, thinking about why Bobby had come here. What reason he must have had. Mason's voice burbled downstairs, bubbling up through the floor like some dark spring. Suddenly, Daniel heard his great booming laugh.

When he found himself staring at the black rubber doorstop screwed into the floorboards, he wondered if what he was thinking might possibly be true. That Bobby had seen that the flask was hidden somewhere in the pantry when he and Bennett had asked him to look for it and had lied to them. He knelt down quickly and grabbed hold of the doorstop and pulled. The small section of floorboard came away, popping free of four magnets attached to the joists below, the brown nail in each corner shorn flush to the underside of the piece of wood.

There, lying in a nest of cotton wool, was a small golden flask, almost a perfect circle about the size of a small paperweight, with a cap screwed on tight. When Daniel looked closer, he saw how beautifully made it was, the fine gold dimpled, looking as soft as tissue paper.

'Oh, Bobby,' he whispered. 'Bobby, what have you done?'

When he heard someone coming up the cellar stairs, Daniel picked up the flask and hid it in his pocket, then slotted the piece of floorboard back down on to its four magnets.

The kettle clicked off as he stood by it and Jiff walked into the kitchen.

'Mason wants his tea.'

Daniel held up the mug with the teabag in it. 'Just coming.'

'I'll have one 'n'all. Milk and two sugars. Like Mason. There's some digestives knocking about somewhere too.' Jiff fumbled with the Tupperware boxes till he found the half-open packet. He stood eating a biscuit, watching Daniel make the tea. When he smiled, little crumbs dropped from the corners of his mouth.

64

A large section of the cellar had been covered with black plastic sheeting, held down at its four corners by cement blocks. It hissed like an angry thundercloud tethered to the floor as Mason walked across it, sipping his tea.

Sitting on a wooden chair in the corner of the room was Rosie, Jiff stood next to her and drank from his mug too and said nothing.

Mason nodded approvingly. 'I'm going to make you chief tea-maker from now on, Daniel. You have many talents.' Mason smiled at Rosie. 'You both do. That's why I'm sure one last push is what we need to find this flask.'

Mason put his tea down on the floor and motioned at Jiff to do the same. The two of them walked across to a chest freezer that was in the far corner of the cellar and both started to put on pair of black leather gloves which had been sitting on a chair.

The tiny red light in the bottom corner of the freezer's front panel was illuminated, as bright as a cherry. Daniel was still wondering what might be inside as the two men stood at either end and heaved up the lid.

They lifted out Lawson's frozen body, the ice cracking and falling from his shirt, his black hair brittle with frost.

Daniel heard Rosie gasp and he went to her and put his arms round her as the two men struggled with the heavy frozen body.

'I've found it. The flask,' he whispered as he hugged her close.

The body bumped down on the black sheeting like a rock when it was laid down.

Blood had frozen in icy pearls around Lawson's mouth. The stump of his arm looked like the end of a frozen joint.

When the leather fingers of the men's gloves peeled up off his body, they made little popping sounds.

The cold flowed like dust over the lip of the freezer as Mason bent down and rapped Lawson on his forehead. 'Anyone home?' He grinned and turned round to look up at Daniel. 'About as talkative as your dad.' Jiff laughed. 'Course he might tell us a few things using the fit. Why don't we give it a try? One big push. I've been saving him in case he might be useful. In case he wasn't telling me everything I wanted to know.'

331

Jiff slapped the lid of the freezer shut. Mason sat down in a rickety wooden chair. He plucked an iPhone from his pocket and dialled a number.

When Frank's face appeared on the screen in a Skype call, Mason beamed. 'Who you got there with you, Frank?'

'Rosie's gran,' came back the tinny reply.

'And what are you doing?'

'Having a cup of tea.'

'So are we! Daniel makes the best, Frank. Even better than you!'

'I doubt it.'

Mason turned the phone round so Rosie and Daniel could see the screen. With a free finger, he pointed at the frozen body of Lawson.

'You don't need him warmed up, do you? To help, I mean? How about the gloves? Do you need them?'

'Stop,' said Daniel quietly. 'Just stop. We think we know where the flask is.' Mason looked at Daniel for some time, saying nothing. Lawson's body was already beginning to melt, *drip-drip-dripping* on to the black sheeting.

'I knew it,' said Mason. 'I knew you were lying.' He chuckled and slapped his hand on his thigh. 'So show me where you think it is. Then we'll figure out what to do next.'

65

Daniel pulled up the false floorboard in the pantry at Ashwell Lodge and took out the silver-plated box. When Mason reached for it, Daniel shook his head.

'There's more,' he said and opened the box, revealing the severed finger inside with the black twine around it. Daniel pointed to the symbol on the wall. 'We think there must be four of these symbols to go with the compartments in the box but so far we've only found three. I'll show you the others.'

And he did.

Mason, Jiff and Rosie followed him through the rooms of Ashwell Lodge, with Frank watching them on Skype as Mason held out his iPhone. 'He's my insurance policy,' said Mason. 'I've got no reason to trust you at all.'

Daniel showed him where the golden wedding band was hidden and the lock of hair.

He put them in the compartments of the silver box and hooked the pieces of twine to the clasp in the centre of the lid in the same way the finger was attached.

'There's one more item to go in,' said Daniel. 'But we don't know where it is. We think it's hidden some-where in one of the downstairs rooms, at least that's what Rosie saw. But we couldn't find it.'

'Which room?' asked Mason.

'We'll show you.'

Daniel and Rosie led them into the room that might once have been the dining room. He pointed at the mattress. 'We sat here for some time, trying to work it out. But Rosie didn't see anything.'

Rosie was watching Daniel. Listening to his every word. She licked her lips. 'I might feel ready to try again,' she said.

Mason's eyes sparkled. 'Go on, Rosie. I'd like that very much.'

When she closed her eyes, Daniel knew she was pretending to make the fit. There was no pain in his chest. No blood from her nose. The strain in her face was an act and, when he realized, he put his hand to his chest as if pretending to feel something, making her performance seem all the more real.

'It's somewhere,' she whispered. 'It's somewhere in this room.'

'Are you sure?' Mason was walking around, inspecting the walls for another symbol. 'I don't see anything. There's nothing here.'

'It is,' she hissed. When she opened her eyes and sat down on her haunches, she looked up at Mason. 'I need a rest.'

Daniel pointed to the fireplace. 'Why don't you go and check that end of the room? I'll look this end while Rosie takes a moment.'

Daniel listened as Jiff and Mason searched the wall and then knelt down and inspected the hearth. He held his breath as he listened to them rooting around like pigs in the dust and the grime.

When Jiff stopped and cursed excitedly, he didn't look round. He waited for them to prise up the loose tile.

'We've found it!' shouted Mason. 'We've got it.' Daniel turned and saw Mason holding up the human tooth by its black piece of twine. 'Give me the box. Let me have it.'

Mason put the tooth in the compartment and hooked the piece of twine round the clasp.

'What do you think happens now?' asked Mason.

He was about to ask again when Daniel pointed. 'Look,' he said.

A misty, shadowy figure was emerging from out of the floor and drifting towards him.

'Who's that? Who's there?' whispered Mason. He gripped Daniel and turned him to face the ghost. 'Can you see him, boy? Can you?'

'Yes,' whispered Daniel. He thought he heard Jiff cursing, but his heart was pounding too loudly to hear properly as the ghost drifted closer, just a dark silhouette in the shape of a man.

'Where's Lawson?' it asked, in a voice that shimmered all around them as if coming from the walls of the building itself.

'We're friends of his,' said Daniel. 'Lawson's dead. We've come to collect a flask. Is it here?'

The figure drifted towards Daniel and pressed its fingers into the boy's chest, making him gasp, then pulled them free.

'A friend indeed,' said the ghost. 'Yes, the flask is here.' It floated towards Mason and looked at him. 'I'm the keeper of the flask. I decide who has it. It's your fate to be the one. You're destined to have the flask. That's what you've always believed, isn't it? That you and this boy met for a reason.'

Mason nodded. Little flecks of spit were caught in the corners of his mouth and he licked them away. 'Yes,' he said in a trembling voice. '*Yes.*'

The cellar was lit by three cross-beams of light from Mason's and Jiff's phones and Daniel's too. There was no reception down beneath the house and, before the Skype connection had been lost, Mason had told Frank to stay with Agatha. But the man hadn't seemed too pleased, worried about missing out on his cut that Mason had promised if they found the flask, cursing and shouting, his tongue flicking out like a viper's over his cleft lip. But Mason didn't seemed too bothered, shouting that Frank was paranoid before clicking off the phone.

The ghost pointed at a section of wall and asked Mason to push in one particular brick. As soon as he did, a trapdoor in the cellar floor sprang open and Mason strode towards it and peered down into the dark hole. The man took a few careful strides down the slippery stone steps until he was low enough to be able to stoop and see what was below, using his phone. A large dark room. Windowless. The walls damp and tinged with green.

Mason waved Jiff and Daniel and Rosie closer and the beams of light from the two phones moved with them across the floor until they were standing above the stone steps beside the trapdoor. Mason beckoned Jiff down a few steps and they panned their phones round the secret chamber.

'There!' shouted Mason. 'Look, right there, on the far wall.'

When Daniel stooped to look too, he saw a golden

flask set into the wall at the end of the chamber. It looked exactly like the one he had hidden in his pocket.

'Daniel,' said Mason excitedly, a big hand sweeping across his sweaty brow. 'I want you and Rosie to remain at the top of the steps and keep your light focused down so I can see where I'm going. Jiff, stay where you are, and keep your phone straight. I want to see what we've got here.'

Daniel stood beside Rosie, shining his phone past Jiff's humped back, and lighting up the steps. Mason walked carefully down and stood on the last step. 'Hello!' he shouted as if expecting someone to be there. 'Hello!' He turned and grinned at Jiff. 'Keep that light directly on the flask so I can see it,' he said and then he turned and stepped down on to the stone floor.

He crossed one flagstone, and then a second, and then a third, walking along the shaft of light from his own phone as if it was a balance beam. The ghost was beside him, drifting above the stone floor, telling him that the flask had been put here by its maker, Francis Green, and that Lawson had known about it and had wanted to keep it a secret from him. Mason was chuntering and cursing, calling Lawson all manner of names.

And then there was a click, like a bone snapping, as he stood on a segment of floor and heard the trapdoor at the top of the stairs flipping up.

As Daniel and Rosie jerked sideways so as not to be

hit by the door closing back down, the last thing they saw was Jiff spinning round, humpbacked, to look at them, his eyes wide, and the phone in his hand lighting up a spot on the ceiling of the cellar.

And then the trapdoor locked shut back into the cellar floor.

Daniel heard shouts. Muffled through the stone. And then he realized he could hear nothing, that his imagination was only telling him that, and he turned to look at Rosie.

Inside the chamber, Mason was whirling round like a devil. He didn't know which way to go, towards the flask or back to the steps where Jiff was lying, knocked out by the trapdoor which had swung over and hit him, his phone beside him.

The ghost was telling Mason things he could barely hear above his own cursing. That Francis Green had made the trap to protect the flask from men like him. That Lawson had discovered where the flask had really been hidden in the house. That he had found the trap and had come up with a plan to get rid of Mason.

'You killed me,' said the ghost. 'Just like I'm going to kill you.'

'I'm not dying. I'm not,' roared Mason. 'You can't do anything to me.' He went to the flask on the wall and reached out for it, only to find that it was a picture

339

drawn with such skilful perspective that it looked real from all angles.

Mason roared again. 'Let me out,' he screamed, like some wild animal caged. 'Daniel!' he screamed at the ceiling.

But then he stopped when he heard the sound of rushing water.

'What's that? What's happening?' The ghost was drifting higher as two sluice gates opened in the walls at either end of the chamber and water started gushing in.

Mason roared again as the cold water quickly started filling the room. But the ghost was gone. Vanished through the walls.

66

The ghost led Daniel and Rosie to a body that was hidden in a priest hole in the wall of a large room downstairs. The corpse was covered with car air fresheners and the hole was full of a sweet chemical smell.

Dust moved in tiny tumbleweeds as Daniel leant down over the curled-up body, his movement disturbing them. Something had nibbled one of the ears. Spiderwebs trailed over the dead man and caught the dust and grime. The clothes had something white and furred growing on them in patches. Daniel put his head to one side and held his breath as he took the flask out of his pocket.

After the ghost had told him what to do, he unscrewed the cap and paused, wondering how much of the liquid he should drop on to the corpse's head. Two drops at first. And then another two. And one for good luck.

They all disappeared. Nothing trickled out of the hairline down the neck or the throat. The body had soaked up every drop.

'This is the secret of the flask,' said the ghostly man. 'This is what Lawson knew would happen,' it said as its outline started to fade away. And then it vanished as if someone had turned off a projector and the image was gone.

Daniel and Rosie waited to see what was going to happen.

But when they heard footsteps running round the paving stones outside the house, and the front door being pushed open, they squeezed each other's hands.

'What's happening? What's going on?' asked Rosie and Daniel could only shake his head.

They stood up and turned to face the doorway as they heard feet frantically running in the hall.

'Mason?' shouted a voice. 'Mason!'

They knew who it was before Frank appeared in the doorway, a black revolver in his hand.

He stared at them. Sunlight glancing off the muzzle of the gun.

'Where is he? His car's still here. What's happened to him? Has he mugged me off? Has he?'

Sunlight mottled the floor.

Daniel heard a sound behind him.

The crick of joints.

The gasp of a breath.

And he looked back round at the body in the priest hole as it started clawing the webs from its dirty clothes, combing the grime and dirt from its hair. Its lungs like paper bags as they crackled.

As the man opened his eyes, he smiled at Daniel. And then he looked beyond the boy and saw Frank moving towards him with the gun pointed, his mouth wide open.

'What the hell are you doing here? You're supposed to be dead!' Frank's tongue whipped round the outside of his mouth like a lizard licking its lips and he fired a shot.

The man put his hands to his chest and suddenly they were leaking red. He tried to push the blood back in, but it was coming too fast and he looked up with bright blue eyes as he fell back into the priest hole, the dust flying and the air fresheners scattering in his wake.

67

Rosie tried pushing the brick into the wall of the cellar again, but it wouldn't budge.

'Give her a hand,' growled Frank, waggling the gun at Daniel.

But it was no use.

'Harder or I'll shoot the girl first.'

The two of them pushed with all their strength and the brick began to move. At first they heard the sound of something opening beneath the floor of the cellar and then water starting to rush away. The trapdoor popped open as the water continued to run.

Wet steps below. Bright and grey.

The water was still going down and all three of them watched the slick walls grow taller, Frank flashing his phone as he told Daniel to wave his too.

At first a black heel, like a fin. And then a trouser leg, bedraggled, pasted to the leg of Jiff, his humped back emerging like a tiny island until the rest of him began to appear. When Mason floated up against the bottom step, they heard the gentle *thock* of his bald head against the stone.

'Go and get them,' said Frank, as the last of the water gurgled away. 'Now!' he shouted and waggled the gun.

Rosie and Daniel struggled to drag Mason up the steps between them, treading carefully on the greasy stones, and laid him in the cellar. But Jiff had slid away from the steps and was lying in the middle of the floor and the two of them were wary of fetching him out until Rosie noticed that the floor was lower than it had been before, because a border of red brickwork was showing all around the wall.

They wondered why until Daniel worked it out. 'I think it must have to be reset, otherwise whoever built this would have had the same trouble as us getting a body out.'

He stepped out on to the floor and walked towards Jiff, one foot in front of the other like a tightrope walker going carefully. Rosie followed him too. And they picked Jiff up and carried him across the floor and up the steps. As they emerged into the cellar, they heard cogs grinding in the walls and the floor began to rise, finally locking back into place, the red section of brickwork gone.

Frank motioned with the light from his phone at the steps out of the cellar. 'Take them upstairs,' he said.

* * *

The two wet bodies were laid in the living room across bars of sunshine on the floor. They steamed like they were gently cooking on a grill.

Frank took the flask from his pocket and threw it to Daniel.

'Now do to them what you did to the other one.'

'I don't know how it wor—'

'Yes you do. That man in the hole, that *body*. He was dead. I killed him first time around a couple of months ago and then he was suddenly getting up. So I know that something happened. What he was doing here, you'll tell me later. But first things first.' He waved the black revolver at Daniel. 'Bring them back like you did the first one.'

Daniel knelt in front of Jiff and tried not to look at his face or his eyes as he unscrewed the cap on the flask and tipped it up over the man's head and allowed a few drops to escape. And then he moved across to Mason and did the same, the droplets hitting his bald head with a smack before seeming to melt and disappear into the skin.

Nothing happened at first.

'More,' said Frank. 'Pour on more.'

But, as Daniel started to unscrew the cap again, Jiff began to move, squirming like a big fish landed on the deck of a boat. He rolled over on to his side and threw up the water in his lungs, rinsing the dust from the floorboards around him.

346

And then Mason began moving too, his body convulsing like he was being shocked, and when he threw up the water it came out green and dirty and Daniel stepped back from it until he butted up against the wall.

Jiff stood up and blinked and then looked at Mason who was still sitting on the wet floor, staring at Daniel. When he pointed at the flask in the boy's hands, Daniel just nodded and Mason began to laugh. He slapped his wet thighs so hard he sent up a spray of water.

68

Rosie and Daniel were driven back to Lawson's house in the blue BMW with Mason sitting between them in the rear seats. He smelt stale and wet. He was jabbering to Jiff who was driving. He wouldn't stop.

Frank drove behind them in his own car.

It was only when they got inside the house that Jiff noticed that something was different. He looked at himself in the mirror in the hall, his clothes half drying on him, and stood sideways. And then he took off his jacket and his shirt and inspected his bare torso.

'It's gone!' he shouted. 'My hump's disappeared.'

He turned to show Frank and Mason and they looked at his back, the spine straight and the shoulders back, the hump gone. Mason took off his jacket too and undid his shirt and checked his stomach.

'That scar, the one I got at Jimmy's . . .' He trailed off, his fingers feeling the skin for any blemish. He cricked his neck. Shook his shoulders. 'How do you feel, Jiff?'

'Marvellous.' Jiff grinned. 'How about you?'

Mason struck a bodybuilder pose. 'More than marvellous.' And he slapped Daniel on the shoulder. 'You little beauty,' he said.

Mason and Jiff took showers, rubbing the dust and the grime from their bodies. Cleaning off what the dirty water had left on them. They put on dry clothes and toasted each other with brandies and then Frank who had come to save them.

And, all the while, Rosie and Daniel sat on the sofa in the sitting room, as Frank kept an eye on them.

Eventually, Mason came and sat next to them, landing on the sofa with a thump. He toasted them too and drained his brandy and put the glass down on the table in front of him.

'You know what you've done and I can't put that behind me. I'm not a good man so I can't forgive. It's your fate to suffer for what you tried to do just as it's my fate to go on living. It's an indisputable fact.' He rapped on his chest. 'Because here I am, better than ever. Just like Jiff there.' He pointed at Jiff on the opposite sofa who raised his glass.

'And that's given me an idea.' He grinned at Daniel. 'Go on, have a guess.'

Daniel shifted uneasily on the couch. Shook his head. But Mason kept staring. 'I don't know,' he said.

Mason nodded, put his hands on top of his head and then went on. 'Well, it's a great idea. And it involves Rosie too. You see this collector is going to pay a lot more when he sees what the flask can do. We can show him. I'll name my price once I've killed Rosie and brought her back to life in front of his eyes.' Mason beamed as Rosie's mouth began to open slowly, her face turning even whiter. 'I'll be gentle, I promise. Don't you want to be cured, Rosie? Get rid of your tumour? There'll be no more chemotherapy then. You'll come back even better, like Jiff and me.'

'I'm a new man!' shouted Jiff and downed his drink.

Mason poured another brandy and swilled it round the glass, making the early evening sunlight spin inside it. 'And then you two'll make the fit whenever I want you to for as long as I want. You owe me that after your little scheme. You're in my debt.' He drank down the brandy in one and then stood up. 'I'm going to give this collector a call.'

69

When Jiff held the brandy bottle upside down, a single golden drop landed on his tongue.

He set it down next to the first empty one and started opening a third bottle.

Sitting on the sofa, Daniel and Rosie could hear Mason upstairs, talking on the phone. He was laughing.

Frank sat back in his chair and raised his glass and then downed what was in it and cleared his throat. He licked the scar on his cleft lip. 'Tell me what it's like, Jiff.'

'What?'

'Feeling so great. Being reborn.'

'What do you think?' And Jiff started laughing as he tugged at the wrapping round the bottle. Then he stopped and looked round. 'Why don't you try it?'

'Nah.'

'Why not?' Jiff raised his hands and pointed at himself and then nodded over at Daniel. 'I could do him and show you how quick it is.'

'Wasted on him,' said Frank.

Jiff nodded. He fumbled at the cap on the bottle when he felt a throbbing in his head and cursed as his fingers slipped. 'I need a drink.'

He poured another brandy for himself and then filled Frank's glass, bending down to study the man's cleft lip. 'You shouldn't be so chicken. I could make you handsome, you know.'

Frank said nothing as he stared at the golden flask on the table in front of him. Then he took a sip from his glass and set it down. He took the black revolver out of his jacket pocket and handed it to Jiff. 'Make it quick,' he said.

'How quick do you wa—' but before he could finish, Jiff raised the gun and fired point-blank at Frank's forehead.

Frank slumped back in his chair, dead in an instant.

Jiff tossed the gun into Frank's lap and finished his drink. Sniffed and admired his handiwork.

He smiled at Daniel and Rosie, and then turned round to pick up the flask from the table beside the empty brandy bottles. He missed it and grinned. 'I'm so drunk,' he said. But, when he went to pick up the flask again, he missed a second time. He looked at his hand

and then at the flask and reached slowly for it, watching his fingers slip through one side and out the other.

When he tried the other hand, it wafted through the flask too. He turned to Daniel. 'Get up! Get the flask open. Get it open!' But Daniel just sat there, watching Jiff's panicked face. He managed to pick up the flask between his elbows and unscrew the cap with his teeth. But, as he spat out the cap, the flask fell straight through his elbows and landed on the floor, spilling the contents into the carpet.

'No,' gasped Jiff, shaking his head 'No!' He kicked out, but his foot went straight through the flask. He bent down and tried to lick the wet carpet, but his tongue touched nothing.

Quickly, he turned to look at Frank and screamed at the bloody mess in the chair as his whole body started to fade.

Mason had heard the gunshot. And he had heard the scream. He came down the stairs and strode into the living room and saw Frank in the chair, his brains sprayed on to the wall behind him.

When he saw the flask on the floor, he picked it up and swilled it round next to his ear. He tipped it up and there was not a single drop left.

'Where's Jiff?'

'Gone,' replied Daniel.

'Gone where?'

Mason bent down to pick up the gun from Frank's lap, but his hand wafted through it. He tried again.

He looked up. 'What do you mean gone?'

When Daniel and Rosie said nothing, Mason stood up and stepped back from them. 'What do you mean gone?' he said quietly, holding up his hands in front of his face and staring straight through them at the two of them sitting there on the sofa, watching.

After Mason had vanished too, there was nothing but the sound of Frank's chin dripping red spots on to his chest.

The Fire

70

When Daniel sat down opposite his aunt, he felt something heavy lurch in his stomach. He just kept staring at his father lying there in the bed.

And then he heard the silence.

The room was much whiter without all the machines.

'Daniel?'

'I'm OK.' He wiped his eyes and the wet tips of his fingers shone before he dried them on his jeans. But then something uncoiled in his throat and he started to cry without being able to stop, losing sight of his dad as he put his hands to his face and stared into nothing.

When he realized his aunt was holding him, he tensed up, but she kept a tight grip on him until he fell deeper into her arms and sobbed until he was spent, his breath hiccuping in dry bursts.

357

She stroked his hair. She whispered things to him. And eventually she held his hand and they sat together in silence, looking at the dead man in the bed.

'I know the things I'm feeling can't compare to what's inside you,' said his aunt. 'But I do care, so much, Daniel. I want you to know that.'

Daniel nodded. 'I know.' He sniffed.

They sat there quietly, saying nothing for a while.

'Can you tell me now?'

'About what?'

'Why you and Dad fell out.'

'Why?'

'Because I'm not sure I want to make the same mistake.'

His aunt smiled and then she shook her head and sighed. 'I'm not sure I can even remember.'

But Daniel squeezed her hand. 'It's important. Because I don't want the same thing to ever happen to us. Remember, we're all we've got now.'

His aunt nodded. Something electric crimped her lips for a moment and she had to look away. And then she cleared her throat. 'It was something to do with the funeral. I don't remember exactly. The flowers, the choice of hymns, something small.' Daniel's aunt stared at a spot on the floor. 'It's the little things that fester and grow, that can break people apart if you don't address them.' She tapped her head. 'They grow into bigger things up here.'

'Dad said you didn't want to see us.'

'Your father was very protective of you. He was in love with your mother and then when she died you were his world. He didn't want to share you with me or anyone else. I think it was his way of coping with his grief. You and he grew together. But no one else grew with you.'

'Maybe you reminded him too much of her?'

His aunt nodded. 'They were very much in love. I've never seen two people so connected like that. You came out of all that love.'

Daniel reached out and held his father's hand. 'How did you let go of Mum?'

'I don't think anyone ever really lets go.'

Daniel nodded and stared at the man in the bed, the man who might have heard everything or who might have heard nothing at all each time he'd come to sit beside him. Daniel could almost hear his aunt's brain ticking.

'You never forget,' she said quietly.

Daniel nodded. But then he looked at his aunt. 'But how do I say goodbye?'

'You can say it whenever you want to, whenever you feel the time's right for you.'

And Daniel just sat there with his lips shut tight.

71

Bennett's little sister had rubbed her eyes red. Her pale face was still puffy. Every now and then, a breath crackled in her chest as she sighed and her lips wobbled.

'At least she's stopped crying,' said Bennett, popping the top off a cold beer and handing it to Daniel. 'It was a drama.'

'What was?'

'The death.' Bennett looked at Daniel and before he could say anything else a little voice piped up.

'Chester isn't dead,' squeaked the little girl as she studied the shoebox which she was busily painting gold. 'He's just in a different place. Like your dad, Daniel.'

'Who's Chester?' asked Daniel.

'Where's Chester seems to be the more relevant question.'

'Chester was our friend. He's in heaven. He was a good guinea pig.'

'You remember him, Daniel. About so high. Nice coat of hair. Partial to dandelions.'

Daniel nodded. Sipped his beer.

'I'm sorry to hear that, Lola.'

'That's OK. I just wasn't expecting it. It was such a shock.' She sighed and picked up the shoebox and dabbed the paintbrush at a couple of spots. 'I must feel exactly like you do.'

Bennett chinked his beer bottle against the one Daniel was holding.

'To your dad. And to Chester.'

Bennett took a swig from his beer and the bottle fizzed. Daniel nodded and took a sip of his own too.

'How's Amanda?' he asked.

'Healing. Like the others. I think you need to keep clear of my brother for a while though.' And they were silent for several moments. 'I'm sorry about what he said,' said Bennett eventually.

The late afternoon sun was still very hot. The beer bottle was strung with cold beads. Daniel rolled it across his brow to keep cool and then he took a large mouthful. And then another.

He took out the golden flask and sat it on the garden table between them and then told his friend everything that had happened, as always.

By the time he had finished, all that was left of his beer was a warm golden disc in the bottom of the bottle.

Bennett picked up the flask and studied it, turning it round. He jiggled it up and down. 'So there's nothing left?'

Daniel shook his head. Bennett unscrewed the top and looked inside with one eye, like peering into a microscope. Eventually, he screwed the cap back on and put the flask down on the table.

'It's yours,' said Daniel. 'To replace your hip flask.'

Bennett nodded a thank you. 'So tell me again what happened after the sinkhole, before you found your way out.'

'I thought I was going to die.'

Bennett necked the last of his beer and didn't take his eyes off Daniel. 'Go on.'

Daniel shifted in his seat. The sun was like a lamp in his face. 'I asked for help.'

'Who did you ask?'

'Anyone who was listening.'

'And do you think someone was?'

Daniel watched as Lola knelt beside the flower bed further down the garden, digging a hole with the trowel, the faint chiming of stone on metal as she scooped and her shoebox a golden brick on the grass beside her. And then Daniel shook his head.

'I don't know,' he said. 'I don't know if that's what matters.'

Bennett nodded. 'We need more beer,' he announced.

He scraped his chair back and headed towards the kitchen door.

'When's your mum back?' shouted Daniel.

'Not for ages yet,' hollered Bennett as he disappeared inside.

Daniel sat there, trying to convince himself he didn't need to pee. But his bladder throbbed all the harder. He sighed because he was perfectly warm. Through the buzz of the beer, he could hear a breeze lifting the leaves in the trees.

He stood up and walked over the grass to the nearest bush, passing like a ghost through a cloud of midges. He stood watching the patch of hard earth turn a darker brown. A waxy foam bristling and popping in the sun.

He looked up when he heard Lola laughing and applauding. And, when her feet thundered over the hard lawn towards him, Daniel zipped up quickly and stepped out, almost colliding with her.

'Oh, thank you, Daniel,' she cried out loud, hugging him. 'Thank you.' Before he could ask, she was pulling him across the lawn to the grave she had dug. The garden moved a little quicker than him and he stumbled and he knew he was drunk. Lola's hand was sweaty and covered in grains of dirt. Suddenly, he remembered the time he had spent hidden away from the rest of the world. A dark shadow passed across him and he shivered.

'There! Look!' shouted Lola, clapping her hands and beaming, then pointing and dancing a jig. Daniel looked down and saw the creature stumbling over the grass, like a wind-up toy. It was breathing fast in the heat.

'He wasn't dead,' explained Lola. 'Chester wasn't dead!' she shouted as Bennett walked smartly over the grass with two bottles, each capped with a nipple of white foam. He started laughing when he saw Chester picking up speed. He handed a beer to Daniel and clinked it and drank.

'What happened, Lola? Did you do magic?' asked her brother.

'No,' she said as if her brother was stupid. She took out the golden flask from her skirt pocket and handed it back to Daniel. 'I just filled it up with water, Daniel, from the garden tap. I did think it might be magic because it looked so pretty.'

When Daniel looked up, Bennett was staring straight at him. Out of the corner of his eye, he could see Chester panting in the heat.

Lola slipped her hand into his and pulled him down to her eye level and kissed him on the cheek.

'But Mummy's gonna be mad if she knows you've been drinking.'

She put her finger to her lips as the gravel crackled and a car stopped out of sight in the driveway. Bennett

364

tossed the bottles end over end into the hedge, tracing arcs like Catherine wheels spun off their posts. They told Lola that Chester had fallen into a coma, just like Daniel's dad, but had woken up. And she nodded back, saying it all made sense, and told them that magic was made up anyway.

72

When the heavy oak door opened, Daniel heard his heart all around him, beating in the cold, empty space of the church.

The coffin was balanced on three wooden trestles in front of the first row of pews. It looked like a magician's prop left behind after a show. When Daniel laid his hand flat on the top, the wood was cold and hard. He said something quietly to anyone who might be listening and then set to work.

The lid was heavy, unwieldy, and the trestles below the coffin creaked as Daniel raised it all the way up. His father was dressed in his favourite clothes and looked exactly as he had done in the hospital, but this time there was something missing. And, as Daniel kept looking at him in the moonlight, he could not work out what it might be.

When he unscrewed the cap from the flask, Daniel waited for the silence to settle again. A few drops were all it took and, when his father opened his eyes, Daniel felt a weight fall away from somewhere inside him because he had been waiting for this moment for what had seemed like an age, ever since the sinkhole had opened.

After helping his father out, they walked down the aisle together in silence, hand in hand, the faces in the windows looking down at them, watching them on their way.

73

'What about the coffin?' asked Bennett as he yanked the gear stick of his mum's red Fiesta nastily, grinding the gears. Rosie was sitting in the front passenger seat.

'We stacked some hymn books inside it,' whispered Daniel as the red Fiesta rattled and bumped over the dirt road. His father leant forward in the back seat and pointed.

'Is that it?'

Up ahead was a huge dark saucer in the ground that grew and deepened as they drove closer.

'Yes,' said Daniel. 'That's where it all started.'

'I don't remember anything.'

'Neither do I.'

Bennett wound the car past the warning signs and manoeuvred carefully round the sinkhole, the wheels crackling over the loose stones, and Daniel and his father peered into the dark pit through the metal grille of the fencing erected around it.

'We made it out,' said his father.

'Yes we did,' replied Daniel.

Daniel and his father set up camp as they had always planned to do, finding a flat patch of woodland floor for their tent, springy with dead brown needles mattressing the ground.

'It's just like you said it would be,' said Daniel's father.

'Yes it is,' said Daniel.

They lit a fire inside a ring of stones and watched the pieces of dry timber burning black and orange, the sparks dancing up around them and disappearing into the dark above. And Daniel tried not to watch them vanishing as he stared into the fire and kept the warmth on his face and his chest.

'Did you hear everything I told you in the hospital?' he asked.

'Some things,' replied his father. 'It was like being in a dream. So maybe it's just that I can't remember it all.'

Daniel poked a stick into the embers and a log sprouted a flame.

'I don't hate you,' he said.

'Of course you don't.' His father took hold of him and held him tight in his arms. 'Your mother and I loved each other so much too.'

'What was she like?'

'She was like you. Strong. Powerful. Brave.'

'We had a good time, didn't we?'

'The best.'

When Daniel noticed his father's fingers beginning to fade, he tried to look up, but his father held him tighter. 'Keep looking into the fire,' he said.

And Daniel kept looking into the light, keeping the heat on his face.

'Tell me the best bits,' he said. 'About what we did.'

And his father began to tell him everything he could remember, laughing about the one Christmas Day the fire brigade had arrived because they'd fallen asleep while the turkey was cooking . . . and about the holiday they had taken in Greece and booked themselves into a nudist resort by accident . . . and about the piglet they had found one day trotting down a lane and tried to catch . . . and so much more.

But the more Daniel laughed, the sadder he became, and he had to try harder and harder to keep looking into the fire and not think about what was happening.

And, when his father's voice had finally stopped, Daniel felt the cold and the dark all around him and he moved closer to the fire to keep warm and smiled and wiped his eyes. Rosie wanted to get up and hug him straightaway, but Bennett told her they should stay where they were, watching on from their own spot

370

beneath the trees, saying that Daniel needed some time on his own.

Eventually, all three of them fell asleep beside the fire.

When the morning came to meet them, the light was pure and clean and fresh, and the trees all around them crackled with dew, their branches steaming as the sun rose higher, and it filled Daniel with a sense of hope.

After packing away the tent and kicking over the hot embers left in the fire, the three of them walked back between the trees and found the track where Bennett had parked the car.

They didn't say a word because there was nothing to be said.

They drove back down the dirt road and, when they passed the sinkhole, Daniel asked Bennett to stop.

He walked to the metal fence around the hole and clambered up it and sat astride the top with the flask in his hand, winking in the sun.

'What should I do?' he shouted.

'Whatever *you* think is right,' said Bennett through the open window.

And Daniel thought about it for some time and then made a decision and climbed down.

74

The early morning had promised a good day and that promise was kept.

When Daniel stood with his aunt and watched the coffin being lowered into the grave, he whispered something that nobody else heard.

And then, as the first shovel of earth landed with a crash, he took his aunt's hand and they turned away, listening to every sound as the hole was filled back in.

When he felt another hand in his, he knew it was Rosie's without even looking.

'It's the what not the why, just like you said,' she whispered as they walked on.

'I know,' said Daniel. 'We can be anybody we want to be, no matter what happens. It's up to us to be whoever we want.'

'And we can be anyone, can't we?' said Rosie.

'Yes, we can be all sorts of possible.'

Acknowledgements

Writing a novel means I spend a lot of time with made-up people but there are lots of real people involved too who are just as important, helping and encouraging me, as I work on the manuscript.

I would like to say thank you to Bella Honess Roe, Nick Roe and Emma Timpany for all their thoughts and comments, and to Matt Wheeler for all his optimism and confidence. Thanks also to Ollie and Noah for reminding me what it's like to be a teenage boy.

Thank you too to my agent, Madeleine Milburn, who is always so enthusiastic, believing in what I write.

I must also thank my editor, Jane Griffiths, for all her patience and good ideas and generosity of thought. Thanks also to everyone at Simon & Schuster involved in the process of bringing the book to publication, especially Paul Coomey who is always so inspired in his cover design.

I am very grateful to my Mum and my sisters, Katherine and Joanna, for all their support.

I could not have written this book without Priscilla with all her grace and understanding and love.

RUPERT WALLIS

THE DARK INSIDE

'If you loved *Skellig* by David Almond, then this is the book for you'
Serendipity Reviews

'Beautifully written... I wanted it to go on forever' **BookBag**
'Gripping and atmospheric' **So Many Books, So Little Time**
'A book that you can't stop thinking about,
that you have to tell people about – the mark of
a truly powerful novel' **Writing From The Tub**
'Intense, dark, brooding and highly adventurous'
Fiction Fascination

Rupert Wallis read Theology at
Cambridge University and holds an MFA in
Screenwriting and Writing for Television
from the University of Southern California.
His debut novel *The Dark Inside* has been
shortlisted for several awards including
the Branford Boase.

You can follow Rupert and his writing on
twitter @rupertwriter.